# Runaway
## to
# Romance

# CATHRYN BROWN

Sienna Bay Press

PO Box 158582

Nashville, Tennessee 37215

www.cathrynbrown.com

Cover designed by Najla Qamber Designs

(www.najlaqamberdesigns.com)

Runaway to Romance/Cathryn Brown. - 1st ed.

ISBN: 978-1-945527-46-3

❦ Created with Vellum

# DEAR READER

Two Hearts, Tennessee, is a small town I created. It's everything I would want if I chose a new place to live. The old homes are beautiful, and the people are friendly. But the town has fallen on hard times.

The wedding in this first Wedding Town romance is Carly and Jake's. You may remember them from *How to Marry a Country Music Star*. She's a star who has lost everything, and he's a wealthy man who hires her to be his housekeeper. He doesn't know who she is, and she wants to keep her job, so she doesn't tell him.

Many thanks go to wedding planners Megan Scurlock, owner of Locklane Wedding & Events, and Sara Fried, owner of Fête Nashville: Luxury Weddings, for sharing their knowledge of wedding planning. Any mistakes are my own.

I hope you enjoy your visit to Two Hearts!

# CHAPTER ONE

*C*assie jumped over the church pew and raced toward the exit, dodging well-wishers. She launched through the church doors and knocked down the groom's best friend. He yelped and scrambled out of her way. She took the stairs sideways so she wouldn't break her neck on the high heels Bella had talked her into and reached the curb at the exact moment the limo pulled away.

Waving her arms and yelling, she hoped the driver checked his rearview mirror. When he turned the corner at the next street and vanished from sight, she knew she had a problem.

Well, two problems.

Her groom had cheated on her. And she had no way to get out of here to save herself from the chaos that would ensue when her mother learned she'd run.

With Sandra Van Bibber, it was all about the show. Southern ladies didn't make a scene. She'd tell Cassie to march her hiney back into that church and marry the man.

A motorcycle roared down the street and stopped in front of her. It was as though God had sent her an exit plan.

The man pulled off his helmet and stared in confusion at the woman in the wedding dress.

"Hi, I'm Michael." He held out his hand. "I hope I'm not late to the wedding."

At her puzzled expression, he added, "Jonathan's boss."

She nodded slowly. He knew her former groom well, so he'd have no qualms about loaning his motorcycle. Cassie glanced over her shoulder toward the church doors as her mother stepped out.

"I need to get out of here." When she made the mistake of making eye contact with her mother, the woman moved swiftly toward her—as swiftly as could be elegantly achieved.

*Now!* She pointed at the motorcycle. "Can I borrow that?"

He gripped the handlebars more tightly and stared at her as though she'd lost her mind. "I can't loan my bike to an unlicensed driver."

Cassie dug in her bag. If her mother had worn flats, she'd be here by now, but thankfully, she'd go to her grave in heels. "Here." Cassie held up her motorcycle license. The one she'd used once for the biker-themed wedding last September.

With one longing glance at his motorcycle, he climbed off. "Okay. I guess I can trust someone who's marrying my top employee."

*Not in this lifetime.*

Cassie climbed on, hiking her dress up to her knees to keep fabric out of the spokes.

He handed her his helmet, which she slipped on as she heard the shouted words, "Cassandra Van Bibber!" No one except her mother called her Cassandra. She hit the gas. Talk about a narrow escape.

An older woman stepped into the crosswalk, and Cassie hit the brakes. The woman glared at her as only a grandmother could before moving again. Cassie waved and sheepishly smiled.

Lesson learned: don't kill anyone when you escape a wedding fiasco.

Glancing over her shoulder, she saw a man and woman running down the sidewalk toward her. Only her mother could wear that shade of green well, so that meant her parents were on their way.

The words "Don't you dare do this to me!" floated to her over the gruff engine sounds.

With the senior citizen safely across the road, Cassie accelerated and left the scene of the crime.

His crime, not hers.

She always felt calmer when surrounded by countryside, so she put Nashville's skyline in her rearview mirror. Her time with Jonathan replayed itself as she headed toward open, green spaces.

After a brief but wonderful get-to-know-you period, the two of them had decided to get married. He'd suggested eloping. Cassie had had problems with that. First, she was a wedding planner, so she would have been setting a bad example. Who wanted a formal wedding planned by someone who didn't believe in them? Second, her mother would have pitched a hissy fit.

At thirty, Cassie had long since stopped trying to please her mother at every turn. But she could already hear her comments at every family gathering through the end of time: "This is my daughter, who didn't think enough of her family to have a wedding we could all attend," or some variation of that.

An image of Jonathan popped into her mind. He had been sweet and loving.

It had all been an act.

"Jerk. Jerk. Jerk!" she shouted as she roared down the street and turned onto a two-lane highway.

Subdivisions became scattered houses, then open fields with

single farmhouses and barns. She could feel her blood pressure dropping as tension melted away.

Then she remembered her morning, and it slammed into her again like a freight train.

~

She'd floated around her condo this morning and fixed her smoothie—the only thing she had felt like eating with the excitement of the day already filling her. Then her best friend Bella drove her and her dress to the church for the early afternoon wedding. Her mother had decided that the mother of the bride should arrive in a limo, but she'd conceded that the driver should return to take the newlyweds to the airport after the reception.

Her bridesmaids crowded around in their pink-confection dresses until her mother had cleared the room so "the bride could prepare." An updo by a hair stylist made her feel special compared to her usual ponytail. Then makeup by a professional had done wonders for the dark circles brought on by the usual nerves. Bella stayed to help her into her wedding gown.

The barely off-white dress suited her vibrant red hair, fair skin, and brown eyes much better than white had when she'd tried on Bella's sample dresses. Her friend's custom design had surprised her with its elegant simplicity. Cassie's mom had wanted a ball gown, but she'd been brought around to the fit-and-flare style her daughter had preferred.

The sheer sleeves gave it a sweet touch, and the beaded bodice with lace added the elegance. The bodice met satin at the waist, and the skirt flared out to the floor, where it had the same length all around instead of a train. And Bella had surprised her with a hidden pocket on each side, "in case you have essentials to carry." You had to love a friend who knew you that well.

That friend stood beside her at the mirror. "You look beautiful!"

Cassie stared into the mirror, and a vision in almost-white stared back. Though the woman didn't look like her, she did look great. Grinning, she spun, tottering on the ultra high heels.

"I'm so happy!"

Bella clapped her hands with glee. "I'm so happy for you. Just the smallest bit jealous, but still happy."

"I'd hug you, but I'd probably mess this up." One more glance in the mirror confirmed that she made a beautiful bride. "I wonder what Jonathan looks like in his tux."

"Girl, he looks good in jeans and a T-shirt. I'm sure he'll knock your socks off. And other things later tonight." She waggled her eyebrows.

"Stop that!" Cassie swatted at her friend's arm. So far, her plans for the day had gone well, but what if her groom was facing problems she didn't know about? The tux might not fit right or a button could have fallen off. She usually knew everything about a client's wedding down to the tiniest detail.

Her wedding-planner tote bag lay off to the side. It held everything she might need for a wedding and had saved her on too many occasions to count. It also had her phone tucked into a side pocket. "I think you're going to try to talk me out of my next idea." She pasted on her best smile. "Isabella—"

"Ooh, that smile and the use of my full first name means trouble is coming."

Cassie placed her hand on her chest in her best Scarlet O'Hara gesture. "Why, whatever do you mean?"

Bella fixed her eyes on her. "Just tell me what the idea is."

"I want to make sure Jonathan's tux fits and that there aren't any problems."

"The groom isn't supposed to see the bride before the wedding." Bella crossed her arms in defiance.

"I don't want him to see me. What if—and give this time to

sink in before answering—I pushed open the door to the groom's room, held up my phone, and snapped a photo without him knowing it?"

This time, her friend's expressive eyebrows shot upward. "That's just wrong. I'm not going to let you do that, Cassie."

"Why is it wrong? It isn't as though I won't see him in a matter of—" she pulled out her phone "—fifteen minutes, anyway."

Bella paced across the room, turned, and came back. After a moment's hesitation, she said, "I'm in."

When she started for the door, Cassie grabbed her tote bag and followed her.

Her friend put her arm out to stop her. "Why are you taking that? Leave that beast of a bag behind."

"No way. I may need to fix a crisis on my way from here to there and back."

Bella chuckled. "Always-Ready Cassie. Remember when the girls in college called you that?"

"At least they meant it in a nice way." Cassie glanced over her shoulder as she stepped into the vestibule toward the group of bridesmaids and groomsmen clustered to the side, talking.

Good. Jonathan should be alone. The groom's room was around the corner and had side access to the front of the church so he could reach it and be waiting for his bride when she walked down the aisle.

Carefully turning the old-fashioned doorknob, she felt the door move as it released. She slowly pushed it open a few inches, enough to hold up her phone in the opening, and scanned the room for her groom.

She found him to the left with one of her bridesmaids, a cousin he'd said was like a sister to him. He'd asked her to make Giselle part of the wedding. Cassie pushed the button to start recording a video and watched as his "sister" leaned closer and kissed him. Not a sweet, sisterly kiss, but a full-on kiss with heat behind it.

Jonathan laughed and wrapped his arms around Giselle, tugging her close. Then he leaned in, put his mouth on hers, and kissed her back deeply.

Cassie's heart stopped, and the phone slipped, but she sucked in a breath, caught the phone, and continued filming.

With Jonathan's arms still around Giselle, he leaned back and said, "You can't be caught here."

"One more." She moaned as she leaned in.

Jonathan stepped away. "We're so close to the finish line. I don't want to mess this up."

Giselle pouted.

"Remember her father's money."

At that, she smiled and kissed him on his cheek, then sashayed away with a swing in her hips. "Just remember the money tonight."

"I'll be thinking about it—and you—the whole time."

After Giselle blew Jonathan a kiss as she exited a door on the opposite side of the room, Jonathan checked his appearance in the mirror and smoothed his recently mussed hair while whistling a happy tune.

Anger surged through Cassie. He'd lied about everything. Nothing about their relationship was true.

She shoved her phone in her bag and raced for the door.

The motorcycle ate up the miles, and she got farther and farther away from the city, Jonathan, and everything associated with him. When a cow moseyed onto the road in front of her, she squealed to a stop. Unfortunately, the cow was in even less of a hurry than the old lady had been earlier.

When Bossy had crossed enough of the road to let Cassie

drive around her, Cassie gave a glance to the dashboard—or whatever it was called on a motorcycle—and saw that the gas tank was dangerously low. She was in the middle of nowhere, as far as gas stations went.

Mile after mile of farmland, pockets of trees, and charming farmhouses passed by, but nothing that resembled a town and modern conveniences. Finally, a green sign with the distance to a town appeared. She slowed to read it: *Two Hearts, 5 miles.*

She'd lost *her* heart, but it seemed they had a lot of love in the next town. She'd be okay if she could put gas in the tank, and surely any place big enough to warrant a highway sign would be big enough to have a gas station. She also hoped there would be someone who knew how to put gas in the tank because she didn't have a clue where the tank even was, let alone how much to put in.

The promised distance later, she slowed again and tilted her head to the side to read the words on the faded wooden sign that hung sideways: *Welcome to Two Hearts.* At least that's what she assumed the barely there words said based on the earlier sign.

The houses became closer and closer together, all of them fairly small and not showing a lot of signs of prosperity. The yards were often overgrown, the buildings covered with faded or peeling paint.

She slowed as a gas station appeared up ahead. Then she saw the boarded-up windows and *Closed* sign on the awning over the pumps. A few blocks later, a small grocery store with a single gas pump out front came into view. As she pulled in to the parking lot, the motorcycle sputtered once, then again, and died.

"Made it just in time." Cassie slid off the back of the motorcycle and tugged her wedding dress back to the ground, staggering on her heels after riding for so long. As she wheeled the bike over to the gas pump, she noticed that there wasn't a soul at the grocery store or anywhere in the parking lot. She checked her watch. Ten minutes after four on a Saturday.

The gas station should still be open, right? Standing in front of the lone pump, she discovered it was not. It turned out that her lack of knowledge about putting gas in the tank was irrelevant. This motorcycle had just become worthless. Worse than that, she needed to take care of it so she could return it to its owner.

Her grandmother had liked talking about the "good old days." Those had included the ability to knock on a stranger's door. They trusted you, would invite you inside, and would provide help if needed. Long before cell phones had brought roadside assistance to almost anywhere, people had relied on each other.

Cassie wasn't sure what she'd discover if she tried that here. She wasn't even sure where *here* was. Was she still in Tennessee? Had she crossed a state line?

She stared at the small store in front of her. No gas. No groceries? She was officially stuck in a small town in the middle-of-nowhere Tennessee. What had the sign said? *Two Hearts.* She wheeled the motorcycle behind the building and parked it out of sight.

Since she had to either sleep here or see what was up the road, she walked ahead. With every step, the high heels got more and more ridiculous. A motel sign came into focus. As she grew closer, she could see that the motel was one of those old-fashioned ones that had a main office and separate cottages. She'd seen one of these once in an old movie with Clark Gable and Claudette Colbert.

When she got close enough to actually see the front of the building, she felt like shouting with glee. A lit *Vacancy* sign in the window welcomed her. Surely no place would be closed if they had turned the sign on.

Cassie dragged her feet the short distance it took to get

inside. Then she took off her high heels and threw them in her tote bag, thankful her dress hid her feet. Her engagement ring sparkled in the sun. She tugged it off and tossed it in her bag, too. That wouldn't be needed again.

No one was at the desk, so she tapped the bell on the counter. *Please, please, please let someone be here.*

A woman's voice called from the back, "I'll be there in just a minute, Earl."

Less than a minute later, a dark-haired woman about Cassie's age stepped through the doorway and froze. "Oh, I'm sorry. I thought you were Earl Finnegan."

"No. I'm sorry I'm not the man you were hoping for."

The woman giggled. "I'm not sure Earl is the man anyone's hoping for." When she grinned, Cassie felt the first moment of lightness since she'd leaped over the church pew. Maybe this woman would be kind and able to help her.

"I guess I need a room for the night."

The woman cocked her head to the side. Speaking slowly, she said, "You're not sure?"

"I'm not sure about a lot of things right now. If there's any place to get gas—"

The woman shook her head. "There won't be anything open around here until Monday at 7:00 a.m."

Jonathan's boss would probably not be happy about having his motorcycle missing for two days—not that there was anything she could do about it. She didn't even have a way to contact the man. Monday might work out better for returning it, anyway, since she only had one parking space at her condo, and she could drive the bike directly to his office building. One piece of truth in their relationship was that she knew where Jonathan worked.

"Then I guess I need a room for two nights."

When the woman sucked in a breath and seemed to hesitate, Cassie said, "Please tell me you have a room, Ms. . . ."

"I'm Randi. And that's not it. Almost every room in the place is available. It's just that I have one room ready for Earl. I'm not sure how long it will take me to get another one ready." She shrugged. "Maybe he won't need it tonight. Why don't I put you in there, and I'll start cleaning another place in case he does stop by."

Why would a man *stop by* for a motel room? Was this a motel where people came for illicit affairs? Glancing around, she found the décor too attractive for the business to be that unsavory.

Either she was exhausted or this woman was confusing. Probably both. Cassie rubbed her eyes and leaned her elbows against the counter. "Anything is fine. I probably shouldn't bother asking this, but is there somewhere I can buy some clothes and other basics?"

The woman leaned over the counter and checked the floor around Cassie. "No luggage?" She asked in a tone that made it sound as if she were questioning Cassie's sanity at the same time Cassie was wondering about the other woman's.

"I left in a hurry. Don't worry. I'm not a wanted criminal." That was the truth. Well, nothing was *wanted* except her money, and it wasn't even hers yet. She wasn't even sure she would accept her inheritance. It would have been a surprise to Jonathan if he'd married her for the cash, and she'd turned her dad down when it had come time to give it to her.

Randi lifted a key off of a rack. "Follow me. You can park your vehicle in front of your unit."

"My vehicle is a motorcycle, and I parked behind the grocery store when there wasn't any way to put gas in it."

The hotel clerk stopped and turned around. "You pushed it down the road and into the gas station?"

"No. I actually ran out of gas as I pulled in."

"This is your lucky day!" The woman continued walking as Cassie stood there.

Lucky day? Make that worst. Day. Ever.

They walked past several buildings, all in good repair, and then the woman stopped in front of one. Randi opened the door to the cottage, and Cassie was immediately charmed by what she saw. It felt like she'd stepped back into that 1940s movie. All the furniture was vintage and in great shape—probably because early owners had bought it new for the motel. There was even a small kitchenette in the corner. She peered into another room and found a tiny bathroom with a shower.

"This is quite nice."

Randi beamed. "I've tried to do what I could with the place. I put on new roofs last summer."

"New roofs? By yourself?"

The woman waved her hand in front of her face. "Of course not."

Cassie envisioned a team of roofers.

"My brother helped me some."

Cassie stared at her, dumbfounded. What strange place had she come to?

"There isn't any food in the fridge, of course. And as you saw, the grocery store is closed."

"That's okay. I can just go out to dinner to get a bite to eat if there's something within walking distance."

The woman didn't dispute that option by saying nothing was open, so Cassie's hopes rose for a decent meal.

"As to your other question: there's nowhere good to shop in this town and nothing open over the weekend. We have a consignment store that's open three days a week. The next one of those won't be until Wednesday." She stared at her. "You can't exactly walk around in that, though, can you." Her words came out as a statement, not a question. Randi stared a little longer before saying in an exasperated tone, "I'm sorry. I just have to ask. Is that a wedding dress you're wearing?"

Cassie shrugged. "It is. I was supposed to get married this

morning." The sadness of the situation caught up with her for the first time, maybe because she was tired now and the anger had held it at bay. "It didn't go as planned."

She could tell that this woman wanted to ask more. Who wouldn't? "By the way, what state is this?"

After an odd look that Cassie couldn't quite put her finger on, Randi answered, "Tennessee. Where did you think this was?"

"I honestly couldn't remember if I'd seen a sign saying I'd entered Kentucky or if I'd driven south and gone to Alabama."

"You didn't have any idea where you were driving?" The woman seemed to be shutting down and putting up barriers against what seemed like an unstable woman not only in her presence but in her motel.

"If you knew the morning I'd had, that would not seem so strange."

Moments later, Cassie watched the door close behind her landlord. Two Hearts seemed to be less than happy right now.

She had a room so she was safe. She couldn't beg Bella to drive here because she was busy. A rideshare or taxi would be ridiculously expensive and leave her alone with a stranger in sparsely populated countryside, which didn't sound wise.

Unless there was a surprise solution to the gasless motorcycle, which she didn't feel like she could abandon, Two Hearts would be her temporary residence.

She was stuck here for days.

# CHAPTER TWO

*P*lopping onto the one comfortable-looking chair—the other two chairs were metal and tucked up to a tiny table—Cassie took in her surroundings. Really looked at them for the first time.

The room had a decidedly masculine feel to it, but that made sense as Earl, whoever he was, often stayed here. A blue-plaid bedspread reminded her of visiting her grandma in the summer as a child. This chair, covered in beige fake leather, and the kitchenette, with its ancient sink and old-fashioned white cabinets that looked from here to be metal, all said her *great*-grandmother may have stayed here and used them.

This was the middle of nowhere for a city girl, but at least everything in the room sparkled with cleanliness.

Cassie wriggled her toes. Standing, she felt the blisters yet to come. Instead of walking anywhere, she lay back on the bed and pulled her cell phone out of her tote bag.

Her finger hovered over her mother's number, then called Bella instead. Mother Van Bibber wouldn't say anything she wanted to hear right now. She'd probably be incomprehensible as she sputtered on about the emotional distress and shame Cassie had heaped on her.

Her friend didn't even say hello. "Cassie! Are you all right?"

She looked around her temporary lodgings. "I'm safe, if that's what you mean."

"Safe as in 'inside your Nashville condo and you're just not answering the door'? Because I went there."

Laughter that sounded more than a little crazy bubbled up inside her. "I'm so far from my condo."

"Your mother and Jonathan's brother told everyone you'd driven off on a motorcycle. Jonathan is beside himself with grief."

Anger returned. She preferred that to being sad.

"He's claiming he's the injured party?" She jumped to her feet, instantly regretted that move, and sat on the edge of the bed. "You saw what happened, right?"

Bella paused. "I saw your face go from bridal bliss to anger."

Flopping backward, Cassie stared at the ceiling as the morning replayed itself. She saw the kiss, but no one would believe her.

"Wait! I have video!" She found the file and forwarded it to Bella. "Watch that."

"Got it." Her friend was silent for a few seconds. "Why was his cousin in there? Wait! She's coming on to him. If this is what upset you, I'm not worried, because he loves you." A growling sound was followed by, "She's kissing him. No, Jonathan is kissing *her*. He's pouring heat into it. Cassie, this doesn't look like it's their first kiss. This is crazy. *He's* crazy, and—"

"Wait until you hear their conversation," Cassie interrupted.

"There's more? Oh, no!"

She fell silent. Cassie could barely make out the garbled sound of recorded voices over the phone.

"He's marrying you for money?"

"It seems so. The thing about the family money is that Dad is young enough still that I'm not inheriting anytime soon. On top of that, I don't know if I even want his business. Why would a woman who is happy running her own wedding planning business choose to give it up and take over operations of a grocery store chain?"

"I know Jonathan works for a company your father's chain does business with, right?"

"That's how I met him. He was the new guy in the advertising company Dad's business used, and was invited to a couple of functions I also attended. We fell head over heels in love. He was supposed to start working for Dad in the Nashville office when we returned from Bali, probably so he could secure his position in line for CEO."

"You said all of that with a strangely matter-of-fact tone."

Cassie thought over her words. They'd been delivered without tears or emotion. "I should be sobbing, shouldn't I?"

"Yes. You should be the one who's heartbroken. Jonathan's getting his emotions—and other things—soothed by Giselle, who I assume is *not* his cousin."

She hadn't considered that. "I would agree. I was set up on every level." In a lower voice, she asked, "Why aren't I upset?"

Bella said, "Don't be sad about not being sad. Why don't I bring over ice cream tonight? We can binge eat until we get brain freeze."

Cassie laughed. "While that is appealing, remember that motorcycle?"

"How could I erase the image of you in a wedding dress trying to get onto the thing?"

Cassie laughed in spite of her angst. "I rode it until it ran out of gas."

"I can still bring the ice cream. Where are you—Springhill, Franklin, White House?"

"Two Hearts."

"Two what?"

"The sign as I entered said 'Two Hearts.' Of course, it was broken and hanging sideways, so I could have misread it."

"Where is that?"

"I'm here, and I'm not even sure. I know it's in Tennessee."

"Since I can drive for hours to the east or west and still be in Tennessee, that doesn't help. What part of the state are you in?"

Cassie sighed. "I honestly don't know. Country roads calm me down, so I drove down them until I ended up here."

Her level-headed friend groaned. "Bring up a map on your phone."

Cassie felt like slapping her forehead in frustration. "That didn't even occur to me. And it doesn't surprise me, with the day I've had." Her GPS showed a map with a dot for her location. "Yes, it's Two Hearts, Tennessee. I'm quite a few miles west of Nashville."

"I guess I won't be bringing you ice cream."

Her mouth watered at the thought of the creamy treat, and she realized she hadn't eaten since her breakfast smoothie. "You've made me hungry. I'm going to find a store and get some ice cream."

As Bella said, "Good plan," Cassie remembered she'd parked the motorcycle behind a *closed* grocery store. There was no question that she needed to freshen up after miles of country roads before she went out to eat. Holding the phone to her ear, she went toward the bathroom.

"This small town closes up on the weekend. I'd better find a restaurant before it's too late tonight." She entered the bathroom and screamed.

"Cassie!" A sound like someone slamming a door came through the phone. "Find your address."

The bathroom mirror reflected a woman with wild hair, specks of something on her face—*please tell me those aren't bugs!*—and a wrinkled off-white wedding dress. Cassie heard another door slam in the phone at her ear.

"I'm okay, Bella! I just saw myself in the mirror." She laughed self-consciously. "I'm glad no one—"

"Don't scare me like that again. I'm already in my car with the key in the ignition."

"Sorry." She plucked at her hair. "I now understand why the motel clerk first treated me like I might be an escapee from an institution."

Bella chuckled.

"Hey, it's not funny. She spoke slowly, like I needed to take time to absorb her words."

Now her friend laughed out loud.

Cassie ran back to the bed and reached for her tote bag. "I'm going to have to fix this before I go anywhere. I'll talk to you later, Bella."

"Call your mother. And let me know if you need anything."

She considered asking for clothes, but she could survive for two days. Bella had her own business to take care of.

As for contacting her mother, she'd wait until she had some food in her system. Nobody should talk to Sandra Van Bibber when they were at less than full strength.

A quick shower washed whatever that was off her face—she shuddered as she considered the options—and brought her hair back to normal. She twisted it into a messy bun secured with a hair tie from her bag.

That same bag had clean underwear and stockings in multiple sizes—she never knew when a client would need the correct pair of undergarments for her gown or have to replace snagged stockings—so she put on the first and left her legs bare. Enough makeup in different shades to stock a small store allowed her to apply mascara to her blonde lashes and gloss to her lips.

The dress couldn't be changed. As she rooted through the tote bag searching for spot remover, she found foldable ballet slippers in her size. She'd put them in there a year ago but hadn't needed them. They would have been removed the next time she'd done a review of her bag, but she was glad that hadn't happened yet.

When Cassie passed the main building on her way out of the motel complex, she considered stopping for directions. She decided there was no point since she saw one road and had already been to the right.

About five minutes up the road, lovely and tree-lined here with somewhat larger but equally neglected buildings, a downtown area began with Victorian era or earlier buildings lining both sides of the road. Some buildings were one-story, some two, and most had large display windows to show the goods inside.

Or would have, if there were any. The first few stores were closed. She would have expected nothing else on a weekend. As she walked, though, she realized that the businesses weren't simply closed for the day; they were shuttered. Some stores she passed had windows covered with sheets of plywood; others had windows with what must be years of dust and grime on them.

The scent of what she hoped was fried chicken grew stronger, and she spotted Dinah's Place. The restaurant's windows were spotless. Looking through the glass door, she saw a small room packed with people. When she opened the door, conversation stopped. Strangers must not come here often.

Then she remembered the wedding dress, which was now rumpled and dragged on the ground because her four-inch-high heels had been traded for flats. She smiled in spite of the awkwardness, hoping to seem less like a criminal ready for a dangerous rampage but probably just looking like a happily crazed one.

An empty table to the left caught her eye as a twenty-something woman, wearing a pink T-shirt, jeans, and a name badge that read *Michelle,* approached her.

"Can I help you?" she asked in a stern voice.

Several men watched them, seeming ready to come to her rescue. The waitress's, not Cassie's.

Since it was obvious she'd come to a restaurant to eat, Cassie wondered just how almost-ready-for-a-serial-killer-movie she looked. "The restaurant smells wonderful. Could I have that table, please?" She used the friendly voice that worked miracles with distraught brides.

Michelle's shoulders relaxed a notch. "Sure." She headed that direction. "The special is fried chicken. Dinah serves it with mashed potatoes and gravy, and a choice of either broccoli or green beans." Michelle leaned closer. "I'd choose the green beans."

"That sounds perfect. And I'd like sweet tea, if you have it."

"We'd have a mutiny if we ran out of sweet tea." Michelle wrote the order on a small pad, gave a nod, and returned to the back.

After a minute or two of her sitting quietly with no unruly behavior, normal sounds of forks clinking on plates joined by voices rising in conversation filled the room. It wasn't long before Michelle returned with a plate piled high with food.

Crispy-on-the-outside, moist-on-the-inside fried chicken, mashed potatoes that must have been homemade, and country green beans with bacon were accompanied by a fluffy biscuit. She may have had a rough start to her day, but dinner helped soften the blow.

She usually stayed away from dessert, but today called for something sweet. Wedding cake had been on her original menu. Had someone taken cake home—a lot of cake—or had they thrown it away? Between the cake, the flowers, the sit-down dinner, and everything else, she'd left a big mess for someone to take care of.

Her mother didn't handle those situations well. Maybe Bella or a bridesmaid had helped. She'd have to call the church Monday morning to make sure it was all as it should be.

Michelle came back to remove her empty plate. "Would you like dessert?" She motioned toward glass-covered desserts. "We have apple or pecan pie and red velvet cake today."

Cassie's mouth watered. By the time she set down her fork, she should have been stuffed, but between missing lunch and her walks, she still had room for dessert. "I'll have a slice of apple pie."

"Whipped cream or *á la mode*?" Michelle's southern accent softened the foreign words.

"Ice cream, please." There. She could tell Bella she'd soothed her sorrows with ice cream, after all.

The homemade pie filled an empty place. Her grandmother had made apple pie every time Cassie had visited her. After, they'd sit on the front porch of her small-town Alabama home and watch the townspeople walk by, sipping sweet tea and talking. She missed those days. What would Grandma have said about today?

Probably something like, "Honey, you made a clean escape. Choose more wisely next time."

A law enforcement officer entered the diner as Cassie stood to leave after paying her check. Handsome didn't begin to describe the chiseled features, dark brown hair, and blue eyes over his fit body.

She moved to walk around him when he reached out his arm to prevent her.

"I like to introduce myself to everyone new here."

She bit back a response that even her tired self knew wouldn't have endeared her to the people in the room. She may not like his high-handedness, but that did make sense for someone doing his job in a small town. "Cassandra Van Bibber. Cassie."

He gave a single nod to acknowledge her words, then said, "Sheriff Brantley. It might be easier if we spoke outside."

Cassie was about to argue that point when she realized that not only were all eyes on them, but every ear must be listening. "Sure." She followed him out the door to the sidewalk.

He looked her up and down. "I have received multiple reports about a woman in a wedding dress. I didn't believe the first one. After a few, I started to wonder."

"I'm sure they all said that woman was law-abiding." Cassie crossed her arms. With the day she'd had, she wasn't going to take much from him or anyone.

"Are you part of a publicity stunt?" He glanced around as though expecting to find a camera crew behind a tree.

She rolled her eyes. "I can assure you I'm alone." *Very* alone.

He hesitated. "Then why?" He waved his hand up and down to encompass her dress.

"Why do women wear wedding dresses?"

At his puzzled expression, her rating of his intelligence went down.

"Weddings." *Yes, she was playing with fire. That was better than admitting that she, oftentimes wedding planner to music stars, Cassie Van Bibber, had ditched her groom seconds before the altar.*

"But you said you're alone?" His confusion seemed to be shifting to annoyance.

"I'm a runaway bride. Okay?" There, she'd said it.

A grin spread over his face. When the smile grew, a dimple appeared in his left cheek. "So, you, uh, ran from a church in a nearby town?"

"Nashville."

His eyes widened. "That's a long way to run. That also doesn't make sense, because my reports said you walked here." He gestured toward the restaurant. "You apparently don't have a car, and buses don't pass through town. Not anymore."

"My motorcycle ran out of gas when I rode into town."

This time he laughed. "I'm sorry, but the thought of you in that dress riding a motorcycle is ludicrous." He glanced around as if checking again for cameras. "Could I see your identification?"

She'd had enough. Her legs were stiff and sore. She just wanted to go back to her charming motel room to lick her wounds. She bit out the word, "Sure." When she shoved her hand in her bag, he snapped back into officer mode.

His hand moved to the pistol in the belt on his hip. "I'd like to check your bag first."

She thrust it at him. "Fine. I've had the worst day of my life." She silently added, *And law enforcement apparently thinks I'm a criminal with a concealed weapon.* Not unless the needle in the sewing kit counted. "My license is in the wallet."

After looking through her purse, he handed it back to her. "You can find it now."

Seconds later, she held up the plastic card with its super-bad photo.

"How long will you be in town?"

"Until Monday morning, when I can buy gas and ride out of here."

"Where are you staying?" He asked that like she'd planned to camp in his backyard.

"A motel." What was the name of it?

He muttered something about Randi not finding it worth mentioning she had a guest in a wedding dress.

Maybe she'd found a new friend in the motel clerk.

"You're free to go."

"Well, thank you, sir." She gave him a salute.

As she marched away, he added, "Dinah's closed on Sundays."

She froze with one ballet-slippered foot in the air. "Is there another—"

"It's the only restaurant in town. We used to have more." He shrugged.

Instead of returning to her sanctuary, she spun around in a turn worthy of the ballet slippers, with just a slight wince from her sore feet, and went back toward the diner. "I'll get something that will keep in the fridge. Is she open for breakfast Monday morning?"

"That she is."

Ten minutes later, Cassie once again left the restaurant, this time carrying a bag with a scrambled egg breakfast wrap that Michelle had assured her would heat well in the microwave for breakfast, and a ham and cheese sandwich for tomorrow's lunch.

The officer was leaning against his car door, scanning his phone, when she went back out. He straightened when he saw her. "I noticed you wincing when you walked. Can I give you a ride?"

She desperately wanted to tell him no and never see him again. But he was right. Swallowing her pride, she said, "Yes, please."

He held the passenger door open for her, and Cassie slid inside. A laptop rested on a stand between her seat and the driver's. An odor she didn't want to identify perfumed the inside of the vehicle.

When he pulled away, he said, "Sorry about the smell."

Her nose twitched as she tried for small breaths that didn't pull in too much air. A criminal must have had incontinence issues.

"My grandfather's golden retriever puppy . . ."

"I bet she's cute."

"He. George. Yep, he's cute, and he's going to get the hang of going where he's supposed to very soon."

She laughed, instantly regretting the swift intake of air. Would she smell like this car when she got out? She'd have to spend the next day in a poop-scented dress. When they pulled into the motel's parking lot, she pointed toward her unit.

He parked in front of it. "Earl's place?"

"This weekend, it's Cassie's place." She reached for the door latch.

"Ms. Van Bibber, I called the motel clerk while you were in Dinah's. She said you arrived with what you're wearing, that oversized purse, and nothing else."

"Correct."

He shook his head. "You didn't have time—"

She leaned toward him. "No. The bridal march was about to begin." She held up her hand when he started to speak again. "Jonathan cheated on me, and I found out with seconds to spare. Now, if that's all, I'm tired, and I'm going in there." She pointed toward her unit.

With a shrug, he said, "I hope you enjoy your time in Two Hearts."

Laughing, she said, "I've run from my wedding, ridden across Tennessee on a motorcycle, run out of gas . . . My day has to get better. There's only up from here." Cassie opened her car door, getting a whiff of fresh air. Turning back to him, she said, "Oh, and you may have found a way to stop crime here."

He raised one eyebrow. "And how would I do that?"

"Release any criminals who have ridden in your poop-mobile. Word will quickly get around that it's disgusting. Crime will stop because no one wants to ride in it."

His startled laughter made her happy inside. "I've already bought the carpet cleaner, and it will soon be back to normal." He shook his head with mock sadness. "Our crime wave will continue."

His words, said in jest, sent a prickle of fear through her. "Do you have a lot of crime?"

"Last week, Mrs. Martinez's Chihuahua chased Mr. Kelly's Doberman. I had to separate the owners, who were nearly coming to blows, and by the time I'd done that, the dogs were side by side and friends."

"No murder, mayhem, drugs?"

He hesitated. "No." She thought he murmured, "Not yet, anyway." He handed her a business card. "If you run into any trouble here, which I doubt, this is the emergency number."

Why would he expect crime to rise?

She tucked the card in her bag, then stepped out, closed the door, and walked gingerly on her sore feet to the door. His car might have smelled nasty, but he had saved her another walk.

At about dinnertime, he received a call from his mother. He hit the button so he could hear it through the car's speakers.

She opened with, "Greg, did you know there's a woman in a wedding dress walking around the town?" Her tone implied the woman was unstable.

"Yes, Mom. I went over to talk to her when Dinah called me from the restaurant."

His mother gasped. "Are you saying you did not give me first dibs on the most interesting thing to happen in this town in the last year?"

He chuckled.

"Did you arrest her?"

"Of course not! She hasn't broken any laws." He turned in the direction of his mother's house.

Her voice dropped a notch and became more serious. "Son, the woman is wearing a wedding dress."

"Mom, she's clothed. You can't arrest a woman for wearing clothing you don't like or approve of."

"Now you know that's not what I meant."

He pulled up the driveway. "I'm here now. If you've got a pot of coffee on, I would appreciate a cup."

"I'm on it."

Walking up the drive, he passed his apartment, which sat directly above his mother's garage. His parents had finished off the until-then empty space for his sister and her new husband several years ago, and they'd long since moved to another state. After a decade in the Chicago Police Department, he'd moved home and somehow fallen into living next to his mother. She was sweet. He loved her very much. But a man in his thirties should be living on his own.

She greeted him at the back door. "Tell me about her." Rushing to the table, she pulled a chair back, pointed to it, and he sat. She seated herself across from him and leaned forward.

"She's very nice. She has red hair. Not a bright-orange red— a little bit darker."

"That's it? You can't give me any more? What did you do, say three words to the woman?"

"Mom, I'm a police officer. I can't go into all the details, and you know that."

The black liquid pouring out of the coffee maker gurgled to a stop, and she went to get him a cup. "You must admit that she's the most interesting thing to happen for a while." She set the mug in front of him and took her seat again.

"I can share a bit more. I'm not telling you anything that everyone at the diner didn't hear. Her name is Cassie. And she's a runaway bride."

His mother jumped to her feet, and her chair flung backward. "You kept that from me? That easily makes this *the* most interesting thing to happen in Two Hearts in at least the last *five* years."

He chuckled. "I wasn't here for most of that time, but from what I've seen of the records Dad kept, I can only assume you're correct."

He got up and righted her chair. Then they both sat again.

"I don't know why she ran away. That's her business." He gave his mother a stern look.

She raised her hands in defeat. "Don't worry. I'm not going to track her down and ask."

"I do know she rode a motorcycle into town and ran out of gas. She's stuck here until Monday when Herb opens the gas station."

His mother muttered, "Because you know that man leaves town every Saturday night to spend Sunday in his cabin on the lake."

"Exactly. So she's at the motel."

"I may need to go over to the diner Monday morning to meet her. Even without that wedding dress, I would still pick out a new woman with red hair."

He shrugged. "She came without luggage. Whatever made her run from her wedding had her running fast." He kept the cheating to himself.

Different expressions chased each other across his mother's face before realization hit. "Are you telling me that this young woman—because I am assuming she is young—has nothing but the clothes on her back?"

He gave a single nod. "I am. It also looked like it had picked up grime of an unknown source as she rode here."

"Yuck. Would Tracy's things fit her?"

Greg thought about his sister compared to Cassie. He had to smile when he pictured her wearing something from his casual sister's wardrobe instead of that dress. She would be beautiful in anything.

"Well?"

His mother's voice pulled him out of his reverie. "I think she's taller, but she's about the same build as Tracy."

"Before or after she had the second baby?"

"Before. But knowing my sister, she'll be out running a marathon as soon as she can and be back to her usual size not long after that. What does it matter, Mom, if she can wear my sister's clothing? Tracy lives in Kansas."

"She left some clothes here the last time they came. I think there's a pair of jeans in the closet. They aren't the newest, but I know I washed everything up. I planned to give it back to her the next time she came." His mother left and returned with a pair of jeans and a purple T-shirt, which she dropped on the table. "Let me grab one of my sleep shirts, too."

When Greg left, he had a paper bag loaded with the clothes and had walked away with his mother's final words ringing in his ears, "Find out anything you can. This woman is interesting." Less than a minute later, she called to him. "Greg, wait!" He turned around to face her. "The restaurant and grocery store are both closed tomorrow."

"If you're asking about her needs, she bought extra food from the diner."

His mother shook her head so hard that her curls bobbed. "It would be rude not to invite that poor woman here for a meal. And I'm not saying this because I want to dig into the woman's private life. I'm a good Southern woman, so I'm going to feed a guest to my town. Tell her you'll pick her up about four tomorrow. I'll make sure I have enough food for a Sunday dinner for the three of us."

He chuckled as he walked to his car. His mother hadn't made a meal small enough to feed only three at any occasion he could remember in his life.

# CHAPTER THREE

*A*s she settled back into her room, Cassie realized that bugs and perspiration from her ride had made this dress—and her—feel grimy, even after her shower. It was probably a good thing the officer's car had smelled bad because otherwise he'd have noticed this in close quarters.

But a wedding dress probably wouldn't survive soap and water. Besides, what would she wear while it dried? She was stuck with it for now.

She'd call her mother now, because it was the right thing to do. Avoiding what she expected to be yet one more unpleasant addition to her day hadn't erased the task. Sitting on the one comfortable chair, she hit her mother's number. Cassie knew she wouldn't look to see who it was before answering.

"Mother, it's Cassie."

Her mother screamed; this one had a bloodcurdling pitch to it that would have had Bella calling 911 instead of running to her car to help.

"I'm fine," Cassie said. The drama would be more about Sandra's feelings than her daughter's well-being.

"You broke that sweet boy's heart." Cassie's scoffing sound

was met with, "I don't understand you. It was a perfectly nice wedding to a boy from a good family. Why did you run away?"

Her mother sighed in a way that Cassie thought might be concern for her daughter. They never talked about personal situations, so how should she handle this?

The truth won out.

"Mother, Jonathan cheated on me."

"Cassie, men sometimes look elsewhere, but that's just their way."

She hoped her father wasn't one of those men.

"Come home and all will be forgiven."

Forgiven? Her or Jonathan? She sent the video to her mother.

"What's this?"

"Watch it. And don't worry about me. I'm resting in a small town outside the city."

"I hit play." Seconds later, a scream much louder than the first one came through the phone as Cassie ended the call. That should keep her mother from singing her former groom's praises for a while.

Never one for naps, she stretched out on the bed, hoping for healing sleep. Staring up at the ceiling, she wondered if she *could* sleep after everything had raised her adrenaline levels.

Cassie jumped when a knock sounded on her door. Blinking, she glanced around the room. The pieces fell into place as she remembered where she was. Two Hearts. She had managed to doze off.

Another knock had her fully awake. She plodded over to the door and didn't see a peephole—the building must be from before they were common—so she pulled the curtain aside on the window beside the door.

Officer Handsome was outside with a stuffed paper bag. He was raising his hand to knock again when she opened the door.

"I was starting to get concerned."

She closed her eyes and slowly opened them. "I fell asleep. I wasn't expecting visitors."

He handed her the paper bag.

She reached in and dug through the layers to see a pair of pants, a T-shirt, and a nightgown. "That was thoughtful of you!" She pulled at the neckline of her dress. "I never planned to wear this as athletic gear."

He shifted on his feet. "I stopped by Mom's house. It didn't take long before she asked about the woman in the wedding dress."

Cassie felt her face grow heated. "Did you tell her you'd seen her in person?"

"Since it wasn't part of a case, I gave her details. She launched into me when she learned the 'poor woman' was here without luggage or a change of clothes." He shook his head as though to clear the incident from his mind. "When Mom isn't happy . . . whew!"

"Please thank her for me."

He rolled his eyes. "You can thank her yourself."

She peered around him, expecting to find a woman twice his age in his car, but it was empty.

"When I told her where I'd met you—"

She grinned. "You also told her I had to buy more food." She pointed to her refrigerator. "I have enough. You can tell her I'll be fine."

His eyes sparkled. "You aren't from the South, are you?"

"Indianapolis, Indiana. But my mother is from a small town outside of Atlanta, Georgia. She says I've lived in Tennessee so long that I'm Southern now too."

"Interesting." He clearly wanted to ask about that, but instead said, "Mom loves to cook for people. She invited you to Sunday dinner." He brushed his hands together as though saying it was done. "There's no getting out of it. At least, no polite way to do that." He tilted his head to the side, perhaps waiting for her to try.

It wasn't enough that she was at this town's mercy for gas. Now she had to accept a dinner invitation from a stranger. Well, she'd entertained many strangers in her role as a wedding planner. This would just be one more event. The strange Nashville woman in the wedding dress would probably be the talk of this small town for the next week.

She blew out a breath. "Fine. What time should I be ready?"

He grinned. "Wise decision. Mom said to pick you up at four o'clock."

"That's an early dinner time."

"It would be *if* we ate dinner then. We don't get many strangers, so I think she just wants to visit with you."

Eating would be easy. Making conversation with the small-town sheriff's mother sounded more challenging. But she didn't want to be rude, especially to someone who had sent over clean clothes, and a homemade dinner sounded better than something she'd reheat. "I'll see you then."

He touched the brim of his hat and gave a nod, turned, and left. The good officer stirred up emotions she didn't want to have just hours after she'd run from her fiancé. Yes, he was handsome. But he was also kind to his mother and cared about this town, qualities she found endearing. She watched his car slowly drive through the motel complex, turn left, and leave.

Stepping back, she closed and locked the door. It had been lonely being in this room alone, and she honestly hadn't been looking forward to a whole day of her own miserable company, so maybe this would be a good thing. Besides, she'd get one more look at the sheriff before she drove out of town.

When she checked the bag, she discovered that the sheriff's mother had a fun streak. The jeans looked a little too big at the waist and weren't as long as she'd have liked, but the T-shirt in a vivid purple made her smile—and actually went with her red hair—and the mid-thigh-length, oversized, pink sleep shirt had the words *Sleep, Sleep, Counting Sheep* on it. The fresh scent of everything stood out sharply next to the dress she'd worn through so much.

Stretched out in bed in the nightwear, she opened a book on her phone and tried to read, but her mind kept shifting back and forth from Jonathan and Giselle's passionate kiss to the sheriff's twinkling blue eyes. Neither image helped her relax. She realized that the officer hadn't even given her his first name. One more oddity in this day.

Taking a deep breath, she tried counting sheep as the shirt instructed. By the fifteenth woolly animal, she did feel a little sleepy.

A rattling sound woke her. The light next to the bed illuminated the room. The rattling sound came again. This time, she thought the doorknob jiggled. Cassie turned off the light and tiptoed over. Peering out the pushed-aside curtain, she gulped when she saw a large man on the step trying to get into her room.

She stepped away from the door. The doorknob twisted back and forth. Even in the dark, she knew the good-sized window to the left of the bed and the small ones on the right and in the bathroom were her only exits.

If she were in the city, she'd call the police. Cassie pulled out her phone and the business card the sheriff had given her back when she'd never expected to need it. She dialed and waited. At three rings, she considered hanging up and trying the window.

"Sheriff Brantley," a sleepy voice said.

"This is Cassie Van Bibber," she whispered.

"Please speak louder."

She went into the bathroom and closed the door. "This is Cassie Van Bibber," she repeated. When he didn't respond, she added, "The woman in the wedding dress."

"Yes? What can I help you with?" His voice clearly meant, *in the middle of the night.*

"A man is trying to break into my unit."

"I'm on my way."

She heard a siren and saw flashing lights five minutes later. God bless the short distances of small towns. The car stopped, and she waited to hear shouting or even gunshots. Instead, she heard calm conversation outside her door. Whose side was he on?

A firm knock sounded, and a voice near the door said, "Cassie?"

Should she open it?

"It's Sheriff Brantley, and it's safe now."

She unlocked the door and slowly opened it. The sheriff was standing on her step, and the man she'd seen was standing with one hand on the sheriff's car as though he needed the support or he'd fall.

"Earl and his wife had an argument. It was late, so he thought he'd let himself into the unit he always uses. Unfortunately, he stopped at a buddy's place for a couple of drinks first and seemed to lose any of the good sense he'd been born with." The sheriff glared at the other man, who swayed and seemed unconcerned.

Her heart rate started slowing back to its normal, steady pace.

"Do you want to press charges? He did try to break and enter." He pursed his lips as he waited for her reply.

"No. Just make sure he won't be back tonight."

He sighed. "Thank you. That's my plan."

When he opened the door to the backseat for Earl, the other man said, "What did you do in there, Greg?"

Cassie laughed as she closed the door. She finally knew the sheriff's first name.

With the door bolted, she crawled back under the covers. A sound outside made her clench up. Then she realized it was a truck on the highway. A few seconds later, she turned the lamp on. Maybe that would make this unknown place better. When an owl hooted and her heart raced, she got up and pushed a small table in front of the door.

What felt like a short time later, Cassie stretched and sat up. Sunlight poured through the side window onto the bed. She checked her watch and was startled to see it was nine o'clock. She hadn't slept so late in years. Even when she worked late-evening weddings, she always had to be up early to make sure all the pieces of the wedding breakdown were done.

But yesterday morning, last night, and everything in between had worn her out, and she'd finally slept soundly. A new sense of energy rushed through her.

She took a moment to give thanks for her narrow escape from marriage to Jonathan. A twinge of sadness tried to wiggle its way in, but she ruthlessly shoved it away. He'd already hurt her enough without her wallowing in it. She needed to find something to focus on to take her mind off the wedding fiasco.

Her sore leg muscles reminded her that she didn't usually spend hours on a motorcycle. Moving slowly, she stood, then regretted that for a moment as she also recalled the heels she'd walked in.

After a shower, she put on fresh underwear and her borrowed clothes. His mother had to be a good three inches shorter than she was, but once she tied a cord around the waist for a belt, her borrowed jeans, now pedal pushers, were fine. With the T-shirt and her ballet slippers, she actually looked presentable. The warm shower had helped her sore muscles and even her feet.

She heated her breakfast burrito and sat at the table to eat it. Then she checked the time. The day loomed in front of her, offering *nothing* to do. Until the dinner she'd rather miss.

But not.

A homemade meal sounded wonderful, and she had to admit that sitting across the table from the handsome sheriff wouldn't be a hardship. She may as well get her fill of that while she was here. The odds that she would ever set foot in Two Hearts again were slim. And she wanted to thank the woman who'd provided the clothes.

Grabbing her bag, she went outside, carefully locked the door behind her, and walked toward town. The spring sunshine felt warm, but in a pleasant way with no burn and low humidity —unlike in the summer.

This time, when she passed the buildings on the main street, she paid more attention. It seemed that every business had been permanently shuttered, with the exception of the sometimes-open consignment shop. She reached the end of the row of buildings, went by the now-closed Dinah's Place, and continued. A white steeple up ahead marked a church. By the time she reached it, people were leaving the building, some stopping to visit outside.

The building itself was a charming white clapboard with stained-glass windows and red brick steps leading up to double doors. Tulips in pink, white, and purple, along with yellow daffodils, bloomed beside the steps and around the sides of the building. The town may have been down on its luck, but the church looked well cared for.

As she stepped nearer, she noticed that the paint could use a touchup. Maybe the problems hadn't left the building unscathed.

A woman waved at her. When Cassie focused on her, she motioned for her to come over. As she moved closer, she still couldn't figure out if she was supposed to know her. Then she realized it was Michelle, her waitress yesterday. She stood with a group of five other ladies.

Michelle asked, "Are you enjoying your visit to Two Hearts?"

She had such a positive tone to her question that Cassie wasn't sure what to say about the depressing town, so she said the first thing that came to mind.

"It's a gorgeous day. And the flowers around the church are so pretty." There, she'd come up with *two* good things to say.

"We have so few visitors." When Michelle sighed, the others in her circle joined her. It was as though Two Hearts had exhaled.

"Not anymore," a woman about Cassie's mother's age muttered.

"Those were the days." Cassie recognized the speaker as the motel clerk.

Did she dare ask what had happened? When everyone seemed lost in thought, she decided she had nothing to lose. She'd be rolling out of here bright and early tomorrow, anyway.

"Why is the town struggling?"

"Our hot spring dried up. Poof! One day it was there, the next day it was gone. Any tourist traffic we had ended."

"Businesses closed."

"The elementary school couldn't stay open once that many families moved away."

Another sigh went up from the circle of women.

Cassie wished she'd kept her mouth shut. "Maybe things will improve." She put as much hope in her voice as she could, even though it sounded like Two Hearts was a dying town.

"Ha!" the motel clerk, Randi, said with such force that Cassie took a step back. "I've expected things to turn around for a decade." She stared at the ground and ran the toe of her shoe through the dirt.

"We can still hope," Michelle said in a barely audible voice.

The raw emotion startled Cassie. "When did the spring dry up?"

One of the older women answered. "We first noticed changes about twenty or thirty years ago, then it faded away."

"There aren't many jobs here." Michelle said the words flatly, without question.

"Have you considered moving closer to the city?"

All eyes turned toward her.

"This is our home. Would you leave your home?"

Cassie's answer was that she would and had, but she didn't think that information would be appreciated.

"Most of the residents work in a town close to an hour away."

One of the older women said, "It looks like my Charlie is wrapping up his conversation. I'll see you ladies next week, if not sooner." Her leaving seemed to signal to the others that it was time to go. Cassie was soon left with only the hotel clerk.

"I just realized that you're wearing something other than a wedding dress."

Cassie laughed. "Yes. Thanks to a kind donor."

"I'm walking back to the motel. Ready to go back?"

Cassie had wanted to explore more, but saying "no" felt rude, so she faced that direction, and the two women began moving.

"I'm Randi."

"Yes, I remember."

"And I already know you're Cassandra."

She winced. "Cassie, please."

"Who was your good Samaritan?" She gestured toward the outfit Cassie wore.

"The sheriff drove me home from Dinah's Place, I think mostly to see if I was safe to allow in his town. His mother mentioned the woman in the wedding dress. He said he knew where I was, and presto! He showed up with a bag of clothes for me to wear."

Randi tilted her head to see the lower part of Cassie's leg. "She's larger than you, so those jeans aren't hers." She laughed. "So what do you do, Cassie?"

"I'm a wedding planner."

"That explains the dress! No, wait. Don't wedding planners work with *brides* in wedding dresses? You don't have to wear them all the time, right?"

"I put the dress on for my own wedding."

"You arrived alone." Her voice had a matter-of-fact tone.

"Yes. But he didn't leave the church alone. I, thankfully, found out about the other woman in time."

Randi stopped and turned to her. "You're an actual runaway bride! I've seen them in movies, but I never expected to meet one." She stared at Cassie as though she were a celebrity.

Cassie had never thought of it that way, but she had always liked that type of romance novel. Living it was different, though. In the books, the bride-to-be finds new love.

Yin to her yang.

Jam to her biscuit.

Her sweet courtship with Jonathan came to mind—and it had been a courtship. He'd brought her flowers, and not just any flowers, but pale pink roses once he'd learned they were her favorite. He'd sent her a box of her preferred dark chocolates the day after she did a wedding. Every wedding. When she'd had to pull an all-nighter for a wedding setup with problems, he'd ordered Thai food for everyone there from a restaurant she loved.

All in all, he'd been the perfect fiancé.

He had wooed her with finesse worthy of . . . a conman. Jonathan had run a con the short time they'd been together like something from a dating playbook.

When they'd kissed, he'd always been sweet. She'd thought him the perfect gentleman. But he'd done that because he had a real relationship with another woman.

Cassie stopped walking and leaned forward with her hands on her thighs, her breath coming in giant gulps.

"Are you all right?" Her new friend turned to her with concern.

Cassie started to nod. Then she said, "No," but it came out close to a whisper.

"Sit down over here." Randi took her by the elbow and led

her to a bench. "You look like you're going to faint. Put your head between your knees."

Cassie did as she was told. She focused on this moment and the sounds of birds singing in nearby trees, pushing her worm of an ex-groom out of her mind. Randi was saying something, but between her position and the blood now rushing to her head, she couldn't understand her words.

When her breathing slowed, she sat up and looked around to find not just Randi, but also a man her father's age. He pressed a cold drink in her hand.

She took what turned out to be a glass of ice water from him and sipped some, feeling better still. "Thank you."

Randi explained. "Albert owns the hardware store that's just behind the Main Street buildings—" she pointed across the street "—so I called and asked him to bring this." She crouched in front of Cassie. "Are you sure you're okay?"

"Yes. Just feeling foolish. I thought over, um, what we were talking about and realized I'd been a fool. That sent me into panic mode."

Randi looked up at Albert. "She's a runaway bride."

The older man's eyes widened. "I've heard about them."

"Me too." A new voice chimed in.

Conversation swirled around her, but she wasn't part of it. Feeling stronger, Cassie stood. "Thank you for your concern. I think I'll head back to my cottage now." She smiled at the group, which now included Randi, Albert, and two ladies she recognized from the church.

Thinking she'd made a clean break when no one followed her, she was startled a minute later by a male voice to her left. "Need a ride?"

Cassie jumped and put her hand on her heart. Sheriff Brantley leaned over in his car to talk through the open passenger window.

"I'm fine. Besides, I'll see you in a few hours for dinner."

Gasps rose from the group, which could apparently hear them.

The sheriff dropped his voice. "Now you've done it. Word will get around that the sheriff and the runaway bride are an item."

Cassie smiled at the group. "The sheriff's mother invited me to dinner when she learned I was stranded here."

Understanding nods from several of them were accompanied by the words, "That's just like Emmaline Brantley. She'd never let a body go hungry."

Cassie put her hands on the side of the car and peered through the window at him. "I'm not getting in here unless I have to, anyway."

"Good choice," he said grinning.

She glanced back at the group, which still watched her. "Besides, I could use the exercise."

Twisting in his seat, he checked the group before saying, "That may be best," he said in a low voice. The sheriff waved and drove away.

When Cassie arrived at the motel's entrance, she realized that going to her room would give her hours with nothing to do except stare at the four walls. Once she'd eaten the sandwich, there would be nothing to do.

She kept going. Her work often kept her running and on her feet, but she rarely had time to enjoy a walk. At the grocery store/gas station, she decided to check on the motorcycle. She found it untouched and safe. Good. The last thing she needed was a teenager with access to a gas can filling it up and taking it for a joyride.

She considered moving it to the hotel, but didn't know if she could do that with such a heavy piece of metal. She'd leave it here and run over when the gas station opened to fill up the tank, then ride it back to the motel to wait until she checked out.

On the way back, spring flowers blooming in some of the houses' front yards, made her smile.

Her work left her with little time for the proverbial smelling of roses, but now that she'd walked this route several times, she noticed her surroundings more. One house looked cared for, and another abandoned. Flowers pushed their way up among tall weeds in yet another yard that had an air of neglect.

It seemed that much of the town had shut down years ago, and only a handful of hardy souls had stayed.

Greg drove through the town and thought about the woman everyone knew as the "runaway bride." He hadn't checked her out before, but he should. Not just because his mother had invited her into his family home, but also because he wanted to know who was befriending the good citizens of Two Hearts.

He pulled his patrol car behind the motel's office, then climbed out and waited for Randi. He'd given up anonymity when he'd taken this job. Gossip would spread like wildfire if people noticed him spending too much time here.

His fiancé, Suzette, had broken their engagement right before he'd decided to move back to Two Hearts and take the job his father had held for decades. He'd lost his father to an unexpected heart attack and been rejected by his fiancée within weeks of each other.

With distance, he'd known that Suzette had done him a favor. But that didn't mean he wanted to put his toe in the dating pool again. He considered it a lesson well-learned. Besides, his dating life had been a dumpster fire since he'd returned.

The town's librarian, Joanna Jennings, had called him several times about her cat before he'd caught on that she was putting her tabby, Cedric, in the tree. The last time, Cedric had given his owner a look of disdain before descending the tree in that graceful, lithe way that only a cat could.

After the second visit, whispers of the sheriff's romantic relationship with the librarian had started working their way around town. With the library only open three days a week, she'd had plenty of time to come up with her plan of attack. He'd asked Albert to help her the fourth time. There hadn't been a fifth.

Randi approached the office and smirked when she saw him. "I wondered when you'd stop by."

He raised one eyebrow. "Because?"

She rolled her eyes and sighed. "Because she's a stranger in town."

"Motels usually have strangers staying in them."

She snorted. "Not this motel. Or this town." After unlocking the door, she motioned for him to follow her and went straight to her computer.

He followed her behind the front desk. His mother had dragged him over here to visit her friend, Randi's mother, on many occasions. Postcards of the hot springs that showed the town in its heyday had been pinned to the back of the desk and faded even when he'd been a child. The color-coded files in perfect order were a newer addition and pure Randi. He moved in closer to see a photo in a frame. "Is this Becky's baby?"

Leaning back, she grinned up at him. "My niece is the cutest baby ever!"

Ignoring her comment because the baby actually resembled a tiny wrestler, he pulled the conversation back to his earlier request. "What do you know about Cassie?"

She typed for a moment, and then reached for a pen and a pad of paper. "I don't know too much about her. Other than the fact that her fiancé was a lying piece of scum." She said the last part with a sweetness that belied her words, and she smiled as she tore off the sheet of paper and handed it to him. "That's all I know."

*Cassandra Van Bibber* followed by a Nashville address with a unit number.

Randi crossed her arms. "Did she tell you what her fiancé did?"

She had, but Greg wanted to see if she'd told a consistent story. "What did he do?"

Standing, Randi leaned against the counter. "He cheated on her with a bridesmaid, a pretty little thing who was supposed to be a cousin but wasn't."

He held up the paper. "If you learn anything else about her, please let me know."

"She's nice and she has been hurt, so you'd better be kind to her." Her concerned expression changed to a smirk. "And you can't interrogate her like you did Timmy Martin."

Memories of his childhood flashed into his mind. Randi was two years younger than him, but she'd been part of the group of kids he'd hung out with. "I was twelve."

"A simple game of cops and robbers turned into an interrogation worthy of a—"

"Detective show. I loved a series that was on TV then. *They* did interrogations."

"Yes, but you had a light shining in Timmy's eyes, and kept telling him to 'come clean' about his crimes. He stayed away from you for months after that."

And there was the blessing and the curse of living in a small town. No one ever forgot *anything*. Picturing the event, an important detail returned. "You were the one holding the flashlight on his face."

With a grin, she said, "We did have fun. And no one was surprised when you moved away to be a cop." She paused for a moment. "Now you're back. Are you glad you returned, Greg?"

He replied without a moment's hesitation. "Never a doubt."

Back in his patrol car, Greg entered Cassie's name and address in his laptop computer. He couldn't legitimately run a background check, but he could go to social media. Photos matched her. Nothing suspicious. She was who she claimed to be. The address turned out to be for a newer condominium complex in Nashville in an area he knew fairly well. She'd paid quite a bit for the condo and probably had a wonderful city view.

He was glad she'd be leaving tomorrow. She might not appreciate even this basic level of investigation.

But he was just doing his job. It wasn't like he was investigating her for personal reasons. He'd never pursued or walked away from a police situation because a beautiful woman had piqued his interest. She *was* beautiful, though. Cassie had sparkled and charmed him when she'd laughed about his car and Grandpa's dog—even when she'd been wearing that grimy wedding dress.

This afternoon, he had to pick her up and take her to the family home. Could it get any more embarrassing than having your mother request that you bring a woman to her house for dinner?

As Greg drove down Main Street and contemplated that question, he came to the conclusion that very few things could top this level of awkwardness. He'd noticed his mother's boredom recently with her attempts at multiple craft projects. She needed a hobby other than his love life, which had been beyond dull.

When the time arrived for him to pick up Cassie, he smiled and realized he liked her more than he should. But she had a boatload of baggage right now *and* was leaving town. After his fiancée had walked away with no apparent damage to her heart and married an accountant in a stable job a few months later, he'd become somewhat jaded about women and relationships.

As much as he'd tried to ignore it, though, something about

Cassie did spark his interest. She'd brought life and vitality into his world that had been missing for too long. It wasn't that Two Hearts was too small to have that or even the town's decline, it was the special something Cassie brought into a room.

But she was here for a short time. And she had just been burned in a relationship and by a man she'd trusted with her heart. That made her unavailable.

As he turned into the motel, he realized that those things would prevent his mother's matchmaking. She couldn't be planning to pair him up with a woman who must be devastated and heartbroken after what had happened to her.

After he'd stopped the car in front of Cassie's unit, he caught himself as he started to lean over to check his hair in the rearview mirror and chuckled. Maybe he could enjoy tonight's dinner, but nothing about this was a date. He needed to get through the evening and push away any ideas of spending more time with Cassie.

Stepping out of the car, he muttered, "Let's get this show on the road."

# CHAPTER FOUR

*C*assie stared in the mirror for longer than she should have. No matter what she did, she had to admit that someone else's clothes in the wrong size were on her back. The overall look wasn't worthy of going anywhere except maybe Dinah's Place, and only then because they'd seen her at her worst. Greg's mother had never met her.

Other than brushing her hair, the one thing she could do was apply makeup. She could manage a decent makeup job, but nothing like the professionals she always insisted a bride hire. Few things stressed a bride out more than her appearance on her wedding day.

Red hair and fair skin made color choices a challenge. She'd crossed the line between enhancing her appearance and clown makeup on too many occasions. After a quick swipe of mascara to darken her blonde lashes, a powdering of blush, and a streak of lip gloss, she decided that anything more would both push her luck and be over the top with her borrowed, oddly-fitting clothes.

A knock at her door a few minutes before four made her cringe, but this time, when she checked out the window, the sheriff stood there. He smiled broadly when she opened the door. The man had a smile that could melt snow.

There was no doubt about it. He was handsome. If she lived here, she'd try to fix Bella up with him.

Gesturing toward herself, she said, "Pretend I'm wearing something lovely for dinner with your mother. Something special for the occasion."

He laughed and shook his head. "You are. You managed to turn my sister's not-quite-your-size clothes into something that looks good. I guess that goes to show you that some people are so beautiful that they look great in everything." As soon as the words left his mouth, his face turned beet red.

The sheriff thought she was beautiful. Interesting. She could admire an attractive man, but she wasn't about to go anywhere near him relationship-wise. Her battered heart couldn't take it now. Maybe not ever again. It wasn't, she realized to her great distress, that she'd been so deeply in love with Jonathan. More that she'd been foolish to trust someone with her heart and her emotions.

With her tote over her shoulder, she went out and locked the door behind her. When she saw his patrol car, she wondered if she should walk instead. "You said your mother lived nearby."

"She's about ten blocks from here." He opened her car door for her.

She sighed, knowing she didn't have a choice. No matter what he'd told her earlier, she still held her breath when she sat. He had the windows rolled down, so she leaned closer to hers as he pulled the car out and drove toward their destination.

"Breathe normally. It's fresh and clean."

His trust-me expression made her inhale the interior air to test it. "Much better. Thank you for doing that."

He laughed. "No one, including my grandfather, the puppy's owner, wanted to ride with me. I quickly became the town pariah."

When they started driving, she decided to put the conversation back on him. "So, Sheriff—"

"Greg, please. Now that I'm back here as sheriff, I have so few people who use my first name."

"So you aren't a hometown boy who grew into the job of local sheriff?"

"I was a Chicago PD officer for almost ten years. I came home about two years ago."

Going from a major city to a town this small didn't sound like an easy transition. "Do you miss it?"

He put on his turn signal, turned, then put on his signal again for a quick right. This man followed the law exactly, even when no other cars were in sight. "I can't get an awesome cup of coffee at two a.m. unless I stop by my own house and make it. I have to drive a half hour for pizza. And don't even ask me about the entertainment here. I went from some of the finest theatrical performances in the world to high school plays. They poured their hearts into a play last year, but..." He shook his head.

Now that he'd mentioned pizza, she wanted it. In Nashville, that would have been easy to get. "It didn't go well?"

He seemed to be fighting a grin and finally gave in. "Juliet forgot her lines when she stepped onto her balcony. We did not hear 'O Romeo, Romeo, wherefore art thou Romeo?' After a long, silent pause, she cried out, 'Where'd you go?'" Greg turned into a driveway in front of a faded blue Victorian house. "Do you know how hard it is not to laugh at that?"

By now he had her grinning, too. "Did everyone else manage to keep a straight face?"

"Right up to the moment the director screamed, 'No!'" Greg was even more handsome grinning from ear to ear. "I scheduled required training for the weekend of the next production. Can you imagine *Hello Dolly*, a musical, by that group?"

Cassie shook her head, then turned to look at the house in

front of them. "Please tell me about your mother. I'm going to the home of someone I have never met." She wanted to ask if she was friendly or if she'd been to the same motherhood school as Sandra Van Bibber.

Not that she didn't love her own mother. She did. But she'd also learned at an early age to maintain strong boundaries so she didn't get her feelings hurt by her proper way of doing things—or Sandra's Way, as Cassie always thought of it.

He shifted in his seat. "She's well liked."

Was *he* nervous about dinner? Maybe he did have a similar mom.

He opened his car door. "Let's do this."

Was the quality of the meal part of his distress? As they walked up to the door, she asked, "Do I need to be warned about the food?"

He stopped and turned toward her. "Is that what you think? My mother's the finest cook between here and Nashville."

A woman who was a cross between her own mother and Julia Child came to mind.

The door flew open, and a plump woman in a floral dress stepped outside and clapped her hands with glee. "It's the runaway bride!"

He muttered under his breath, "*This* is what I'm concerned about."

Cassie froze in position. Her choice was to be rude and leave, or to go with the flow. She *could* tell her story one more time.

"Cassie Van Bibber, I would like you to meet my mother, Emmaline Brantley."

Instead of a polite nod of the head as her mother would have given, the woman pulled her into a tight hug. "I'm so happy to meet you, my dear." Then she set her back on her feet, leaving Cassie reeling. This definitely wasn't Sandra Van Bibber.

Mrs. Brantley stepped back to allow her son and guest to

enter. Cassie found a room out of a country design magazine. The fading paint on the outside had made her wonder what to expect. The savory scents of dinner in the oven and those from a dessert that must include cinnamon and other spices mingled.

"Please sit down, Cassie. We have about a half hour before dinner will be ready."

The unspoken words were clear: *...to find out everything I can about your situation.*

Cassie chose a chair upholstered in a happy, spring-floral pattern and took a deep, slow breath. The people in this town were wonderful, but she wanted to forget about yesterday, Jonathan, and everything to do with her own wedding.

That would probably be impossible.

When it had come time for her own wedding, she'd pulled out her folder of favorites—her accumulation of best favors, flowers, and cake designs from over the years. Since there was no way a future bride wouldn't request pink roses in a bouquet or an orange cream cake, she would have to revisit her own choices again and again for other weddings. She winced inwardly at the thought.

Mrs. Brantley sat down on the edge of an overstuffed chair. "Tell me *everything.*"

"Mom." There was a warning tone in Greg's single word.

The older woman frowned. "Am I being pushy? If I am, I apologize."

That broke the ice. Cassie's shoulders relaxed, and she smiled for the first time since she'd walked in the door. "I'll begin with that morning at the church. My best friend helped me into my wedding dress."

"The one with the pearls and beading I've heard so much about?"

"That's the one. After makeup and hair, I wanted to check on the groom."

She raised an eyebrow, as her son often did. "You suspected him of something?"

"No. No." Cassie shook her head. "I wanted one last look at him before we got married. I slowly turned the doorknob on the room he was in, held up my phone to take a photo through the opening, and poof! My wedding went up in smoke." The story felt like someone else's. Perhaps telling it over and over again was helping.

"What happened?" Greg's mother leaned forward and asked the question, but he looked just as curious.

Cassie pulled out her phone. "I caught him with one of my bridesmaids."

"On camera?" The woman eyed the phone, then glanced at her son. She clearly wanted to see a photo but didn't want to ask.

Cassie hadn't shown the video to anyone but her best friend and mother. Something about Mrs. Brantley felt safe and comfortable, though. Without taking time to overthink it, she found the video and handed her the phone. Greg stepped behind his mom and leaned over. His mother hit Play.

As they watched, Cassie's anger amped up, along with humiliation at being played so well. But she felt strangely free. Her wedding had been planned to every detail, and she'd focused on it so intently that maybe she'd missed what her emotions now said: she hadn't wanted to marry Jonathan.

Mrs. Brantley's stricken expression when the video ended caught Cassie off guard. Cassie slapped her hand over her mouth to stifle her sudden giggles. Instead of anguish, this time laughter bubbled up. They'd really wonder about her if she started laughing.

Mrs. Brantley rushed over and pulled her into a hug. "I'm so sorry about what happened." Cassie heard the muffled words against her ear, and a warm sense of peace replaced her embarrassment. A stranger cared about her.

Fortunately, the rest of the evening was pleasant—happy, even. They ate a wonderful meal of poppy seed chicken casserole and had apple crisp for dessert.

When she and Greg walked to his car later—after a big hug at the door by his mom for each of them—Cassie said, "You shouldn't have worried. Your mother is wonderful. You're a lucky man."

Stopping at her car door, he leaned against the vehicle and sighed. "I know you're right, but sometimes it takes a newcomer to point out what's around us every day. I bet your mother's just as sweet."

Cassie grinned. "You'd lose that bet."

He stood and opened her door, stepping back so she could climb inside. "I'm glad you came to dinner tonight."

"I am too." More than that, she realized that she'd rather be here right now than anywhere else.

Cassie stretched and pictured the new day in front of her. Birds chirping outside her window reminded her of her present small-town location. Tonight, she'd be in her own bed with traffic noises the most prominent sounds.

After another hour and a half on the back of a motorcycle, she'd be back in her own condo. If only she wanted to climb back on that beast and ride it again. And she'd have to manage city traffic to drop it off at Michael's office. A taxi would bring her the last leg of her trip.

Since Jonathan's boss hadn't heard from her, he had probably pictured his beloved motorcycle in a ditch, or maybe he figured she'd headed for the border after he'd found out she'd run. She hoped Michael gave his wife adoring glances as intense as the one he'd given his bike. Cassie grabbed her phone off the nightstand and called his business.

As soon as she identified herself, he jumped in with, "Cassie? Where is my motorcycle?"

She addressed his unasked question first. "It's perfectly safe." At least she hoped it still was safe parked behind the grocery store. "I'm in a small town."

Sounds of movement came through the line. "Text me the address." He rattled off his cell phone number.

Was he planning to come here? "But Michael—"

"I'm on my way." Footsteps were followed by words he must be saying to his assistant. She caught "cancel," "appointments," and "afternoon."

"I was planning to ride it back today."

"That isn't necessary. I have someone ready to take me wherever it is."

"Fine. I'm in Two Hearts."

Silence greeted her for a few seconds. "Two what?"

Everyone had the same response. "Two Hearts, Tennessee. It's about ninety minutes outside the city."

"I'll find it. Where's my bike?" He didn't ask where *she* was.

"At the Two Hearts Motel. I'm in unit Four."

He said, "Got it," and hung up.

She'd still have to put gas in the tank and ride it a few blocks, but after that, she'd be free of the torture device. She breathed out slowly as calm settled over her. No more dodging cars and trucks while on the back of that thing. No more bugs hitting her.

She bounded out of bed and went to take a shower. As she toweled off and thought some more about her day, she realized she had a huge problem.

How would she get back to Nashville? She would still be stuck in Two Hearts.

Maybe Greg would drive her home. Then she remembered he was the sheriff and didn't have time for such a long detour.

Bella would pick her up—if she had time. Last weekend,

Bella had two weddings she'd created gowns for and both brides had requested that the designer be on site for final adjustments.

Cassie had given her friend a key to her condo so she could water the plants during the honeymoon. That certainly wouldn't be necessary now. But she'd be able to bring clean clothes. Clothes that fit.

Breakfast at Dinah's Place first. By the time she'd finished, Bella would be awake.

Her steps held a bounce today. She'd be waving goodbye to Two Hearts this afternoon and would probably never have a reason to set foot in it again. The city beckoned. She'd order her favorite latte and finally get that pizza.

As she walked, she debated eggs and bacon or pancakes. Her usual boring plain yogurt and berries just wouldn't cut it after the last few days. She found the place busy, but a couple got up to leave as she entered, so she scurried over to grab their table before it had been cleared.

Michelle smiled and motioned that she'd be there in a moment. Cassie almost felt like a local. As she set the menu in front of Cassie a few minutes later and poured a cup of coffee, the waitress said, "Dinah's making her pancakes with homemade strawberry syrup today. That only happens a few times a year."

Cassie's mouth watered. "Sold. With bacon." She may as well get the luxury plate.

Waiting for her meal, she looked at the people around her. Albert sat at a table with an older woman. Another of the women who had taken care of her when she'd felt faint yesterday was polishing off a stack of pancakes.

They'd stuck around Two Hearts because it was their home. Unless he'd always owned the hardware store, Albert probably received a pension by now, as did the other woman, so they wouldn't need to earn an income here. What about the others? That woman at the church had said that most people commuted elsewhere, so maybe the ones here worked afternoon or evening shifts. And there must be a doctor, a lawyer, and other people in professions like that. You had to feel passion for a place to stay as it devolved into this half-abandoned state.

She hadn't felt loyalty to Indianapolis, and she certainly didn't feel it to Nashville. Not that it wasn't a great city, but she hadn't bonded with her current residence the way these people seemed to have with Two Hearts.

In minutes, Michelle brought her a plate with three large, butter-topped pancakes stacked on it, a small pitcher of the syrup, and a separate plate with three slices of bacon.

She couldn't eat this much food in two breakfasts.

The scent of her pancakes with the syrup brought a smile to her face. She would have eaten luxuriously on her honeymoon, but this kind of homey food beat fancy meals almost every day.

Greg walked in about halfway through this deliciousness. *My, he looks good in his uniform.* She told herself sternly, *You are grieving over one relationship. You have no business ogling any man.*

It was hard to ignore her own advice. She noticed that Michelle had no such qualms.

"Mornin', Sheriff." Michelle's smile said more than "Welcome to Dinah's Place." The waitress leaned on the counter, pushing herself closer to him. "The usual?" Even that had a sultry undertone.

He set a thermos on the counter, leaving his hand on it. "Yes. What's the special today? And not something I have to sit down to eat."

Michelle put her hand on his. "Dinah made strawberry scones."

"I'll take two." He slid his hand from under hers, then checked his watch. "I have to be in Prineville in an hour."

A woman Cassie guessed to be in her early forties and who must be Dinah brought out a pie under a cover and set it to the side of the bar while Michelle filled the thermos.

As Greg waited, he turned and noticed her. A smile lit his face. "Cassie! I thought you would have left town by now." His long strides quickly brought him to her side.

Once again, all eyes were on her, and she felt the heat of a bright, red blush. Rudolph had his nose, and she had her fair skin. They both sometimes glowed.

"I'm waiting for the motorcycle's owner to pick it up, and for a friend to pick me up." She hadn't talked to her friend, of course, but she knew Bella would help her.

"Mom said to tell you that if you were ever in this area, you had an open invitation to come to dinner again."

A gasp from her right told her someone hadn't known about their dinner. She noticed a phone being pulled from a purse. Before she left here, news would have circulated among those few who hadn't already heard about her and the sheriff—not that there was anything to say.

"Please tell her again how kind it was to feed me when the restaurants and grocery store were closed." Maybe that would defuse any ideas about the two of them being an item. Once she left, Michelle would be free to pursue him. "I enjoyed myself." Without meaning to, her eyes lingered on him seconds longer than they should have.

"Here you are, Sheriff." Dinah held out a white paper bag and his thermos. He took them, then gave Cassie a nod.

"Stop by soon, Greg," Michelle said as he passed her.

"Down, girl," Dinah said, as Greg went out the door.

Cassie would have turned bright red again then, but Michelle shrugged. "There are only a few handsome men my age in this town."

Dinah looked toward Cassie. "But he may be otherwise engaged."

Cassie gulped and turned away. Thankfully, she'd be leaving Two Hearts in a matter of hours and wouldn't be in the middle of a tug-of-war over Greg.

Michelle surprised her by smiling widely when she refilled her coffee cup. "Need anything else?"

Startled by her lack of concern, it took Cassie a moment to untie her tongue. The other woman must truly be fishing in the ocean and hoping to catch the sheriff or any other eligible male. But it looked like she didn't have any emotional bond with Greg.

Unfortunately, when Cassie's tongue loosened, it said something stupid, given the number of pancakes she'd already inhaled. "I'd like one of those scones for later." She'd need to walk back to Nashville to whittle off the weight if she kept eating like this. Then again, maybe it would be worth it. At least she hadn't asked for two.

# CHAPTER FIVE

*T*he barren Main Street's air of despair deepened each time she passed by. These empty storefronts should have been filled with businesses. If the citizens of Two Hearts brought Main Street back to life, maybe tourists would make the trek here. Locals from the surrounding area certainly would.

This time, the brick buildings screamed that they had potential. She could mention it to Greg. But they would need store owners with enough money to move in and take the huge risk of failure. That seemed so unlikely that she decided to look straight ahead and ignore the hollow storefronts.

That was easier said than done when she noticed a wedding dress on a sign on one of the buildings. Nothing spoke to her more loudly than something from her field. Two Hearts had once been prosperous enough to not only have the basics but also support specialty shops.

A mewing sound caught her attention when she reached the last building. Where had it come from? Looking around, she didn't see a cat. Then she heard it again, coming from above.

Leaning back, she found a tiny kitten perched on a

decorative row of bricks sticking out above the store window. How it had gotten there was a mystery. Cassie reached up, but it was too high. When the kitten took a few steps and wobbled, she held out her hands and caught it as it fell.

"Hey there, little one. Are you all right?" It looked barely old enough to be on its own. "Where's your mother?" The kitten snuggled against her chest and purred as she petted it.

She went down the alley in back of the buildings, back toward Dinah's Place. A dog barked at her from behind a fence in a yard that backed up to the alley, but she didn't see any other cats. Dinah herself stepped out her back door, carrying a bag of trash.

Cassie called to her. "Is someone missing a kitten?"

Dinah threw the bag in a trash can. "Martin Dunlow's cat got out and ended up having a litter of kittens. He gave them away to anyone who would take them last week, but couldn't find one. Is it gray-and-white-striped?"

The kitten started working its paws, kneading her arm. "It is."

"Then it doesn't have a home." Dinah stepped closer and dropped her voice. "Don't give him back to Martin. He's approaching ninety, and I think his older cat is almost more than he can take care of. That's why it got out in the first place." With those words, Dinah returned to her building, leaving Cassie with a homeless, but adorable, kitten.

She couldn't set it down and walk away. What would happen to it? It had used up one of its nine lives when she'd caught it as it fell.

"I'm your temporary mother. We'll find you a good home."

Where? All of her friends lived in the city and worked as hard as she did. He mewed again.

"I bet you're hungry. We can find you some food at the grocery store. I'd better get you settled, then fill up the motorcycle and move it to my place before its owner gets here."

Michael would have a fit if he knew his precious motorcycle had been left unattended for days.

After a quick trip to the store, she fixed up a temporary box she hoped the tiny kitten would know how to use and opened a can of food for him, which he gobbled up.

"If you'll wait here for a little while, I'll be back."

He made that little mewing sound again as she closed the door.

Walking past the manager's office, she realized that Randi might not want a kitten in the motel room, but she'd be out of here in a few hours, and hopefully the little guy would have a new home by then.

The reason for her second trek to the grocery store today put pep in her step. As she arrived, a man pulled up to the pump and got out of his vehicle. Cassie's eyebrows raised. His well-fitting suit and tie didn't quite meet the town's usual casual clothing standards.

With great effort, she wheeled the motorcycle over to the pump. Then Saturday's dilemma returned. The man at the opposite pump didn't look like the type to know where you filled a motorcycle, so she searched its top and sides.

"It's there." He pointed.

She checked and saw the gas cap. "Thank you."

"I'm Micah Smith." About thirty and with dark brown hair, green eyes, and a build that said he worked out, this man vied with Greg for Two Hearts' most handsome award.

"You're a little overdressed for the occasion, Micah Smith."

He laughed. "I'm an attorney for this county. The only attorney." After a shrug he added, "People expect an attorney to wear a suit."

"The *only* attorney?"

"Yes, ma'am."

"'Ma'am' is my mother. I'm Cassie Van Bibber."

His gas pump clicked that the tank was full, so he removed

the handle and screwed the cap back on. "I've never seen you before." His voice suggested that he might like to see her again.

"I was here for the weekend."

She saw a light bulb go off, and a slow grin spread over his face. "Your red hair should have clued me in. You're the—"

She groaned. "Please don't say it. Yes, I'm that person."

"You wore a wedding dress while you rode that motorcycle?"

"Desperate times called for desperate measures." She inserted her credit card into the slot on the gas pump. "I wouldn't recommend it."

He grinned. "I'll remember that if I ever decide to wear a wedding dress."

"Or ride a motorcycle," she added, because the more she talked to him, the less she could see him on the back of a bike. She put the pump nozzle into the tank and started filling it.

"I have a motorcycle, but it isn't as nice as yours."

Laughing, Cassie shook her head. "This baby is borrowed and will be returned to its owner today. Then I hope to never ride on another." Ever. "I hadn't spent more than twenty minutes on one before this. Just enough to learn what I needed to pass the test for the license, and to ride in the wedding."

He gave her a puzzled expression—something that had happened a lot lately—opened his car door, and leaned on it. "Nice meeting you, Cassie."

When he drove away, Cassie wondered about what Michelle had said earlier. There were a few handsome single men. Greg was obviously one of them. Not only had Micah not worn a wedding ring, but he also hadn't acted like a married man. If she were a woman looking for a man, this town had at least two solid specimens to choose from.

Next question: how did one start a motorcycle? She'd done that once for the biker wedding. Chewing on her lip, she sat on the beast and tried to remember. If this bike wasn't waiting for Michael when he arrived, he would be even more upset. Closing her eyes, she pictured the lessons she'd had and was soon on her way.

She parked it in front of her unit, glad she didn't see any new cars there. When a high-end car turned into the lot, she realized she'd made it with seconds to spare. Pasting on a smile, she greeted the unsmiling man who stepped from the passenger door as the car rolled to a stop. When he closed the door, the car left as if the driver had an urgent appointment.

Michael hurried over to his motorcycle and checked it over. When it apparently passed the test, he turned to her. "How dare you let me believe you were running an errand when you were running away from your wedding with Jonathan? You broke his heart." He punctuated every word by shaking his finger at her.

"Excuse me?"

"What kind of person are you? You're so unfeeling."

What was her former fiancé telling everyone? *She* was the victim.

"Are you finished?"

"I put him up in a luxury hotel for the weekend at the company's expense. He couldn't bear to go to the honeymoon destination and didn't want to see reminders of you at his home."

Her annoyance shifted. "Michael, you're the most gullible man on the planet."

His sputtering didn't slow her down.

"First, I have to thank you for loaning me your motorcycle."

He tried to speak, but she raised her voice. "I have a video to show you."

She'd planned to keep the video private, showing it to a select few, but letting Greg and his mother see it had been healing. Anyway, she couldn't let Jonathan ruin her good name. She queued it up and held it in front of him. She didn't trust him not to throw her phone to the ground if she handed it to him.

When his mouth dropped open, she knew he'd gotten to the kiss.

"She kissed him. That doesn't prove—" Now he was at the passionate point of their little escapade. His expression hardened. "Jonathan played me."

She had to bite her tongue to not say, *Like a master.*

"He said his cousin was like a sister, and he needed her nearby, so I got them a suite."

Cassie fought the battle against a grin and lost. "Don't feel bad about that. I fell for that 'cousin' line, too."

A contrite man looked up from her phone. "I owe you an apology."

"Thank you."

When he climbed on his bike, he said, "Wait! I'm taking your ride back to the city. If I'd known, Hugo could have driven you there."

Ninety minutes with a stranger sounded less than fun. "Thank you, but a friend will pick me up."

"If you're sure?"

She nodded, and he started the engine. He gave a solemn wave and drove away, leaving her alone in Two Hearts.

The kitten reminded her that she wasn't actually alone as soon as she opened the door. She picked him up, holding him closely while she dialed Bella.

"You're back! If you've already dropped off the motorcycle, I can meet you for lunch. I have enough time at about noon."

"I'm not quite there. And the only lunch I'll have is at Dinah's Place—unless you can come get me." She didn't believe in the power of crossed fingers, but she crossed them anyway.

"Ahh, Cassie! Today's a bear. I have two fittings back to back, with barely time to breathe between them, and a first meeting with a client who can only meet in the evenings at seven. If I move the second fitting—"

Putting her fingers back to normal, Cassie snuggled the

kitten closer. "Take care of your clients, and they take care of you. I can still hear Professor Mallery saying that."

Bella groaned. "You're right, but I hate it that you have to spend another night there."

The breakfast she'd had and the nice people of Two Hearts that she'd met came to mind—unfortunately for her character, in that order. Food shouldn't have come first. "I'll be fine." And she would, but she might have to at least wash this shirt and hang it to dry. At this point, clean clothes that fit would rock her world.

"*If*—and that's always a big if—the second appointment is short, I could be over there and back before my other appointment."

"Bella, I'm somewhere beyond the middle of nowhere. You're looking at an hour and a half each way. There's no way you'll have enough time."

"But I can't leave you there!"

"I'm safe. I may be gaining weight from the great food." *And there's a handsome sheriff I'd like to see again.* Yeah, she should be too brokenhearted to be interested, but she'd enjoyed spending time with him. She could have a handsome friend, right?

"My stressed-out brain missed a detail earlier. You drove *that* far on the back of a motorcycle?"

Cassie held the phone away from her ear.

"What were you thinking?"

Therein lay the problem. "I drove until the gas ran out."

"Speaking of motorcycles, why didn't you ride it here this morning like you'd said?"

Cassie told her what had happened with Michael. Then she heard paper being moved.

"My schedule is open tomorrow morning. You know, if I move one short appointment, I could take the day off." Cassie was about to argue with her friend when Bella followed the words with a deep sigh. "I like the idea of a whole day off."

"Then I will welcome your company here. We can have lunch at Dinah's Place, but don't expect a light salad."

Bella chuckled. "When I take a day off, I go for the gusto. I'm looking forward to it."

Cassie pictured herself greeting her friend the next day. "Could you please stop by my condo on the way and pick up some clothes for me?"

"Sure. Text me the name of the motel where you're staying. I'll see you at about eleven a.m."

Cassie hung up the phone, realizing she'd be completely stranded in Two Hearts for the first time. Even with an empty gas tank, the motorcycle had felt like a way out. As sudden panic climbed, so did the kitten, who distracted her enough that she could relax and smile.

She needed to find out if there was a veterinarian in town. Her guess would be no, based on the shuttered businesses, but this was a rural area, and people needed large-animal care for cows and horses.

Before she did anything else, she first needed to make sure Randi had space for her for tonight. Since she'd only noticed a car at one other unit this whole time, she didn't expect to have any trouble.

Instead, Randi hesitated and frowned. Cassie's heart leaped into her throat at the prospect of being evicted from her unit while being stuck here.

"Would you mind moving to Cottage Two?"

Cassie held onto the edge of the counter to steady her wobbly legs. "I can do that if it helps you."

A big smile burst out. "Thank you. Earl's been using your unit once a week or so for years."

After Saturday night's escapade, Cassie considered herself happy to go where Earl wasn't.

"Having you here made me realize we could get a tourist

now and then, so I freshened one up that I think you'll like. Now, I'll make sure two units are always ready."

Randi thought being ready to rent two out of ten cottages would be a step up? This town needed to be brought back to life.

Randi reached behind her for a room key and handed it to Cassie. "I keep Cottage Four basic because I know that's all Earl would want, but Two is much girlier." She giggled.

Cassie's shoulders tensed. What did that mean? Lace and ruffles?

Randi handed her the keys.

A while later, with her wedding dress draped over her shoulder and her tote bag stuffed with her usual supplies plus cat food, she tucked the kitten in the crook of her right arm and picked up the cat box with her left. It was a bulky load, but Cottage Two was just across the courtyard.

After some juggling to get the key in the lock, Cassie pushed the door open on her new cottage, unsure of what she'd find. To her surprise, she discovered a charming room with white painted furniture, a pink-and-green bedspread with matching floral drapes, and an overstuffed checkered-print chair—all of it appearing to have come right out of the 1940s.

The décor was feminine and historically accurate in the way of good antiques. She could imagine one of the movie stars of the era staying here on a cross-country trip.

The kitten struggled to get down, pulling her out of her reverie. She set everything, including the cat, on the floor. "Let's settle into our new place."

A short time later, she relaxed in the upholstered chair, and the kitten jumped in her lap. Petting it, peace descended over her. Cassie closed her eyes, wanting to hold on to that emotion for as long as she could.

## CHAPTER SIX

*A* short time later, the kitten jumped down, and she stood. What was she going to do with a whole day to herself in Two Hearts? Saturday, she'd been too upset to care. Sunday, she'd at least had the dinner to look forward to. Today?

Cassie checked on her phone to see if she could find a veterinarian and, much to her surprise, did. The office was about as far away from her as it could possibly be while still remaining in the town. The April sun shone brightly but not too hot, and since neither she nor the feline in her care had anywhere else they needed to be, she gave the vet's office a call. They'd had a cancellation and could fit her in an hour from now. She wrapped the kitten up in a towel and started walking.

She went the direction Greg had taken her to his mother's house, made turns, and walked past his family's house. There were only so many blue Victorians with beds filled with pink and purple flowers. A glance at the map on her phone showed that she was only about halfway to the clinic.

A park with overgrown grass, a few picnic tables that had seen better days, and majestic old trees appeared to her left as Cassie continued on. She was starting to get a little nervous as the houses thinned out and the countryside started. The Heartfelt Veterinary Clinic sign appeared on the left, and she breathed a sigh of relief.

As expected, the sign said that the vet took care of all animals from small to large and whether they "walked, slithered, or flew."

An older woman greeted her when she went inside. "Welcome." She leaned to her left to peer around Cassie. "I don't see an animal with you."

Cassie set the towel on the counter and opened it. The kitten stood up and stretched. He must have slept the whole way.

The woman rubbed under the kitten's chin. "Aren't you a cute one. Hey!" She stopped with her hand still on the kitten. "Martin Dunlow lost a kitten like this a few days ago."

Cassie nodded. "Dinah told me that when I found him. She said he really couldn't take care of a kitten. That I shouldn't take this one back to him."

The woman looked thoughtful for a moment. "You're right about that. If he says anything about it, I'll tell him we saw a stray gray-and-white-striped kitten who has been adopted." The woman held a pen ready. "And what is your name and address?"

Cassie gave it to her. The woman's eyebrows shot upward and disappeared underneath her bangs. "You're a tourist from Nashville?" She said it as Cassie imagined one would address an alien from a heretofore unknown planet.

"Let's just say that I've been visiting for a few days."

"Oh. I should have put the pieces together. They said the runaway bride had red hair."

She should be used to this by now. The bad thing about a small town was that everyone knew your business. "That would be me."

"If you have a seat, the doctor will be with you in just a few minutes."

About five minutes later, a door to what she assumed was

the exam room opened and an older man in a white coat leaned out. "Erma, please bring me—"

A pink piglet darted between the man's legs and toward Cassie.

"Persephone!" A man she guessed to be about twenty darted around and past the surprised vet. "She got away from me. Sorry, Doc!"

Cassie raised her feet off the floor to avoid getting her legs tangled up with the pig's, but Persephone turned at the last minute and raced toward the exit.

Erma stepped around the check-in desk, scooped up the piglet, and handed her back to her owner.

"Thank you." The man held his pig close and returned to the room she'd escaped from.

The vet said, "I'll just be a few more minutes, Miss. What do you need?"

"Kitten," Erma called from her post.

True to his word, man and pig left less than five minutes later, and Cassie was called back.

She picked up her furry bundle in the towel and carried it into the exam room. "I found this kitten and want to make sure it's taken care of."

The doctor examined the kitten. "He's healthy. Have you named him yet?"

*It* was male, then. "Romeo," she said, the first name that came to her. It must have been at the top of her mind because of the discussion with Greg about the play.

The vet chuckled. "That's a cute name for a kitten. You have to get a female one so you have a Juliet."

"Oh, but it isn't my kitten. I just found it. Him." Cassie leaned against the table and went through her list of friends and acquaintances again in her mind. No one stood out as a possible cat lover. "Is there a shelter nearby?"

The man stood upright. "This is the country. We don't have

an animal shelter in our small town. And I know that someone in Two Hearts was giving away kittens not long ago. We did manage to find homes for them, but it wasn't easy, so I don't know if we could place another one."

Romeo ambled over to her and rested his head on her hand. She absentmindedly started petting him, and he began purring. She picked him up and held him in front of her face. "You are a cute little guy, aren't you, Romeo? We'll find a home for you."

"Are you sure he hasn't already found one?"

Cassie held the little kitten close to her chest. She'd never had a pet. Her mother didn't allow such things in her home or to disrupt her life. When she'd been nine or ten, Cassie had cut out pictures of cats and dogs and put them on a bulletin board in her room so she could pretend she had one. They'd ended up making her sad because she'd known she never would, so she'd taken them down a month later.

Maybe having a furry friend could be fun, but she was clueless on how to care for one. "Do you have directions for new cat owners?"

The man seemed to relax at that. "I can point you to some great websites filled with information. The important thing is to put your cat on a quality diet. Otherwise, just keep him safe and love him."

The furry, purring animal in her hands seemed eminently lovable. Maybe that's what she needed right now. She held the kitten in front of her face again. "Are you okay with the name Romeo Van Bibber? That's a mouthful."

The vet chuckled. "That is a mouthful. I have a cat carrier that would make it easier for you on the way back."

She was about to tell the man she was fine, when she remembered she had to somehow transport her kitten back to Nashville. "That may be a good idea. You can have the carrier added to my bill. You don't happen to have any food so that I could take care of all of that right now?"

"We only have special diet food here. But there are some quality ones you can get at the grocery store in town. I'll write down a couple for you."

With the strong suggestion of having Romeo neutered soon and the payment of her bill, Cassie left with her new kitten.

Over the last few days, she'd lost a fiancé and gotten a new guy in her life. When an image of Greg Brantley popped into her mind instead of the kitten, she firmly pushed it away. She would be leaving here quite soon. As quickly as a ride came to get her.

Walking by Mrs. Brantley's home, she spotted her out in the yard, pulling weeds. Cassie wasn't sure if she should just keep walking and not interrupt her or if the polite thing would be to greet her.

She was saved from the decision when Mrs. Brantley looked up. "Cassie! It's great to see you." Her eyes went down to the carrier in Cassie's hand. "I didn't realize you had a cat." She came closer and peered into the carrier. "Cute little thing. What's his name?"

"Romeo."

The woman chuckled and put her finger through the screen of the door. The kitten immediately trotted over, sniffed her finger, and bumped his chin on it.

"I didn't have a kitten until this morning. He kind of dropped into my life."

"We've always enjoyed having pets in our family. I lost my last cat probably about five years ago. I'm going to need to get a new one, I think. I'd forgotten how cute they were."

For the flash of a second, Cassie considered handing Romeo over to her, but sometime between this morning when she'd caught him and now, he'd become hers.

"We're on our way back to the motel from the vet, where he was given a good report. Then I'll head over to Dinah's to get something for lunch."

73

"You don't need to do that. If you don't mind soup and a salad, I put on a pot of chicken vegetable this morning, and it should be ready about now."

Cassie didn't say no to homemade anything. "That would be great. But can I help you in some way? I can set Romeo down, and he can watch us weed."

"Oh, I'm sure you don't want to weed my garden. You must have to do that at your place."

"I live in a condo, so there is no garden. I have a balcony large enough for a tiny table and two chairs. I've never worked in a garden before." An image of her mother kneeling in a garden and putting her hands in dirt almost made her laugh out loud. Grinning, she said, "I'd like to try it."

Mrs. Brantley gave her an odd look. "Meaning that you've never weeded?"

Cassie shook her head.

"I'm going to give you a quick lesson on what's a weed and what's not."

"That's probably a good plan."

When she'd gotten the hang of it, they worked in the yard for about an hour. Cassie sat back on her heels and admired her work.

Romeo meowed from his carrier, and then the meows became more insistent.

"I hadn't thought of this, but he may need to use the potty."

"Oh my goodness, you're right. Do you think he can be trusted not to run away if we set him down somewhere?"

She looked at her little kitten. "I'm really not sure. But I think we have to give it a try."

"Then follow me." She led Cassie to a sandy area in the back of the yard. "The kids played here when they were little. That's been quite a while, but I know he'd enjoy a sandy spot."

Cassie placed the mewing kitten on the sand. He scratched

and scratched, did his business, and looked up at her like, *What's next, Mom?*

She picked him up and held him close. "You are mine now, aren't you, Romeo?"

He began purring again. Something tugged on her heart in a way she hadn't known was possible.

Inside, over lunch, Mrs. Brantley asked, "I thought you would have gone home by now. Isn't that what you said?"

"Things didn't work out quite as I thought they would. I have a friend coming tomorrow to pick me up."

"Is that so?" Mrs. Brantley looked at her as though Cassie was a prize specimen she had been looking for. "If you'll excuse me for just a moment."

Cassie sat back in her chair. "I'm happy to enjoy the quiet here."

The woman went down the hall, where Cassie heard a door close and whispers of conversation. She returned a few minutes later, seeming frustrated. "I had an idea, but I'll have to let you know about it later."

Cassie walked home soon after, and this time the walk seemed shorter, probably because she knew where she was going. When she stepped into her new cottage, it felt a lot more homey and welcoming than the last one.

Today, he'd relax, maybe head to the lake to fish. Then Greg stopped. He needed to do the yard work he'd been promising his mother he would take care of.

A short time later, Greg stepped back and checked his progress. Winter storms had wreaked havoc on parts of the garden, but he'd cleaned up the mess. After stowing the tools in the garage, he went upstairs to take a shower.

Clean and dressed in jeans and a T-shirt, he opened his door to run up to the store and almost tripped over his friend Micah, who was sitting on his top step.

"What are you doing here?"

Micah stood. "I stopped by to see you and figured you were inside taking a shower."

"And you figured that out how?"

"The car is sitting in the sun, and the doors are open. When I peered in and it smelled fresh as a daisy, I figured you'd cleaned it earlier. Thus, you would need a shower."

Greg chuckled. "I did that yesterday, but I thought airing it out more was a good idea."

When his friend didn't say why he'd come, Greg's eyes narrowed as realization dawned. "You're here about Cassie!"

Micah had the good grace to blush. "She's pretty. And I also heard you'd driven her to the motel."

"You probably also heard she left town today. She went back to Nashville."

"Yeah. Wouldn't you know it? The first woman our age to step into town in forever, and she's already gone."

"There's Michelle. And Randi. I know there are a couple other women." He couldn't think of their names right now, but he knew there had to be.

"Michelle has always been like a sister to me, Randi even more so since she's a couple years younger than me. And before you get all mushy with that friends-to-lovers kind of thing, there's no chemistry with either of them. And I rather liked it that Cassie had the guts to ride a motorcycle when she really didn't know how."

"What do you mean? I know she's licensed."

"I was filling up my car when she was putting gas in the motorcycle. She said she'd gotten the license to be part of a wedding. I didn't understand that part."

Greg muttered, "She's a wedding planner."

Micah's eyes widened. "Now, that makes more sense."

"She's already left Two Hearts, so why are you asking about her?" Greg heard what sounded like sadness in the tone of his words and hoped his friend hadn't noticed.

Micah shrugged. "In case she decides to pass through town again, I want to express my interest."

Greg chuckled. "I don't think that's going to happen." Besides, Greg wasn't sure if *he* was interested or not, so he wouldn't be passing on Micah's message even if he had the chance. He knew he shouldn't be . . .

He reached for his phone when it rang. "It's Mom. Just a sec."

His mother spoke in a low voice, "Greg, that young woman stopped by to visit. Why don't you take her out for pizza tonight?"

He glanced over at Micah. "She'll be in Nashville tonight, Mom." Was his mother pushing for grandchildren so hard that she wanted him to date a woman who lived almost two hours away?

"No. She's staying another night."

Did he want to spend time with Cassie? Without hesitation, he answered, "Tell her I'll pick her up at six."

"She's a nice girl, Greg. I think it will go well."

Micah was watching pretty closely. Greg cleared his throat and shifted on his feet.

"Your mom is setting up a date for you?"

"Hey, wipe that smirk off your face." Before he realized what he was doing, he said, "Cassie decided to stay longer, and I'm taking her out for pizza tonight."

"Then I take back my earlier words." Micah clapped him on the back. "I would like to be best man at your wedding, though." As Greg sputtered his response, Micah chuckled. "Do you want to come over to my house and play a little pool? I don't have any clients this afternoon, and I know Monday's your day off."

Greg embraced the change of subject. "Let me grab my jacket."

# CHAPTER SEVEN

$\mathcal{C}$assie answered her phone not long after she got back from a run to the grocery store for Romeo's food and some snacks for herself.

A voice she recognized as Mrs. Brantley's said, "Greg is going to pick you up at your cottage tonight at six."

Cassie felt her eyes widen. "He doesn't have to do that."

This woman was trying to fix her up with her son. That had been Cassie's suspicion yesterday, but she'd ignored the idea because she was leaving.

"There's a great pizza place about a half hour away."

Cassie had been about to open her mouth to protest, but it started watering. "I've been thinking about pizza—"

Mrs. Brantley said, "Ever since he talked about it. You mentioned pizza two or three times last night."

Cassie felt her skin warm. "Did I really? I didn't even notice. You're right, though. Greg told me what he couldn't get in this town, and that's all I've wanted." That and to spend more time with the sheriff.

They ended the call, with Cassie wondering if she should

have said no. But then she would have disappointed Mrs. Brantley, maybe Greg—and possibly herself, if she was honest.

After a fun afternoon with *her* kitten, she put on fresh makeup—the one improvement she could make. A tap at her door told her that the sheriff had arrived. She pulled open the door and found him standing on the step. "Sheriff—"

"Greg."

If she used his title, she felt more distance between them, and that was good, given the current situation. The last thing she needed was anything that looked like it could be a relationship when she'd just gotten stomped all over by Jonathan.

So why had she jumped on Mrs. Brantley's offer to set them up for dinner? Was she secretly harboring feelings for the handsome sheriff? Or was she just desperate for melty goodness with her favorite toppings? She hadn't eaten so much hearty food since college, so it was probably a good thing Bella was coming to pick her up tomorrow.

"Greg. I'm looking forward to dinner tonight." She meant the words to be polite, but as she said them, she realized she actually was looking forward to the evening. She wanted to reach around and grab a jacket for the slightly cool evening, then realized she didn't have one.

He held up a bag. "Mom sent me with a new shirt. She says she's sorry she doesn't have any other pants that might fit. She offered to ask some of her friends if she could borrow some."

Cassie cringed in humiliation. It was bad enough that one person was lending her clothing, but asking around felt even worse. "Thank your mom, and if you wait just a moment, I'll go change into this clean shirt. I'm sure you'll appreciate my not wearing something to dinner that I've had on for forty-eight hours plus." She passed her kitten on the way. "Greg, this is Romeo."

She heard him say, "What?" and then "A kitten!" as she closed the door.

In the bathroom, she pulled off the other shirt, which had fit reasonably well, and pulled on the new one, a T-shirt in a pretty shade of green. When it settled over her, she realized it was about three sizes too big. It looked like she was wearing a tent. This was obviously one of his mother's shirts and not one that belonged to his sister. But she desperately wanted to wear something clean.

Cassie rummaged in her bag and found a hair clip, so she bunched the fabric at her left hip and snapped it on. The result turned out better than she'd expected. Sure, she'd had to make last minute adjustments to wedding dresses with pins, clips, and tape, but she'd never had to be this creative with fashion.

When she opened the door, Greg did a double take. "That looks better on you than it ever did on Mom." He laughed when he seemed to realize how that had sounded. "I love my mother, but you understand."

She picked up her kitten and snuggled him close. "You be good, Romeo." After setting him down, she turned to Greg and said, "Moms and pizza dates aren't the same kind of people."

They went out the door, and she thought she heard him mutter the word "understatement" when she turned and locked the door.

After driving for about a half hour and making small talk about his family, where they lived, and what his niece and nephew were doing, Cassie asked about Chicago. "Why did you leave?"

"I'd seen too much. I needed small-town life again." His words were curt and pitched so low she almost missed the last few.

She decided to change the subject. "And there was no lovely Midwestern girl to bring home with you?"

He gulped and ignored her question. *Way to go, Cassie.* She'd become way too personal in a hurry.

He pulled up in front of Pete's Pizza. Without saying any more, he opened his car door and came around to open hers. She did enjoy a chivalrous man.

"Pete makes a decent deep dish pizza," he said with a forced lightness in his voice. "Now, it isn't as good as in Chicago, but I'm not in Chicago."

She could certainly roll with a major subject change since she was the one who had caused the awkwardness in the first place. "What's his best pizza?" she asked as she stepped out.

"I haven't had a bad one yet."

As they walked inside and Cassie saw the board behind the counter listing all the varieties of pizza, ham and pineapple caught her attention. "I haven't had a Hawaiian pizza in years."

Greg grimaced. "I have never seen the appeal of ham and fruit on something as wonderful as a pizza."

"Chicken?"

"As in chicken on a pizza? I have never committed that pizza crime either."

"*As in* are you afraid to try something new and different?"

His eyes narrowed. "I have faced down gunmen and been in too many dangerous situations to count. I accept your challenge."

Cassie grinned as he ordered a large Hawaiian pizza.

When the pizza arrived at their table, Greg narrowed his eyes at the pieces of yellow fruit poking out of the cheese. What had he gotten himself into? He normally loved pizza, but this was a different thing entirely. He reached for a piece and slid it onto his plate.

He stared at it. Maybe he should just concede and go order pepperoni.

Cassie said, "Chicken?" again and started making clucking sounds.

Laughing, he picked up the slice. "I'm going to taste this. If I don't like it, I'm going to get a different variety, and you are not allowed to call me a chicken at that point, agreed?"

She held up both hands. "I surrender. Just give it a try."

He moved it slowly toward his mouth and took a small bite off the end, getting some of the ham and the pineapple. Chewing, he realized it wasn't bad. Then he took another bite. When he swallowed, he looked up at her. "Cassie, this is good!"

She laughed and leaned back in her chair. "I wouldn't steer you wrong. Of course it's good. Why do you think people order it?"

"I must say that I always wondered." He took another bite. "I really like this."

Conversation became thin as they ate. Then he said, "Do you mind if I ask about Jonathan?" He inwardly winced. Why had he asked about her ex? That's the last thing you mentioned to a woman on a date. But was this a date? Or were they simply friends sharing a meal?

Cassie set her pizza down. "Make it quick. I don't want to lose my appetite completely."

He tried to find words to have this make sense to her—and to himself. "I just wondered what you saw in him. I'm usually a good judge of character—a skill honed from years in law enforcement. From what you said—and from what I saw in that video—he seemed very slick, perhaps with no substance." He could face down criminals, but talking over pizza with her clearly unnerved him even though she seemed fine. Maybe she was used to eating with people she didn't know well from her wedding planning work.

Cassie seemed to be mulling over his words, and not be

aware of his turmoil. Good. "That's probably a true assessment. Honestly, I'm an unmarried wedding planner. I clearly love weddings. I think about weddings from the moment I wake up until the time I go to sleep. If I go on vacation, I'm probably going to end up considering that spot as a wedding venue. Before you know it, I'm in the hotel manager's office setting up a tour of the property. I love what I do. Do you know what it's like, though, to not be able to have your own wedding?"

He did.

"Have you ever had someone special? Been engaged?" She stared at him intently, and her brown eyes seemed so genuinely curious and kind that he decided to answer.

But it was his turn to set down the pizza. "Suzette. We dated for a couple years and got engaged. A few months before our wedding, my work partner was injured. It didn't kill her, and she was able to come back to work in about a month. But Suzette told me she couldn't live with the thought that I could be injured or killed on duty. She walked away from me." He stared down at the table.

That was more information about his relationship than he'd shared with anyone, including his mother or his best friend. What was it about Cassie that brought out this side of him? Maybe it was that she made him feel comfortable talking because she would be leaving soon and that made her safe.

She put her hand over his, and warmth soared through him. Or maybe he had more interest in her than he should.

"I'm sorry I brought it up. Let me say she was foolish for letting you go."

He looked up from his plate and into her eyes. "I agree about your relationship with Jonathan. You deserve better than that for sure."

"Then we have a pact. Nothing but the best for us, right?"

He smiled and reached for his pizza again. "Only the best. We won't settle for less than the real thing next time."

# CHAPTER EIGHT

"*Y*ou're not going to want to hear this." Bella spoke without saying hello first.

Cassie closed her eyes. After a restless night spent replaying the moment she'd seen her groom cheating, over and over, she wanted this to be a good day. She'd had a perfectly pleasant evening with a perfectly pleasant man, so why had her brain spent all night going back to her rotten con artist of an ex?

"What now? Did my condo burn down?" That would pretty much be in line with everything else that had happened to her recently. The next thing that popped into her head was that she had landed in a pretty sweet place, so maybe something positive had happened back home.

"There are three notes on your door from Glorious Blooms saying they tried to deliver bouquets to you."

"It doesn't say who the bouquets were from, does it?"

"Nope. The shop's phone number is on here, though."

"I don't need it. That's one of the florists I recommend brides use. I know you've met Henri, the owner."

"I do remember now. He's about my mother's age? Wears very formal tailored suits?"

Cassie smiled. "That's Henri. I'll call and see what's going on, and I'll call you right back."

"Wait! Is there anything special you want from here?"

"I don't think so. I'll get back to you in a couple minutes." Cassie hung up the phone and dialed the florist. She explained who she was and the messages that had been left for her.

"Yes, ma'am." Clearly, this was someone she had never met. Nobody who knew her personally would give her the "ma'am" treatment. "They are three bouquets. All with gorgeous pale-pink roses."

Cassie's heart leaped into her throat. Pink roses. "Are they all from Jonathan Albach?"

"Yes, they are." The woman's voice perked up. She obviously thought she was delivering excellent news. "He was most insistent that a bouquet be delivered to you every morning and afternoon."

Those bouquets were never going to enter any home she was in, but it was a shame to let them go to waste. "I'm out of town, so please cancel that order."

The woman started making sputtering sounds.

"Don't worry about Jonathan being upset with you. I'm actually a much better customer than he is. Henri does the weddings I plan."

This time there was a gasp. "Wait! Are you *the* Cassandra Van Bibber, the wedding planner?"

"Yes," Cassie said slowly.

"Oh my goodness. I read about your weddings online. They're fabulous!"

Cassie rolled her eyes. She appreciated the compliment, but, at this moment, it seemed a little over the top. Who knew there was such a thing as fangirls for weddings?

"Please send the bouquets Mr. Albach already paid for to a local senior home. I want to make sure they're enjoyed."

"Yes, Miss Van Bibber."

Cassie hung up the phone and stared at the screen. What was Jonathan's game? When she wasn't home, he'd decided to send flowers? Maybe he thought she would come home at night. She certainly didn't want to be there to answer any questions from him.

The phone rang, and she answered without looking at the caller ID. "Bella, I hadn't even had a chance to call you back."

Silence greeted her. "Is this Cassandra Van Bibber of Just for You Weddings?" a man asked.

Cassie held the phone out and checked the screen, noticing an unfamiliar number on it. Holding it closer to her mouth, she said, "Yes, it is. What can I help you with?" She hoped this was about a future wedding and not the one that should have taken place last Saturday.

"I've noticed a lot of interest online about a wedding planner being a runaway bride. *Bridal Dreams* would like to interview you for a story."

The magazine she'd wanted to get featured in now wanted to write about her—for the wrong reasons. If only she hadn't trusted Jonathan. And what about the scandal when the world heard about the runaway bride wedding planner? She could be ruined if potential brides thought of her as someone who couldn't even get to her own wedding, let alone manage theirs.

No. Jonathan couldn't be allowed to hurt her any more.

"I'm sorry, but I'm not interested in doing an interview at this time."

"It could be good for business." The man had hope in his voice.

*Or it could end my career.* "I'm not interested. I don't want to go over the details of it again right now. I'm sure you understand."

"Yes, ma'am." There went the "ma'am" again. Why did that bother her so much? "If you change your mind, please give me a call."

Cassie said, "I will." But she had no intention of following through.

What should she do? If she went home, she could have Jonathan pounding on her door, wanting to see her. Not to mention a reporter—or two or three. It had to be a pretty juicy story when a well-known and respected wedding planner was a runaway bride. Her worst nightmare had come to life.

As soon as she ended the call, she stepped outside to clear her head. She walked in front of her cottage, turned and walked back, and did that again, and again, and again. Finally, she sat on the front step.

She could go somewhere else for a week. She was supposed to be on a honeymoon, after all. No one expected her to be doing anything for them right now. Maybe she should book a flight to somewhere tropical. Hawaii. The Caribbean. That would be nice. Maybe a beach in Mexico. She got up, walked again in front of the cottage, and came back and sat down.

"Get a grip, Cassie. You can't let these people control you." When she leaned back, she thought about her condo. If she could go there and lounge around and read books all day, that would be heavenly.

A meow from inside her cottage brought her back to reality. Romeo. She couldn't go running off to the tropics. Not right now. She had a little mouth to feed. She stood and brushed herself off. This was as good a place to hide out as any.

There was a kitchenette, and if she stocked up on food, getting through Sunday would be easy this time. She might not be much of a cook, but she could certainly boil water to make pasta or something else super easy. A salad didn't even require the stove.

Yes, she would stay here just a bit longer. She marched over to the office. Randi was lounging in the back, as usual.

"Randi."

The motel clerk looked up, startled, then came toward the front. "Is something wrong? Please don't tell me the toilet is overflowing or the sink is stopped up."

Cassie shook her head. "None of those things. I wondered if I'd be able to stay for another week."

A grin spread across Randi's face. "Absolutely." She leaned on the counter. "Did our town charm you?"

The answer she clearly expected was a resounding yes.

"Honestly, the attention I could get because I'm a wedding planner who's a runaway bride has made me realize I need to hide out for a while. But I do like my new room."

Randi chuckled, then caught herself. "I'm so sorry. That isn't funny." She bit her lip as she tried to not laugh.

"It is funny. Just not from my side."

"I'd be thrilled to have you stay."

Cassie started to leave, then realized there was one thing she still needed to ask.

"Yesterday, I found a kitten. After talking to Dinah and the vet, I decided to keep him because he needs a home. I didn't think it was a big deal for one night. But for a week, I need to ask if it's okay if I have a kitten in my cottage."

Randi brushed the comment aside with a wave of her hand. "Of course. If he shreds something, though, I'll have to charge you."

"I understand. Thus far, he's been a good little guy, so I think we're safe."

Cassie raced into her unit so she could call back Bella before she left her condo.

"I have something else I want you to pick up, after all."

"You caught me just in time. I was about to head out the door. I've got a change of clothes. What else would you like?"

"I want enough clothes to last a week."

"A week? What's wrong, Cassie?"

Only a true friend would know that meant there was a problem. "The flowers were from Jonathan. He's clearly trying to reach me."

"You're not letting that weasel keep you from your own home, are you?" Defiance seeped through her friend's words.

"And a reporter from *Bridal Dreams* called because they want to interview a runaway bride wedding planner." She couldn't keep the sarcasm out of her voice.

Bella gasped. "You've been trying to get an article in there for years, and now they want you because of this? Don't worry. I'll get together enough stuff for you and be out there in a couple hours."

"And grab my laptop, too. I might be in the mood to do some work, and I hate using my phone for anything more complicated than simple searches online."

Bella chuckled. "We need to make a modern woman out of you."

Somehow, Bella could always make her grin.

"I'll see you soon. And lunch at Dinah's is on me."

"It's a deal. I'll see you soon."

Cassie stretched out on her bed with Romeo beside her. He crawled up onto her chest, curled up, and fell asleep. She didn't have the heart to disturb him, so she picked up her phone and started reading a book that she'd been curious about but not taken the time to read yet. The story was good, but her restless night must have caught up with her, because she dozed off.

She jolted awake when Romeo meowed in her ear. Checking her clock, she saw that it was almost time for Bella to arrive. She picked up her kitten and set him on the floor so he could get to his food and box.

"I'm going to be outside waiting for a friend. I won't be far at all."

He watched her as she spoke as though he understood every word. He probably did.

Cassie walked over to the motel's entrance and sat down on the bench in front of the office. About fifteen minutes later, Bella came around the corner, driving Cassie's car. As Cassie tried to figure out what was going on, another car pulled in after her, one that Cassie recognized as Bella's.

She stepped over to her car, and Bella rolled down the window.

"What's going on?"

"I'll explain in a second. Where should we park?"

Cassie pointed to her cottage, and the two cars drove over there. Bella stepped out, wearing her usual impossibly high heels, which made her petite frame taller. Another friend, Simone, the cake baker Cassie used for most of her weddings, followed. Simone could make cakes so gorgeous they took your breath away, and they were delicious, too.

"I realized you were going to be stuck here with no wheels if I just brought your stuff and had lunch."

Cassie slapped her forehead with her palm. "Oh, my goodness. I would have thought of that later. I guess I'm so used to being here with no way to get out that it didn't even occur to me."

"So I recruited Simone, who, I will have you know, set aside a cake she was working on to do this."

Simone gave a cheeky grin. "Bella promised you'd buy me a wonderful homey lunch at a restaurant here if I came."

"I can do that and go one better. Dinah makes the best pies you have ever tasted."

"Ooh! I love homemade pie. Show me the way."

"Before we go, there's someone I want you to meet. Come inside."

She went in first and scooped up her kitten, snuggling him close.

"Bella and Simone, meet the new guy in my life. Romeo."

"Oh my goodness, he's so cute!" Bella rubbed him under his chin.

"I think so." Cassie knew she had a silly grin on her face. Then she told them how she'd saved him.

Simone shuddered. "I don't want to imagine what would have happened if you hadn't been there."

Bella said, "He's a cat, so he might have landed on his feet and walked away. But I'm glad we won't know. Speaking of walking..." She put her hand on her belly. "Can we walk out to my car and go to this Dinah's Place you keep mentioning? My stomach wonders where lunch is."

"Sure." She set Romeo on the floor. "But it's a short walk to the restaurant."

Bella tilted her head and stared. "You're willing to skip driving? Aren't you the same woman who said, 'Why walk when you can drive to a coffee shop a block away'?"

Cassie grinned. "I am. I haven't had a car for the last few days, so I guess I'm used to it now."

"I'm willing. Simone, how about you?"

"Sure. I have my comfortable cake-decorating shoes on. Let's go."

Cassie looked down at her friend's shoes and laughed. "You didn't buy those with pink and purple spots on them, did you?"

Simone held up one foot. "These babies are completely custom. Each pair begins as white, but food coloring and frosting give them flair. You should see my work shoes by the time I need a new pair."

"We'll give them a walk outside today. Let's go."

"Wait!" Bella put her hand on her arm. "You're forgetting something."

Cassie shrugged.

"I brought you clothes. You haven't become so used to wearing that outfit that you aren't going to change, right?"

*Clean clothes.* "I am ready to put on something that fits, anything that fits." She almost added, *And that I haven't been wearing for days already*, but she didn't want to bring attention to the fact that she'd been wearing these jeans since last Saturday.

They went outside. Bella still had Cassie's car keys, so her friend opened the trunk and hauled out two large suitcases. More than Cassie would have brought for a month.

"I'm here for a week. Remember?"

"Hey, you asked *me* to pack, so I did it my way. You have coordinated outfits, including shoes and accessories, for two weeks. I even included a special outfit for an event."

Cassie raised an eyebrow. "I'm in a small town and don't have any elegant events planned."

"You never know when you'll need something for a different occasion."

Cassie laughed. "So far, my social life has been limited in Two Hearts."

"That could change. What if a handsome man interests you? Dinner out requires appropriate clothing."

Cassie knew her face burned red as she remembered the night before, so she reached for the luggage and turned her back to them as she stumbled toward the door with the heavy suitcase.

"We'll wait out here. Those suitcases will fill up the center of your room."

Cassie wanted to comment on the fact that a small bag would have worked, but she knew Bella had gone to extra effort for her. Besides, her friend had years of experience in fashion— first with everyday clothing in a shop, and now with wedding dresses—so asking her to stuff jeans and T-shirts in a bag would have been futile.

Cassie did find jeans, so she took out that outfit, which included one of her favorite tops and coordinating earrings.

Dressed, she admired her outfit in the mirror. Bella had chosen a green shirt, silver earrings, and a simple necklace.

Cassie closed the door securely behind her. When they were passing the motel office, the sheriff drove by. He pulled to the side and stopped, rolling down his window.

She gulped. If her friends thought she'd run away and found a new romance with the local sheriff, they would never let her live it down.

"Good morning, Sheriff," she greeted him, in a tone she hoped sounded small-town friendly.

"I think it's afternoon," he said. She hadn't noticed it before, but now, she wondered how she'd missed the smooth texture of his voice. It made her melt even when she didn't want to—like now. "Are you bringing more visitors to our small town?" His comment sounded appropriate, not too friendly. He tilted his hat back on his head, and she saw his handsome face better.

Simone said in low voice, "Whoa."

Cassie hoped Greg hadn't heard.

"My friends Isabella and Simone brought my car and some clothes."

He looked her up and down. "Very nice. I'm sure you'll be glad to be wearing your own things when you go back to Nashville today."

"She's staying for another week." Bella's smirk said that Cassie wasn't fooling her.

"That's great." His blue eyes lit up, and he smiled, bringing out the dimple in his cheek.

Simone whispered in Cassie's ear, "Are you kidding me?"

Cassie nudged her friend's arm. "We're on our way to Dinah's Place. I'm sure I'll see you around."

"I had the leftover pizza from last night for lunch. I'm still amazed that you were right about the ham and pineapple."

He'd kept the conversation small-town friendly. Bella could guess all she wanted, but Cassie wouldn't give her any confirmation that they hadn't been eating dinner with a large group.

"Have a great lunch, ladies." He waved. "I'll call you about going out again for pizza, Cassie." He drove down the street.

Simone stared at her. "You landed in a town with a sheriff who looks like that? I can't find a man who looks that good in all of Nashville."

"We're just friends." And they were. "Jonathan stomped on my heart. I enjoyed the pizza, but that's all it was."

"Believe that all you want, Cassie. That man's interested."

Cassie's heart did a dance at the thought. Then she pushed any ideas of interest in him aside. "Do you think so? I haven't encouraged him."

They continued down the sidewalk, and Bella replied this time. "I do. And you may be more interested than you realize."

Cassie wanted to argue that point, but she wasn't sure she could. She'd have to do better with her wayward heart. Now wasn't the time for romance.

The three of them soon stood in front of what had once been the wedding dress store. Bella turned in a circle slowly, her gaze going from empty store to empty store. She stopped, facing Cassie and Simone.

"It's hard to imagine this as a happy place."

Simone shuddered. "I don't know about you, but I get a creepy feeling from all these empty buildings. Are you sure you want to stay here even one more night?"

"You haven't eaten at Dinah's Place or met the people."

Simone's expression changed to a smirk. "We met the sheriff."

Cassie felt her face flush. "I told you. He's just a nice guy helping a stranded traveler." She warmed to that idea. "It's part of his job." There. That should make them see the situation right.

Bella and Simone burst into laughter.

Bella hugged Cassie. "I'm glad you found some happiness while you were here." When she stepped back, she put her hand on Cassie's back and nudged her forward. "I need that food you promised."

Up the street a short distance, Cassie caught the scent of Dinah's Place. "I can't tell what she's cooking today, but I'm sure it's great."

"Chicken soup." Bella and Cassie turned to Simone after she spoke. "It smells like my mother's homemade chicken noodle soup. Hers was the absolute best."

Bella picked up speed, something Cassie marveled at with her friend's high-heeled footwear. "If you're even close to right, I'm happy," her friend said.

A short time later, they were seated, and Michelle placed bowls of chicken soup in front of each of them.

Bella took a spoonful and sighed. "Yum. This was worth that long drive down country lanes."

Cassie paused with her spoon halfway to her mouth. "I honestly remember very little of it beyond open fields with horses and cows, and some forested places. Was it an unpleasant drive?" She took a bite of the soup, then eagerly scooped up another spoonful. "This is so good. You know your soups, Simone."

"Food is my life."

Bella and Cassie stared at her.

"What? Did I drip broth down my chin?" She wiped at it with her napkin.

"That sounded so profound."

"It has been a profound day. I'm designing a cake for a painter marrying an engineer. She's all about the colors and artistic balance. He needs to have symmetry or it offends his very existence."

Bella snorted. "Perhaps a little dramatic?"

"You aren't in the middle of it. At least you don't have the groom involved with dress design."

Cassie laughed. "She may not have the groom, but she has the mother, mother-in-law, sisters, bridesmaids . . . the list goes on. I've sat in on some wedding gown design discussions that shocked me. And after eight years in this business, very little can do that."

"Hey, Cassie." Bella leaned closer. "Have you noticed that everyone's watching us?"

"They did that with me when I came here Saturday."

"Yes, but you were wearing a wedding dress. Simone and I are normal."

"Nope. You're not. You're visitors to a town that sees very few of those."

Bella sat back and had another bite of soup. "I see your point." She pushed her bowl away when she finished. "Much better. Now, tell me why you like it here?"

Simone choked on her soup. Once she'd recovered, she said, "You met the reason. She may never leave."

Cassie laughed. "I have a life in Nashville, one that I've worked hard to build." She dropped her voice. "I'll tell you why when we're outside."

Both of her friends looked like they wanted to argue that point, but remained quiet when Cassie gestured with her head to the people around them. Several of the people were regulars at lunchtime; she'd seen them before. An older man she recognized sat in the corner and seemed to be nodding off.

Michelle came over. "I know Cassie wants dessert. Anyone else?"

Bella laughed. "You have dessert every time you come here?"

Michelle answered. "You haven't eaten a slice of Dinah's pie. She made strawberry pie—she apparently got a great deal on fresh strawberries."

Once they'd all placed orders, Cassie asked, "Who is that man in the corner?"

Michelle turned to look. "That's Two Hearts's mayor."

The elderly man had fallen asleep and now had his head on the table over folded arms.

"Did you say *mayor*?"

"No one else wants the job. He's had the position for decades." She looked thoughtful. "I think he's ninety on his next birthday, so someone's going to have to step up soon. I'd better wake him up. Someone will help him home."

When their pie arrived piled high with whipped cream, Cassie's mouth watered.

Simone took one bite, then another. "Oh, my goodness! This is amazing!"

Michelle cruised by. "Coffee?"

Simone pointed to her cup as she shoved in another bite.

Grinning, Michelle said, "Dinah says the best compliment is when people enjoy her food. I think I can tell her you're enjoying it."

Cassie nodded. "She seems to have her mouth full, so I'll say it. Please tell Dinah that she's outdone herself today. And my friend is a respected wedding cake baker from Nashville, so she knows her baked goods."

"Do you also do something with weddings?" Michelle asked Bella.

"I make wedding gowns."

"Ones like on those TV shows?"

"Better than that. Mine are custom made for each bride."

Michelle set her pot of coffee on the table. Glancing at each of them as she spoke, she asked, "Have you ever done a wedding for someone famous?"

Cassie tried to distract her. "Nashville has a lot of famous people."

"I mean someone in country music."

It couldn't hurt to say a little more. "That, other kinds of music, actors. I've done weddings for all of those."

"Me, too," Bella said.

"And I made a cake for a former astronaut. That one was interesting."

"Cassie's planning the wedding for one of the country music greats right now." Now Bella had opened things up.

"Ooh. Who is he?" Michelle's small-town life probably included few of the people she saw in movies or heard on the radio.

"I can't give you a name. I signed a non-disclosure agreement," Cassie said.

The waitress's face dropped.

"But I can tell you it isn't a he, it's a she."

Michelle's eyes narrowed, and she stared off into the distance. Then she snapped her fingers. "I know. You're doing Carly Daniels's wedding!"

Cassie swallowed hard. Client confidentiality was huge in her industry—and that went double for Carly, who had surprised fans last year with her announcement that she was leaving the music industry.

"I can't say who my client is." She hoped that would send Michelle away happy but not able to spread rumors.

Instead, Michelle smiled and gestured with her fingers to turn a lock on her mouth. "My lips are sealed. No one will hear it from me." She walked away with an expression that said she had news for the Two Hearts Gossip Express.

As they finished their pie, Cassie realized that the waitress didn't seem to be sharing her news. Yet.

Once she'd paid the check for the three of them, as promised, they went out the door, this time turning left so she could show them the charming church.

As they walked, Bella asked, "How *is* Carly Daniels's wedding going?"

"Couldn't be better. All guests have been instructed to keep the wedding location secret. One month from now, Carly's farewell tour will be over, and she and Jake will be on their honeymoon on a private island in the Caribbean."

"I love their story." Simone sighed. "They were so cute when they came to me for their wedding cake. He'd make a suggestion, and she'd find a way to turn it into something . . . well, good." Simone laughed. "Their design is one of a kind. It's right for them."

"Are there hot-pink cowboy boots on it?"

Simone laughed. "No. Jake actually suggested that, but Carly coaxed him into doing roses that color instead."

"She came in for her final fitting last week, so that's a go, too. It's always nice when a wedding comes together without problems."

# CHAPTER NINE

𝒞assie stopped in front of the church with her friends beside her. "Isn't this adorable?"

Simone pointed to the front of the building. "Those wide brick steps with the white church behind them would be perfect for wedding photos."

"I agree. Right now, with the spring flowers blooming, it's quite special."

Bella ran her hand over the outside of the building. "Like other things in this town, it needs to be painted."

"Yeah." Cassie sighed. "They have so much potential here. I wish they could bring the town back to life. If only I could figure out a way to help."

"Cassie, when it comes to planning anything, you're nothing short of genius. But I don't think even you can come up with an idea to solve this town's problem."

"I wish you could."

A male voice behind them made Cassie jump, and she put her hand over her racing heart. She turned to find Albert holding the leash of a small brown dog.

He looked up at the church. "When I was young, this town

had a lot going for it. I'd like to live long enough to see that happen again. We keep talking about painting the church."

"It would cost a lot in paint alone."

"We have enough money to buy the materials. We *don't* have enough money for the labor."

"What about having townspeople do the work?" That seemed to be an easy answer to Cassie.

"Sandy Meyer tried to pull something together a year or two ago. But people didn't have the enthusiasm they needed for the project. I think it's because the town in general needs to be fixed up. This seemed unimportant in the grand scheme of things."

Cassie turned toward the church again. It looked to be in great shape as far as the structure went. "The building is protected when it's painted. The more raw wood that's visible, the more the building is exposed to the elements and will deteriorate."

Albert nodded. "I know that from a construction standpoint. Fifty years in a hardware store taught me as much. But it wasn't communicated to the people well."

She had a week here. Could she do this in a week?

Bella stepped in. "Cassie can plan and convince people to do things you would not even imagine."

Cassie put her hands on her hips. "Hey, I do good things with my work."

"I never said they weren't good. I just said you could get the job done. I've seen you talk bridezillas down from ledges and mean mothers-in-law-to-be from their high and mighty positions so they see your take on things. Albert, if anyone can do this, it's Cassie."

Cassie took a step back. "Bella, are you suggesting that a newcomer organize the town to paint their church?"

Albert eyed the church and gave a nod. "I think that's an excellent idea."

"But won't people be angry if somebody they don't know

tries to do this? If *I* do it?" Cassie pointed at her chest.

Albert went silent for a moment. "I think most people will be fine with it once it gets going. I'm not going to lie to you, though. It's possible some people may not like it."

*So I get more stress on my vacation?* Cassie's next thought was. *But I also love getting lost in a project. Never have I wanted to lose myself in a project more than I do now. This could be perfect. Maybe.*

"I think everyone will be excited about the results," he added.

Cassie leaned back to see the steeple over the church. As she did, the sun came from behind a cloud, catching the stained glass in its rays. This church deserved to be saved. "I'll do what I can."

Cassie waved goodbye to her friends. As she watched Bella's car head down the road, loneliness seeped in. Should she get in her car and follow them? She hadn't unpacked yet beyond the clothes she wore.

The second she pictured her condo, she also imagined Jonathan at the door with flowers in his hands and a lie in his mouth. Then there was the writer from the magazine.

Besides, now she had a project in Two Hearts. She would begin work on the church in the morning. She'd buy supplies this afternoon. After some time with Romeo.

When she entered her cottage, she found him curled up on her pillow—and a trail of shredded toilet paper from the bathroom to the bed. What a mess!

"Did you get bored?" He opened one eye and stretched, then curled back up in a tight ball. "This must have been quite a workout. A nap is certainly called for." Crouching, she gathered up the mess and threw it away. Then she took the roll off its holder and put it on the bathroom shelf, far higher than a kitten could reach.

After going through her luggage to see everything Bella had packed, she chose several items to hang up and gleefully put her favorite shampoo and other toiletries in the bathroom. Knowing she had work to do, she put on ankle boots her friend had paired with a summer dress. Bella may have assumed she'd wear them with a dressier outfit, but they would do the job as work boots today.

"Since you seem happy to sleep right now, Romeo, I'll go to the hardware store. Would you like to watch a movie with me tonight? I have my computer now."

Romeo's tail twitched. She took that as a yes.

When she went out, she started to walk away, then turned toward her car. She might have supplies to carry. But it was such a glorious day, and she'd come to enjoy her walks here. Maybe Albert would drop things off if she bought too much to carry. Or she could pick it all up later.

She set off, crossed Main Street, and took a left at the next street. Albert had pointed in this direction when he'd mentioned the hardware store, so it must be here. She could look it up, of course, but roaming until she stumbled upon the building had a ridiculous sense of adventure to it.

This was a new street to her. Homes lining it looked to be from the 1920s or 1930s instead of from the Victorian era like the houses where Mrs. Brantley lived. Maybe there had been a fire or something that had destroyed this street's houses from the earlier period.

Each house had cute details, like a curved brick wall on the side or an arched front door. One stood out from the rest. The yellow cottage's picket fence had lost most of its white paint, but the graceful curve of each section of pickets and the crisscross pattern of wood on the gate made it stand out even now. The house and yard had an air of neglect, but, like the church, it seemed that it wasn't beyond rescue.

She imagined the property with a fresh coat of white on the

fence and yellow on the house, the yard mowed and weeded, bright blooms spilling out over the window boxes, and old-fashioned lace curtains billowing out of windows on a breeze. Even though she'd never imagined herself in a house like this, something about that peaceful image spoke to her. She could see herself coming home to it after a busy day at work. She snapped a few photos to remind her of this simpler way of life when she was back in the city.

Turning away, she continued down the sidewalk. Too bad she couldn't do a ninety-minute-plus commute twice a day. Her business would wither and die if she missed three hours of work every day.

A few blocks later, she entered an area with more shops. A bank that had closed its doors and now only had an ATM. What had been another restaurant, if the cup-of-coffee symbol on the front was any indication, was also shuttered. A half dozen other businesses of unknown history were empty.

The hardware store, a brick building with a faded advertisement for nails on the side wall, seemed to be the only thing still open. A sidewalk she hadn't noticed when she'd walked down Main Street connected these buildings and that main road.

Opening the door under a sign that said *Two Hearts Hardware*, she heard the tinkling of a bell, and Albert greeted her from a worn, wooden front counter.

"Miss Cassie, you're here!"

His words surprised her. "I told everyone I wanted to help."

He hurried around the counter. "I thought you'd be too busy, you being a city girl with no ties to this community."

She smiled. "I do what I say I'll do." Unlike a certain man in her life.

His lips twitched like he wanted to say something. When he cleared his throat but still didn't speak, she realized the problem.

"I ran away from my wedding because my fiancé cheated on me. He didn't meet his obligations to me. I didn't run because I got cold feet."

"The man must be blind! Why, no man in his right mind would do that."

Grinning, she said, "I appreciate that. Now, let's get started. I have a date with a scraper."

Albert went around the hardware store, grabbing a few scrapers—"in case someone else wants to help"—sandpaper, and dust masks. Then he piled them on the counter. Cassie was relieved to see that she could easily carry everything.

"I can order the primer and paint when the building is ready."

She hoped she could get her part done before she left next week.

"I'll drop off a ladder in a little while."

Why hadn't she thought of that? Stepladders were fine by her. Staying at her height or below didn't bother her. She only freaked out when she went higher.

This church had a lot of area to prepare that was up high.

There was no way she would go back on her word, though, so she was just going to have to get over it.

Ten minutes later, she looked up at the church and gulped. What had been a charming steeple mocked her. Her love of old buildings had stolen her good sense when she'd offered to help with this project.

Cassie carefully stepped around the tulips and daffodils to get to the church building. She hoped the amount of work she had to do would appear better up close.

It looked worse.

Peeling paint would need to be scraped off of every board on this side of the building—probably on the whole building. She might be in trouble here. Alone, even if she worked from dawn until dusk for the next week, it was unlikely she'd finish this.

But the weather was great, and she enjoyed being outside, so she'd do what she could.

By the time Albert arrived with the ladder, she'd worked her way all the way down one board and back up the one above it. She had scraped and scraped, and her arm had already started to get tired.

He stopped his pickup truck—a red beauty that was probably from the 1940s or '50s—in front of the church and carried the extension ladder over, propping it against the side of the building. "I can't stay to help you right now because the hardware store is open, but I can come back after work and on the weekend."

"Aren't you open on Saturday and Sunday?"

"Emily Ponder's son helps me out. But he's going to finish up high school here in a couple months, and then I may be in trouble."

"Don't worry about me, Albert. I'll just keep working."

She sensed him standing there for a couple more minutes, then heard the plodding of his footsteps moving away and the roar of the engine as he brought it to life and drove away.

It surprised her that no one else had come out to see what she was doing. She had a big problem, though. To do the building alone, she'd have to climb the ladder. That meant she'd have to climb more than a few feet off the ground.

She turned toward the street. Maybe if people saw her working, they would decide to help. With that in mind, she decided to scrape the most visible part of the building: the front of the church.

As she walked away from her position, the ladder seemed to mock her. *You're afraid to climb up on me, aren't you, Cassie?*

"Yes. Yes, I am," she replied, feeling foolish as soon as she did.

She'd done so many things in her life, jumped over so many hurdles and through so many challenges, including last

Saturday. Having a fear of heights seemed silly. As long as she held onto the ladder, she would be safe, right?

Or would she? Unless she put a rope around her waist or something like that, if she fell, she'd hit the ground. Hard. She spotted a length of rope in the extra goods that Albert had brought. What he intended it for, she had no idea. Although maybe it was to be a new bell pull for the bell in the steeple. She tucked her scraper in her back pocket. Holding the rope in her hands, she envisioned how a lasso would look, twisted and knotted the rope, and came out with something that looked right. She could slip it over her head and hope it would tighten at her waist.

Looking upward, she decided to tie the other end of the rope to the building. That would protect her. "And no one will need to know I'm the biggest baby on Earth when it comes to heights," she whispered as she took the next step.

If she kept going up, did this one time, she'd be safe after that. A decorative support on the corner would work perfectly for the rope. Climbing slowly higher, the air getting thinner with every step—or maybe it was her fear making breathing harder—she reached the support, wrapped the rope around the chosen wooden piece, and knotted it.

Taking a deep breath, she dared a glance to her right and then her left. "This isn't too bad. I can do this."

Setting the rope loop to her side, she decided to scrape the paint here where she wasn't so high that she felt a need to tie on the rope. If she'd climbed up this far, she could conquer her fears and do the work in front of her.

After scraping the wood to each side of the ladder, she felt a rush of triumph. "I can do anything!" she shouted, then shuffled her feet together in a gentle version of a happy dance.

And instantly regretted it.

Her foot slipped into the rope loop, which she must have tied in a genius way, because it immediately cinched around her ankle when she tried to pull it free, more like a noose than a lasso. She grabbed the ladder to catch herself but leaned back at the same time, and the ladder pulled away from the church.

Screaming, Cassie scrambled against the wall, hoping to find a handhold. When nothing presented itself, she felt herself sliding downward. She was falling. When she hit the ground—because she would—she would break bones.

The rope tightened around her ankle, and she yelped with pain as she spun from upright to hanging upside down.

The boots she'd worn were protecting her ankle, but that didn't stop the blood from rushing to her head.

She dug in her back pocket and pulled out her phone. Gleeful for a second, her grip on it slipped, and she watched it land on the tulips. At least *it* had a padded landing and had probably survived.

Would she?

She saw a tan patrol car coming down the road as it must many times during the day. Unfortunately, its windows were up.

Cassie waved her arms in the air and shouted at the top of her lungs. "Sheriff? Sheriff? Greg Brantley, over here!"

He slowed his car and rolled down the window.

"Sheriff, I'm over here."

Greg parked the car and got out looking around for the source of the voice.

"Greg, here!"

This time he turned to face her, and she waved her arms in the air.

Greg hurried over to the church. "Cassie, what are you doing?"

"It should be obvious to anyone that I'm hanging upside down by a rope from the side of the church."

He propped the ladder against the building and climbed to her foot's level. Then she heard the crackle of a radio. "This is

Brantley, I need a rescue team over to the Two Hearts Church immediately."

"I see that Two Hearts and embarrassment go hand in hand. First the dress, now this. They'll never forget the woman who hung upside down and broke her arm. Or leg." Her voice cracked with desperation.

"Cassie, I don't see a way for me to do this alone. But I've got some guys on their way to help. If they can support you while we loosen the rope, we can get you out of there without any damage."

She nodded, and the movement made her swing back and forth.

He steadied the rope with his hand.

"Thanks." She choked back a sob.

"Uh, Cassie, can I ask why you were on a ladder in the first place?"

She choked back another sob. "I was scraping the church to prepare it for painting."

After a silent pause, he replied. "Are you telling me you wanted to help us out, while visiting here?"

"Yes. Probably not my best plan."

Three trucks pulled up to the church. The men inside all moved into action, and a few minutes later, Cassie was sitting on the ground with her leg stretched in front of her, and the rope was dangling from the church with no one attached to it.

"Thank you, everyone."

Greg knelt beside her. "How did that happen?"

"I'm not sure. I meant for the rope to support me when I got higher up the ladder." She looked up to the top of the church and gulped.

"Cassie, are you afraid of heights?"

She sighed. "I'm sorry to say that I am. I fell off a ladder when I was adding a 'congratulations' banner to the wall of a church hall and ended up with a hairline fracture in my wrist.

In the early days of my career, I was stuck doing a lot of the decorating. Even so, I had someone else do the climbing after that."

"Then please don't get into your scared zone. You do all the stuff you can reach comfortably, and we'll have other people do the rest." He stood and looked around at the men, which had now increased to a group of six. "Will we, guys? This is our church in our town, after all!"

They looked at the ground, and a couple of them scuffed the dirt with their feet.

One of them spoke up. "You're right, Sheriff. If this woman is going to come out here and do this, we should be out here, too."

"That's right. I'll be out here this afternoon, and I expect to see some of you here then. And spread the word."

Greg drove Cassie back to her place. When she stepped out of the car, she yelped in pain.

He hurried around to her side. "Did you injure your ankle?"

Cassie hobbled over to the step to her cottage and rubbed her ankle. "I don't think so. Not seriously, anyway. But I can tell you that I don't want to hang off the side of a building again any time soon."

He chuckled. "Let's hope not."

Cassie looked up at him, and even though he didn't understand what was going on between them, he didn't want to say goodbye to her yet. "Let me help you inside."

She surprised him by not arguing. "Careful when you open the door. I don't want to let my roommate out."

"Short guy? Gray and white hair? Likes to sleep a lot?"

She grinned widely. "That's the one." She stood, being careful not to put too much weight on her right ankle, and opened the door. When he heard a meow, she said, "Honey, I'm home."

The kitten hurried over to the door to greet her. She scooped him up in her arms and turned around.

He rubbed the cat under his chin, just as Cassie had. "You're a cute little guy." Then he cocked his head to the side as pieces of the story came together. "Don't I remember that Martin Dunlow lost a kitten? I'm sure I do."

Cassie snuggled the kitten as though to lay claim to it. "Both Dinah and the vet's assistant said I shouldn't return it to him. He was giving his kittens away when this one escaped, and he's having trouble taking care of the adult cat he does have because of his age and health."

Greg stared at her and the kitten as he sorted out which direction to go with this. Did he follow the straight line of the law and take her kitten away from her, or go with what made sense for everyone involved?

"You're right about Martin," he said at last. "His neighbors are helping him more and more. There's a woman a couple doors down who is cleaning for him, and another one making sure that both he and his cat get fed every day. If he mentions it, I'll tell him I saw a kitten like his that had found a good home."

"As long as he doesn't want him back. Romeo is mine." She held the purring kitten up to her face and put her nose against his.

"Mom called me and said she was making lunch and would love company, but I have to go back to work. Can I take you over there?"

"I'd love to have lunch with your mom. I'll drive. I don't think hiking is a good idea today." She laughed.

"I'll see you later at the church?"

"Try to stop me."

He walked toward his car. "Cassie, I may not have known you long, but I know not to do that."

# CHAPTER TEN

*W*alking up to the Brantleys' back door, she realized that Greg had figured something out in a matter of days that Jonathan never had. If she believed in something, she'd do whatever it took to do it. Everything with her ex-fiancé had been an act, so he didn't care if he knew her well. She was a means to an end.

How stupid could she be?

Sounds of someone working in the kitchen filtered through the screen door. Taking a deep breath, she knocked. She'd forget about Jonathan for now.

Over lunch, Cassie asked about the cute house she'd seen. "There's a cottage on the way from the motel to the hardware store. It's yellow, and the yard is overgrown."

Mrs. Brantley shook her head. "You'll have to give me more than that. So many homes here are either abandoned or neglected." She frowned. "Our town used to be beautiful. Our historic homes are fading away. Soon, no one will be able to save some of them."

"I think this one is abandoned. Grass completely covers the

sidewalk to the front door. No one has walked there recently. The picket fence and gate are unusual." She described it.

Smiling, Mrs. Brantley said, "You're talking about Mabel Murth's house. Her son moved her to his home in Nashville because she was starting to need help and would be closer to her children and grandchildren there."

"Her house was left empty?"

Mrs. Brantley smiled sadly. "What else could be done with it?"

"No one wants to buy it? Or even rent it?"

"Not here, Cassie. Two Hearts is a dying town. We're too far to reasonably commute to the big city every day, and we lost the one reason we had for people to come all the way out here." She stood. "Can I get you another glass of tea?"

Cassie looked down at the empty glass beside her. She'd drunk the tea without realizing it. "I need to get back to work at the church."

She moved her right arm and did her best to hide a wince from sore muscles. "I said I'd do this job, and I will." At least she hadn't had to explain about her earlier rope disaster.

"Then I'm coming with you. Let me get my gloves and scraper."

Cassie wouldn't turn down any help. "I appreciate it."

Cassie winced when she stood, and Mrs. Brantley gave her a look much like her son had. "Did you walk or drive here?"

"Drive. I'm saving my standing time for the project."

They climbed into her car. On the way, Mrs. Brantley said, "Cassie, this town needs to thank you. We should have fixed up the church two or three years ago. Maybe longer ago than that."

"It's a charming building. I simply want it to survive."

The other woman stayed silent for a minute or two. "I want all of our buildings to survive. Please let me know if you have any ideas for saving them, too."

She wished she did. Today was Tuesday. A week from now, she'd be at her desk in Nashville, and life would be back to normal.

Without a fiancé. Without a husband.

*And,* a little voice said, *without this town's sheriff.*

The church came into view with Greg and the group of men —and now, women—clustered around it. He'd traded his uniform for a worn blue T-shirt that showed off the muscles of his arms and jeans. Goodness, he was handsome. Not that it mattered. She wasn't sure what was going on between him and her, except for the fact that nothing should be.

She and Mrs. Brantley approached the group Greg was leading. Or *trying* to lead, would be more accurate. He clapped his hands, and most of the people turned toward him. "Everyone take a place at the building and begin working."

How had he pulled together so many people on a weekday afternoon?

An older woman Cassie thought she recognized from the diner asked, "Doing what? I don't know anything about renovation. This is men's work." She looked up at the building like it presented an impossible task.

Cassie cringed at the idea of work for men versus women. "Anyone can scrape paint off a building."

One of the men spoke up. "Maybe the men *should* do this."

Another woman stepped a few feet in front of him. "Frank Harrison, if you think you can scrape paint better than I can just because you have a—"

Cassie interrupted with an idea. "Sheriff, what if we had a friendly competition?"

Several of the people perked up at that.

Greg nodded vigorously, obviously glad to hear anything that might stop the escalating confrontation.

Cassie glanced at Greg, hoping her idea would be accepted. "Ladies, we can do this job as well as a man, right?"

A woman said, "You bet we can!"

Cassie smiled. "Then let's see who can get the most done this afternoon. Sheriff, you take photos of what it looks like now on all sides. At five p.m., we'll compare. Whichever group gets more done wins . . ." But what would be the prize?

A teenager she hadn't noticed spoke up. "Free lawn mowing for a month for everyone on the winning team."

Everyone seemed excited at that.

The woman who'd spoken earlier said, "Justin can out-mow anyone. Will you include weeding?"

He held up his hands. "Hey, some of your yards haven't been weeded in years. It's going to take a while just to mow a bunch of lawns."

"Mowing is fair," Mrs. Brantley said.

The woman who'd challenged Frank Harrison agreed. "Time's a-wasting. Set the alarm on your watch, Sheriff, for five o'clock."

Another woman rubbed her hands together with glee. "Let's beat them!"

Frank said, "Hey, now. What makes you think you can beat us?"

Greg interrupted another possible fight. "Choose your side of the building."

Justin said, "I'm going to get some friends together for the teenager side."

"We'll wait for you."

He said, "That's okay. We'll be back soon. You can get started. Just save us a side."

There were more men, so they divided into two groups. Cassie motioned to the women to follow her around to the back. She'd already done the lower boards on the other side and didn't want to have to climb another ladder today.

As they worked, more people came over to the church to help. By the end of the day, there were about thirty people with scrapers in their hands. Greg's alarm went off to end the competition, and people hurried toward him to hear the results.

"Everyone, gather round while I compare the amount done with the photos I took earlier. Albert, you're good with construction. Why don't you verify that I'm doing this right? Is everyone okay with Albert giving the final answer?"

"Yeah, sure." Dinah spoke up. "Albert is as honest as they come."

The two men circled the building, checking each side, with Albert bringing out a tape measure and Greg making notes on a small notepad. When they returned to the group, Albert said, "There's a clear winner." His eyes narrowed. "I don't want anyone complaining about the results. Agreed?"

"Sure, Albert," said Frank, the man who'd been certain men were better at this work. He winked at the fellow men from his group. "Give us the answer." He leaned back on his heels with a smug expression and crossed his arms.

"The winner is . . . Team Four, led by Justin."

Frank sputtered, but he held his tongue. That made Cassie like him. A little bit.

"Congratulations, Justin!" Everyone crowded around the teenagers and clapped them on the backs.

"Hey, Justin," a woman called out. "Whose lawns will you mow?"

"Let me talk to my team." They went into a huddle, then high-fived each other and broke apart. "We've agreed to mow our own lawns, and every week for a month we'll each mow one of your lawns. That will be like a runner-up prize."

As everyone laughed and gathered together, Cassie felt a lightness in the community that hadn't been there before.

Greg walked over to her. "You've done something good here today."

She turned toward him and looked up, immediately

regretting it. His eyes always caught her attention and tugged at her heart. "We all did."

"But it wouldn't have happened without you. I think we can finish this project before you leave."

"I'd like that, Greg. To know that I helped bring some joy to Two Hearts."

"Pizza?"

Her stomach growled before she answered. "We can have pepperoni today."

He chuckled. "Is that a yes?"

"It's a yes. This time, I'm not getting ready to leave town, so I get the leftovers. Deal?"

He thought about that. "Maybe we'll split them."

When they got to the street, she realized they both had cars. "Can you go anywhere without your police vehicle?"

He frowned. "I can. I'm just used to driving it everywhere."

Should she give in or should he? Did it matter?

"Cassie, I'm so used to having everything I need in an emergency—"

"Say no more. We'll go in yours." She couldn't argue with a man who wanted to help people.

After dinner—and with half of a small pizza for each of them to take home—he brought her to her cottage. As always, he stepped out and opened her car door. The moonlight reflected off the golden strands in his brown hair. When he turned toward her after she'd unlocked the cottage's door, he stood on the parking area with her on the step, making them the same height.

His gaze went from her eyes slowly down to her lips. Cassie nervously wet her lips, and his eyes turned to fire. She put her hands on his chest to push him away, but his warmth seeped into her and she rested her hands there.

"Cassie, I know I shouldn't, but . . ." He leaned forward slowly, as though waiting for her to stop him.

Cassie slid her arms up his chest and around to the back of his head.

Their lips met tentatively at first, a breath of a touch before he pulled back. When he leaned forward again, she met him halfway. Nervousness became heat when his lips touched hers again.

He leaned into the kiss and groaned. "We shouldn't," he said when he leaned back for a moment, but he kissed her again.

Minutes later, the sound of Romeo meowing through the slightly open door brought her back to reality.

She glanced around to see if anyone had been watching, but the parking lot was empty. "I'd ask you inside, Greg, but I don't think—"

"That would be a bad idea." He put his hand on her cheek. "Will I see you at the church tomorrow?"

"Try to stop me."

When he'd driven off, she went inside and picked up her kitten. As she got ready for bed a few minutes later, she realized he'd driven off with all the pizza. And her car had been left at the church.

Greg left Cassie's still feeling the touch of her lips on his. What was happening between them? This was craziness. The woman had driven into town a few days ago, and now he couldn't wait to see her again. What were they going to do?

When he'd parked his car in his driveway, he reached for his pizza and found two boxes sitting there. Chuckling, he grabbed them and climbed out. As he walked toward his steps, a voice called out to him.

"I hope that's you, son."

He stopped, hoping his mother was not waiting up for him

to get home from a date. Then he realized she didn't have any idea where he'd been. "It's a beautiful evening out here." He walked around the corner to an area with chairs set up around an unlit fire pit.

"It is that. Sometimes I miss your father at times like these. I miss him many times, if truth be told."

He sat down next to her. "I miss him, too." Right now, he would have liked to ask his advice about Cassie. Then he shook away that thought. She was just somebody who was passing through.

His mother turned toward him. Even in the evening light, he could tell that her expression was speculative. "I would ask if you brought me pizza, judging by what you've got in your hands, but those are probably leftovers."

He shifted in his seat. His mother could be very observant. "Yes, they are leftovers. I went over to Pete's for pizza tonight." *Less is more.* That was an important motto with his mother that he'd learned when he was a teenager: Only tell her what she needed to know. He'd never gotten into any serious trouble when he was growing up, but he'd skirted the edges a few times only to be reeled back by her and his sheriff father.

"Cassie likes pizza."

"Yes, we enjoyed having pizza the other night." He kept his expression neutral.

"Okay, just spill it. Did you take her out again?"

"Mom! I don't have to give you all the details of my dating life. I'm an adult male in my thirties."

She clapped her hands with glee. "Does that mean you're dating Cassie Van Bibber?"

He had put his foot in that one so deep that he wasn't sure how he could pull it back out. "I don't think you can call it dating when someone has been here for a few days and only plans to stay a few more before returning to a city further away than I'm comfortable commuting. We had dinner together tonight. She's alone and she barely cooks. That's my understanding, at least."

"She's led me to believe that she can make a meal or two. She's a nice girl, though."

He couldn't argue with that.

"Are you going to take her to dinner again before she leaves?"

He groaned.

"It's a simple question. If she's just visiting, then it doesn't matter." She put her hand on his. "I know I encouraged the first date."

"You set it up!"

"While that may be true—"

He snorted. "You pushed us together. Don't try to back away from it now."

"Well, I don't want to see you hurt. She made it clear that she has a life in the city."

That made sense. "I don't have any plans to take her to dinner again. She will be working on the church every day either until it's done or until she leaves." He decided a subject change away from his dating life would be best. "Are you going to work on the building again tomorrow?"

She chuckled. "I helped today, but I'm more of an organizer than I am a paint scraper. If you want to pull together any projects, though, you let me know."

That was true. They'd tried to have a farmers market here a few years back, and she had gone all out organizing it, setting up the tables, and turning it into a very nice-looking event. The problem was that there weren't enough people here who cared about things that came from a farm, and most of those who did already lived on one. Many of the locals were fine buying whatever they found at the grocery store. The rest didn't have any extra income to spend on a special variety of tomato or squash.

He stood. "I'm going up to bed now, Mom. Do you want one of these boxes of pepperoni pizza? One was supposed to be Cassie's and one mine. I ended up driving away with both of them."

She took it out of his hands. "I thought you'd never ask. I do enjoy cold pizza as a late-night snack."

He cringed. "I've never understood why anyone liked cold pizza." He leaned forward, hugged her, and kissed her cheek. "But I do love you. In spite of that," he whispered.

As he walked away, he heard the box being opened and the shuffling sound as she pulled out a piece of the pizza. He trudged up the stairs, tired from the work they'd done, but also energized from his time with Cassie. What would his mother say if she knew about that kiss? The bigger question was, was there any way he could talk Cassie into an encore?

He felt pulled toward her in a way he wasn't used to. Even with Suzette, theirs had been more of a gradual relationship. They'd met through a friend, hung out together in groups, and eventually gone out on a date. They were on a path to marriage, so he'd proposed. There had been moments when he'd wondered if that was what he really wanted, but their relationship had seemed like a runaway train by then. And he really had cared for her.

Right up until the minute she'd ended it all because he was a cop.

Would Cassie do the same thing if she *were* here and they actually could have a relationship? It seemed like any woman with an ounce of good sense would. Why would you want to be close to someone you could lose at any moment? These days, though, his career held a lot less danger.

As he put the pizza in his fridge, he thought about tomorrow and smiled. Any spare time he could get, he would be over at the church helping out, making sure that no one else did something silly like hang upside down on a rope.

He chuckled. It had scared him so badly, but she'd been fine. He had a feeling that it took a lot of energy and resilience to be a wedding planner, and that Cassie was able to do her job with no shortage of either.

# CHAPTER ELEVEN

he next few days passed in a blur. Cassie took a shower each night to clean off dust and grime, then, in the morning, she simply walked to Dinah's for breakfast and went straight over to the church. Two out of the three days, someone else was already there and hard at work when she arrived.

Saturday morning, she found a crowd there, which included the attorney. She thought for a moment—Micah. Around back, the group of women had doubled, and several of them were on ladders, scraping the upper boards. Cassie could picture it painted and beautiful again, as it must have looked decades ago.

Greg wandered over, as he seemed to do often. She hoped no one else noticed that.

Cassie said, "At this rate, we may finish the prep work today."

"I wonder if we could get some paint and start the next step soon." His words echoed her thoughts.

"Albert said he'd have to do a special order for this quantity."

Phone in hand, Greg stepped away from the group and toward a massive oak tree at the side of the church, and she followed him. They stood facing the street, along which most of the volunteers had parked. Another helper arrived and went to work.

A few minutes later, he hung up, grinning. "If we can find someone with a pickup truck and a strong back to drive over to get it, Albert says we can have paint in a few hours."

Cassie faced the street, where the truck-to-car ratio was about two to one. "I don't think that will be a problem, do you?"

He chuckled. "Nope. I'll ask someone I trust. Albert has also volunteered to ride along with that person to take care of the purchase details. His truck is vintage, so he'd rather not use it."

Tucking his phone in his pocket, he added, "As soon as I've done that, I'm going up with a friend to work on the steeple."

"No! That's not safe!" She stared up at the towering death trap she'd viewed as charming before her accident.

He put his hand on her arm. "Don't worry. I will have a rope around my waist tied to the building. And I won't hang upside down if I fall." His mouth twitched as if he wanted to laugh.

Cassie rolled her eyes. "Even I can see the humor in it. Now. I probably have a different view of the church than everyone else." She smiled. "Just be careful." For a second, she wanted to lean forward and give him a gentle kiss. She caught herself and stepped back. The darkening of his eyes made her wonder if he realized what had almost happened.

"Sheriff, Albert and I are going to get the paint," a man said from their left.

The spell broken, they both put on smiles and turned toward the speaker.

The thirty-something man faced back toward the church. "You know, Greg, I never thought I'd see anything in this town looking good again." He paused. "We even managed to work around Arlene's flowers." The flower beds had been disturbed but overall were still beautiful.

"I know what you mean. It will make me happy to drive by this building."

"That's what I think too, Greg. It took a stranger to see what we didn't. Thank you, ma'am." The "ma'am" coming from someone her age didn't bother her as much, but giving her credit for this did.

"I'm not the one doing all the work." She motioned toward the building.

The man wore a serious expression when he faced her. "We knew it needed to be done, but we ignored it." He sighed. "I think that's the problem with a dying town like ours. At some point, everyone gives up." He turned toward the building again. "You wouldn't let us do that."

Greg said, "This gives me hope."

"Me too," the other man agreed.

Cassie smiled. Maybe this town could make it.

Mrs. Brantley arrived as the two men were leaving in Albert's truck.

"Mom, I'm surprised to see you here."

She gazed at the church with a smile. "I decided I needed to be part of this."

"I can get you a paint brush."

She laughed. "Maybe I should say that I wanted to see what was going on."

Greg held up his paint scraper. "I'm ready to work on the steeple."

Cassie wanted to stop him, but that was ridiculous. Not only did someone have to do it, but he was a professional when it came to danger and helping others in danger. Even his mother didn't try to talk him out of it.

As promised, he tied a rope around his waist before climbing the ladder. Once on the roof, he went around to the back of the steeple and seemed to fasten the rope to something. She watched as Micah did the same thing, and both men started working.

Mrs. Brantley sighed. "It looks dangerous."

"Agreed. I hope he—they—don't fall." Cassie shouldn't have more interest in the sheriff's safety than the other man's. That might make it seem as though she had a personal interest in him.

"Greg's been climbing trees since he was old enough to do it. Micah is on the volunteer fire department, so he's been trained to do worse than this."

Cassie felt some of her concern lift. "It's just that I've hung upside down on a rope from this building. I know what it's like."

The older woman turned toward her. "You what?"

Cassie felt her cheeks heat. "I thought everyone had heard my story already."

Mrs. Brantley shook her head. "I haven't, but I need to hear it now."

She should have kept quiet. "I was going to tie the rope around my waist"—when she got the nerve—"but my foot caught on it on the ladder. In a strange twist, it tightened on my ankle, and I fell."

"Upside down?"

"Well, that's what happens when a rope is cinched around your leg."

The older woman gasped. "You weren't hurt?"

Cassie answered, "No. Well, nothing besides my pride."

"I can't believe no one told me this." Mrs. Brantley grinned. "But I can picture you and that rope."

"Thankfully, no one took a photo." At least she didn't think anyone had. She hoped that was true.

Cassie leaned back to watch Greg again. No, not just Greg: him and Micah. "They do seem comfortable up there."

"They'll be fine." Mrs. Brantley glanced around, then she leaned closer and said, "I'd be careful about how much extra attention you give my son. People are starting to notice." She nudged her head toward Cassie's left. "Unless you don't mind them thinking that."

When Cassie did her best to appear casual and turned slowly, she found a group of five women watching her, including Michelle from Dinah's Place and a woman who looked like she might give birth any second. One of them pointed at Greg and nudged the woman to her side.

Cassie needed to do damage control. Fortunately, that was something she was very good at.

She walked over to them, smiling. "I've met Michelle, but not the rest of you."

They made introductions, then Cassie turned and looked up at the men on the roof. "Ladies, it makes me nervous when anyone is high up. Are any of the rest of you afraid of heights?"

"I wouldn't go up there," Michelle said.

"Me either," Cassie agreed.

The pregnant woman said, "I've spent so much time in haylofts—" She gasped and put her hand over her mouth, giggling. "That may not have sounded as I meant it to, especially in my present condition." She rubbed her hand on her belly.

The other women laughed.

"On the farm, I mean, I have to work in the hayloft. When I first married Levi, I was nervous climbing the ladder. I got stuck on it once when I couldn't look down or up, and it took me an hour to talk myself into going to the top. Then I got used to it." She patted her belly. "And now, he won't let me climb the ladder at all."

The women had been diverted from Cassie giving too much attention to the sheriff. She'd been here only a week, so why was she so interested in a man she barely knew? His laughter filtered down from the roof, but she kept her eyes focused on the flowers beside the church.

Saturday. One week ago, she'd been ready to marry

Jonathan. She had no business wanting to spend five minutes with anyone male right now. Except maybe Romeo. Her gaze drifted upward. And yet she did.

Checking her watch, she realized she hadn't had anything to eat for hours. Neither had anyone else, from what she'd seen. Dinah could make some money off the crew. Cassie raised her voice. "I'm taking orders for lunch from Dinah's Place. Please give me your order and your cash."

She ended up with more than a dozen orders. A teenager offered to help her carry them.

When they'd finished cleaning up after lunch, Mrs. Brantley said to her, "Don't forget that the restaurant and grocery store will be closed tomorrow."

Cassie frowned. "How did I manage to forget that? I guess I'm used to being able to get anything I want most times of the day in a city."

"Of course, you have a car now, so you can go somewhere else."

That much was true. But she wouldn't want to drive a long distance for breakfast.

"I make a big Sunday breakfast before church. You're welcome to join me."

Greg must be there for every one of those.

"Pancakes, bacon, and scrambled eggs are on tomorrow's menu," Mrs. Brantley added.

Of course, being around Greg wasn't a problem. She just didn't want people to think they were an item. But this would be in a private home.

"I think I'll make blueberry pancakes."

Cassie laughed. "You know my weakness."

Mrs. Brantley grinned. "I know you love food."

"Good food. And that's what I have every time I'm at your house. *Sold.* What time should I be there?"

"Church is at ten a.m., so I like to have breakfast about eight-thirty."

Cassie caught herself as she almost grimaced. "My first thought was, 'No!' But I'm getting used to early mornings. My normal schedule usually includes a lot of late nights because of wedding receptions."

"That's understandable. Can you make it at the crack of dawn?" The big smile on Mrs. Brantley's face made Cassie like her even more.

"For a homemade breakfast, yes, I can."

Greg got up for church the next morning, took a shower, and stared at his clothes in his closet, debating about which shirt to wear. Cassie would be there this morning. When he realized what he was doing, he grabbed the first shirt he saw and put it on without even looking at it. Thankfully, it was a dark blue one that went well with the tan pants he'd already put on.

He went to his mother's for her usual Sunday breakfast and found Cassie sitting at the table with a cup of coffee.

Her gaze went to his and then to his mother.

His mother turned with a spatula in her hand and an innocent expression on her face. "Isn't it lovely that Cassie could join us for breakfast before church?"

Greg battled against rolling his eyes, but couldn't stop the scoffing sound he automatically made. "Mom . . ."

Cassie picked up his mood but misunderstood. "I can eat a snack bar for breakfast." She started to stand.

He shook his head. "You're welcome here, Cassie. My question isn't about you. My mother may be trying her hand at matchmaking." He stared at his mother in a look that he hoped said, *You told me you were worried that she was leaving.*

Cassie blushed fiery red and stared at him wide-eyed.

His mother set a platter of blueberry pancakes on the table. Not addressing the elephant in the room, she simply said, "Sit and eat your breakfast, son." When she placed plates with scrambled eggs and bacon next to the pancakes, he pulled out a chair.

He hugged his mother. "You know how to reach my heart."

He heard her mutter, "I hope she knows that, too."

Cassie reached for her coffee and took a big gulp with amusement dancing in her eyes.

After breakfast, they went to church separately, since he needed to go to work after the service—technically he was on duty even while there—Cassie wanted to help paint, and his mother wasn't sure what she would do with her afternoon.

He drove his police car over there and waited inside the church for Cassie to arrive. She stepped through the door a moment after his mother, then hesitated.

"Cassie, I'm glad you're here." Mrs. Brantley hooked her arm through hers. "You can sit with us." When they arrived at an empty pew, his mother slid in first and tugged on Cassie's sleeve to follow her in.

Greg crossed his arms and watched. That left him sitting next to Cassie and the scene looking less like she had joined him and his mother and more like the two of them were a couple. When he sat next to Cassie after a pause of a few seconds, he leaned forward and around her. "Could your plans be more obvious, Mom?"

Cassie glanced at Greg to her left, then to her right.

His mother dramatically put her hand on her chest. "Me?"

Greg glared at her.

His mother reached around Cassie and patted him on the knee. "You'll thank me in the future."

Everyone stood to sing before he had time to object to his mother's words. He felt the eyes of at least half the people there on them. This had to be the most embarrassing thing that had happened since he'd moved home.

Not that he didn't want to sit beside Cassie. He did. But his mother would get tongues wagging in Two Hearts if she kept this up.

# CHAPTER TWELVE

*A*s she took her shower and got ready for bed that night, Cassie pictured the work they'd accomplished. The two men had finished preparing the steeple for painting, and most of the church had a coat of primer on it. The minister had declared a painting potluck for the following Saturday, and Cassie thought they'd finish it then. It would be a shame she wouldn't be here to see the final result.

There had been times when she hadn't been sure they would band together to get it done. She certainly couldn't have gotten this far alone, no matter how big she had talked in the beginning.

She climbed under the covers and reached for her phone to read a book, but her thoughts kept wandering back to the day's work. She'd done weddings for the famous, almost-famous, and average, unknown couples, but none of those moments compared to this.

After all their hard work, the town now had . . . *one* building.

The gravity of the situation enveloped her. These people were changing a single building. They might be grateful now, but it hadn't brought new businesses, jobs, or income.

They still had a town with too many abandoned houses and stores. Most of the townspeople drove miles to work—if they could find a job. A high percentage of the young people moved away when they were old enough.

All of that was out of her power. Maybe, if a few people or even one strong person took the next step, they could save the town. It would take more than one adorable church, that was for sure.

But she'd keep working on this building until she left. That was her contribution to Two Hearts's future. Then she would drive toward Nashville and her normal life.

Another beautiful day greeted her the next morning, so she decided to take a walk. She went across the highway and looped around the block to see the cute yellow house. Leaning against the sagging, weathered fence, she wondered if anyone would love this house again.

She sighed and moved on. It would probably be empty for years, and that was a shame. A house like that deserved to be somebody's home. *Home* meant something special to her, and she couldn't help missing hers. She'd be glad to get back to her Nashville condo with its city view.

Mrs. Brantley called to her from her front door when Cassie was walking past. When Cassie stopped, the older woman said, "Come inside."

As she neared the door, Mrs. Brantley added, "I glanced out the window and thought I saw you walking by." She stepped back and motioned inward. "Have you had breakfast?"

Stepping inside, she inhaled deeply of the sweet air.

"Where's Greg?"

The other woman glanced over her shoulder at her. "He sleeps in when he's called out in the night. Go on through to the kitchen, and pour yourself a cup of coffee if you'd like one."

Cassie did that and sat in a chair at the table. "I hope the call wasn't anything serious."

The screen door squeaked open, and Greg entered, wearing plaid pajama bottoms, a T-shirt, and with messy sleep-hair. Oh, my, he looked good in the morning. "I can answer that. A couple of teenagers got into a fight. I broke it up, and everyone's fine." He sat beside her at the table. "What's for breakfast, Mom?"

Mrs. Brantley listed off pancakes, bacon, and fresh fruit, then she set a cup of coffee in front of him. He held it up to his nose and inhaled deeply. "This is what I need. Thanks!"

She placed platters of food on the table and sat down with a mug of coffee. After they'd served themselves, the room became quiet except for the sounds of forks tapping plates.

Cassie stared at the platter of pancakes. "I shouldn't have another one."

Mrs. Brantley laughed. "There isn't anything wrong with two pancakes."

"I've already eaten two."

Greg said, "It takes a lot of energy to walk everywhere."

Cassie turned toward him. "That's true."

"You may need another pancake."

Cassie cocked her head to the side as she looked at him. "If I gain weight while I'm in Two Hearts, it's your fault."

Greg picked up his glass of orange juice. "You look amazing now, and you'll stay that way."

The room went silent. Cassie met his gaze and bit back a smile.

Mrs. Brantley looked from her to him, then stood. "I need to finish getting ready. I'll go to my room now and do that." She vanished down a hallway and through a door, closing it behind her.

"Mom is always dressed and ready when I arrive every morning." Turning toward Cassie, he said, "I apologize if I crossed a line with my comment."

She'd been startled at first, but flattered after that. "I'll thank you for your kind words, and we can leave it at that."

He gave a single nod of his head. Continuing with his breakfast, he said, "Are you planning to leave tomorrow?"

Cassie tugged her plate to her and added the pancake, but she was conservative with the syrup. "That's my plan. I'd only expected to take a week off. I'm working on a major celebrity wedding that takes place in a few weeks. Planning weddings takes more hours than you would expect."

By the time his mother re-emerged, they'd both finished eating, and Cassie had loaded the dishes into the dishwasher.

To Cassie, she looked exactly as she had before. Smiling at them, Mrs. Brantley said, "I assume you're driving, Greg. Let's go."

A short distance from the house, the police radio went off. Greg listened, then said, "On my way." To them, he said, "I'm going to drop you off at the church. Cherry Malone called 9-1-1. They answered the call, but she never spoke to them." He'd become a cop in a second, and had a concerned but in-charge expression.

"Oh, my!" Mrs. Brantley put her hands on her face. "Is Levi there?"

Greg frowned. "He said yesterday that he'd be gone until late today. He went to Nashville to buy a baby bed to surprise Cherry."

They neared the church. The last thing Cassie wanted was to get involved in something beyond her skill level, but if Cherry had gone into labor, she might be a good assistant to him. "I may be able to help."

"I'm sure you're a great wedding planner, Cassie, but—"

"And I have some emergency medical training. A wedding planner needs to be able to handle whatever comes her way."

Greg stopped at the church. "I know the basics, and I've had to use them, but I'm not going to turn down someone who can help while we wait for the ambulance."

"The whole church will be praying that the baby and mama

are healthy." Mrs. Brantley patted Cassie on the shoulder before climbing out of the car. Cassie waved at her as they drove away, hoping her training would make her ready for whatever they encountered.

They drove north out of town, a direction she'd only gone at night when they'd had pizza. In the daylight, fields with crops barely above the soil lined the road. A farmhouse now and then, and a treed area, added to its beauty. A field of pine trees in rows must have been part of a Christmas tree farm. She did love country roads, but it was difficult to enjoy them with her heart racing in concern for Cherry.

Greg turned onto a gravel driveway, and they approached a white farmhouse with a barn to its left. Beyond the house, a field of colorful flowers added a stunning pop of color. What did they grow that was so different from the other farmers?

He seemed to read her mind. "They grow flowers for flower shops." He parked the car and had the door open a second later. "Cherry?" he loudly called as he raced toward the house.

Cassie, following him, heard a sound she couldn't identify coming from the barn. She knew it could be that a cow had mooed or a horse had nickered, but she ran that way, anyway. The dim lighting in the barn made her blink and wait for her eyes to adjust. Once they did, she saw a woman lying on the floor—the same pregnant woman she'd met when they'd been working on the church.

"Cherry!"

When the woman moaned, Cassie hurried outside. She shouted, "Greg! She's in the barn," then went back to the woman's side. Brushing the hair off Cherry's face, she asked, "What's going on?"

"Water broke," she gasped out, then winced and began the quick in-and-out breaths Cassie recognized from being at a friend's side when she'd given birth.

Greg crouched beside her.

The woman relaxed a fraction as the pain seemed to subside. "I thought I had plenty of time to feed the animals and get to the hospital." She gulped. "I thought wrong. Sheriff, my contractions are coming fast."

Cassie grabbed the woman's hand as she went into another contraction. "We're here with you."

Greg left and returned with a first aid kit, blankets, and towels he must have found in the house. When Cherry relaxed again, he said, "The ambulance is on the way, but I'd like to get you on a clean surface. Cassie and I are going to slide this blanket under you." He stretched it out and nodded at Cassie. When he lifted Cherry, Cassie slid the fabric. They got it under Cherry in time for another contraction. Greg put the other blanket over her, then motioned for Cassie to step to the side with him.

When they were away from Cherry's hearing, she leaned forward. "Greg, that baby is coming soon! My friend was like this a few minutes before she gave birth."

He nodded. "I know. That's why I moved her to somewhere cleaner. Did your training extend to delivering babies?"

Cassie closed her eyes for a moment. "I studied the emergency medical techniques I thought I'd need at a wedding. We touched on birth, but barely. I know we need to keep her calm."

"I helped a cab driver deliver a baby once in Chicago."

"Then you're way ahead of me." She tugged his arm. "Let's do everything we can for Cherry and her baby."

Cassie went back to Cherry, took her hand again, and decided to distract her between contractions. "Your field of flowers is so beautiful."

Cherry gave a slight smile. "Having a cutting farm was my idea. It's only our third year doing it." The other woman looked up at Cassie. "Tomorrow's our third anniversary. I hoped our baby would be born that day."

Cassie did not think this baby would wait that long, and he or she made a point of that when a new, harder contraction hit.

When Cherry breathed more easily, Cassie said, "Tell me about the flowers. What do you grow?"

"So many! Spring, summer, and fall, we have something blooming all the time. The sunflowers are one of my favorites. I love seeing the field of them with their faces all pointed at the sun."

"That does sound beautiful."

Cherry gasped and squeezed Cassie's hand, hard, but this time she also writhed and twisted in pain.

She and Greg would need to help this baby into the world. Before they could move into action, the faint sound of a siren filtered through Cherry's screams. Cassie glanced up at Greg, but he was already on his way out the door. The sirens grew louder and louder.

"I need to push!" Cherry grunted out between breaths.

Trying to remember everything from her friend's birth, Cassie pictured the mother's legs being bent at the knee. She helped Cherry get in that position as a uniformed man and woman hurried into the building.

They quickly assessed the situation and took over.

Cassie fled to where Greg watched from the side of the barn.

Greg had never been more grateful to see anyone in his life as when Gerry and Tom had come into view. Cassie stood beside him, shivering—whether from the chill of the barn or the tense situation, he wasn't sure. He put his arm around her for warmth and pulled her to his side.

As soon as he did that, he wondered if she'd misinterpret his motives and push away. She surprised him by leaning against him as they watched the miracle taking place in front of them.

When, not five minutes later, the paramedics clipped the cord on the baby, Cassie gasped. "We almost had to . . ." Her words drifted off as the thought sank in.

He gulped. "I know." He rubbed her arm when she shivered again. "I think we could have done it." At least he hoped so. Law enforcement officers had to make life or death decisions all the time. He was glad that today, they had life.

The paramedics soon lifted Cherry onto a stretcher and drove away with her and the baby. Greg had kept his arm around Cassie through the birth, but now it was only there because he wanted to be closer to her. Something about her made him want a relationship, even though he knew she couldn't be interested in anything long-term with him. Other than their one kiss, she'd treated him as a friend and nothing more.

Considering the fact that she'd almost gotten married a week ago, that was understandable. Since she would be driving out of Two Hearts tomorrow and probably wouldn't ever be back, that saved him the pain of losing her.

He couldn't lose what he'd never had. He needed to keep telling himself that. They were friends, and that would be fine.

She stepped away from him and rubbed her hands on her arms. "I need a nice, peaceful day after all this excitement."

"Maybe Mom can whip us up lunch. What would be relaxing to you?"

"Let me think about it." She seemed to consider it as they went back down the driveway. Halfway back to town, she said, "I need to spend some time with Romeo this afternoon. He's still new to me and needs to have me around."

*Well, she brushed you off nicely, didn't she, Brantley?*

"Do you have a board game we could play at my cottage? Is that too sedentary for you?"

When he glanced at Cassie, her eyes said she did want to spend time with him. His heart gave a leap as he pushed aside his noble ideas about not getting involved with a woman who was ready to leave town.

"I'm the board game champion and will take you down."

She laughed. "You can try."

They entered his mother's house, laughing.

His mother asked, "Are they okay?"

"Mother and daughter are fine. They should be in the hospital by now."

"A girl! Cherry told me yesterday that they wanted the baby's sex to be a surprise. She's always loved ruffles and lace, so she will cover that little girl in pretty things. Wait. You said the two of them were in the hospital *now*. Did you deliver that baby?" She gasped and put her hand on her chest.

"Almost," Cassie said as she smiled up at Greg. "That baby came a few minutes after paramedics arrived."

"Oh, my."

"Cassie and I watched from the sidelines while the experts did the hard work. I have to say, though, that Cassie knew what to do up to that point. She held Cherry's hand during the contractions and kept her talking between them."

"Believe me, I used everything I learned from being in a class and my experience with my friend when her baby was born. We were reaching the end of my talents."

He put his arm around her and squeezed her shoulder.

When Cassie went to wash her hands, his mother whispered in his ear, "She's leaving tomorrow."

"I know."

He thought she muttered, "Do you really?" but he ignored her. He would spend today with Cassie without worrying about the future.

∼

Cassie went into her cottage first, and Romeo greeted her with meows and head bumps on her ankles.

"I don't see any messes, so you've been good, haven't you?" She picked him up. "We're going to spend the afternoon with you. Romeo, you wouldn't believe the morning we had."

Greg's chuckle at her words warmed her from her toes up. When she turned to Greg and he seemed to fill the small space, she knew she may have a problem. Inviting him here had been a mistake, but she seemed to specialize in them recently, especially when it came to men.

With a board game on the small table and Romeo on her lap, they began what turned out to be one of the most fun afternoons of her life.

"No! You're cheating!" he cried out after she won the second game, having already won the first.

"Who's a poor loser?"

He pouted, but she could see the smile behind it.

"I have cheese and crackers if you'd like a snack."

"Have you cooked many meals since you arrived?"

It was time to make a confession. "Um. Stoves and I don't spend much time together. It isn't that I can't boil water like a champ or toast a slice of bread you would love to slather with butter—I can. It's when we get more complicated that there might be a tiny problem." She held her thumb and forefinger an inch apart. "I do two meals well—aren't cooking videos wonderful?—and I make one of those whenever I have company."

Watching him now, she wondered if he'd like to come to Nashville to sample one of them.

"The two of us are quite a pair."

Cassie silently considered what he'd said. They made a pair?

He rushed to add more. "What I mean is that I cook to survive. It's basic. We would get bored quickly if we were together long."

Together? She was reading emotions into his words that he probably didn't intend. Cassie focused on his words, which meant she focused on his lips . . . and that was a mistake.

Greg kept talking, seemingly oblivious to her obsession. "In Chicago, it was easy to find great restaurants, so I didn't have to do much beyond a bowl of cereal for breakfast."

He had such lovely lips. Would they kiss when he left?

"Cassie?"

Her eyes moved to his. The fire in them told her he felt it too. She pulled her eyes away from him. What had he said last? Something about restaurants in Chicago. "Um, you probably had your favorite places to go."

Still focused on her eyes, he continued speaking. "One in particular. They knew what I wanted when I walked in the door." As he spoke, he stood and walked toward her. She hoped he wanted to kiss her as much as she wanted him.

Swerving at the last minute to move around her, she heard him release a big sigh. "How are you doing, Romeo?"

As much as she'd wanted to spend another moment in Greg's arms, she knew he'd made the right decision.

He returned with the kitten in his arms. "I'll set up the next game. And I would like cheese and crackers."

Cassie could hear purring across the small table. They'd both miss Greg. Cassie put together a plate, adding some grapes. By the time she returned to the table, Greg had set up a new game, and the mood had shifted to fun again.

When the light started to dim from outside, Cassie knew that this day with Greg was coming to an end. She both wanted the day to go on forever and knew it couldn't because her life was not here. And she still needed to pick up the pieces from the wedding she'd run away from.

They wrapped up the final game, with him winning this time. He sat back with a smile, but the sadness in his eyes probably mirrored what was in her own. When he stood, she followed suit, the small room suddenly smaller still. Her tumble of emotions about him and Two Hearts filled the room.

"It's been a good week here."

He nodded. "Maybe sometime when I'm in Nashville for training—"

She shook her head. "Maybe. But I live there. You're here. Our lives are tied to each place. Besides, I need to pull my life back together, and I think that's going to take more than this one week."

Greg nodded again and quickly walked to the door. She stayed in place, drinking in her last memories of him.

Romeo, seeming to sense that something was not well with the situation, meowed from where he'd decided to curl up on the bed.

Then Two Hearts's sheriff went out the door and closed it behind him without looking back.

"And that closes this tiny chapter of my life," Cassie said softly to the cat. "Although between you and me, it feels huge right now." She'd lived almost thirty-one years, but one week of simplicity in this small town with its good people and sheriff would stay with her forever.

## CHAPTER THIRTEEN

*C*assie decided to avoid rush-hour traffic, so she and Romeo had a leisurely breakfast before their drive into Nashville. She moved so slowly that she went straight to her office, arriving at ten a.m. She'd made the wise decision to avoid her apartment in case a reporter or Jonathan was there.

One good thing about Bella packing for her was that she'd packed complete outfits for almost all occasions, including a day in her office. What her friend thought she was going to need those for in a small town, Cassie had no idea. But Bella was a city girl through and through. Even Nashville was small-town compared to the big cities in Texas that she'd grown up in.

Cassie disguised Romeo's litter box by covering it with pages from a newspaper she'd bought at her office building's entrance, and hurried up the stairs to her tenth-floor office. By the fourth floor, she was panting, and by the eighth, she had to lean against the wall for a couple of minutes to catch her breath.

With Romeo's box in an alcove in her office that most people wouldn't notice, she took the elevator downstairs, picked up his carrier, food, and bowls from her car, and grabbed her mail.

This time, she paid attention to her office door when she got there. Her "Just for You Weddings" sign always made her proud of what she'd built. Below that, the door was papered with parcel delivery notices. Most of them, if not all, would be business-related.

Jonathan had rarely visited her office. Come to think of it, he'd rarely visited her condo. They'd eaten out most of the time. Why had she thought they should be married?

She tossed the mail on the desk and let Romeo out of his carrier. Then she sat down, leaning back in her chair to stare out the windows at the city. The second she'd seen this view, she'd thought it would convince potential customers that she knew what she was doing. That she knew the city and was prosperous.

It probably had worked, too, because she had done very well since she'd moved here from the less-than-spectacular office she'd had before. With a big sigh, she scooted her chair forward and opened her laptop, ready to go to work. Romeo jumped on her desk, batted a pen onto the floor with his paw, and then jumped down to the floor again to send it flying across the polished wood floor.

Her first call was to Bella to check progress on upcoming weddings, including Carly's.

"Are you back in the real world?" Bella asked.

Cassie stared out the window at the city again. "I'm back in Nashville." It used to feel like the best place on Earth. Now she wasn't as sure.

"Are you okay, Cassie?"

"I guess so. Maybe I'm just not looking forward to dealing with everything from my wedding."

"Or maybe you're more than a little bit attached to that handsome sheriff from Smalltownville."

There was some truth in that. It was time to get on with her life, though. "I'm here and ready to go back to work. What's the update on the dresses you're working on for my clients?"

Bella filled her in. Everything seemed on track, but she didn't mention their country-music-star client.

"And Carly's wedding dress? Have you made all her alterations?"

"It's perfect and ready to go." Her friend sighed. "Cassie, I've been noticing whispers on social media, though, the last couple of days."

"I haven't even signed in to social media for almost a week." Her real life had been busy enough. "Did I miss something important?"

"Well, there may be a little problem."

Cassie rubbed her temples. "I don't want any problems. I want easy."

"You know that sometimes celebrity weddings aren't the easiest."

Cassie laughed. "I've had celebrity weddings that went really well, and I've had weddings for regular people that were a mess. Remember last year when the father of the bride ran off with the maid of honor? They'd been complete unknowns online before that."

"Their story did make a splash on social media. Okay, you're right about famous versus not. But I'm not sure what you're going to do about this. People are starting to talk about Carly's wedding. The venue."

Cassie jumped to her feet. "They *know* the venue?" She paced across her office, turned around, and returned. "No one was supposed to tell." She looked at the ceiling and huffed out a breath. "I warned Carly that this could happen if she told anyone. She was so sure that no one in her small number of wedding guests would leak it that she put it on the invitation. I advised against that because she's been a media darling this year."

"That's so true. I love when she tells the story about how she and Jake met and he thought she was a cleaning lady."

"That always makes me smile, too." Cassie focused on the situation at hand. "Where did you see this?"

Bella told her, and Cassie went to that site.

"No. No. No! There's a photo of the front of the church where she's getting married. You said 'a little problem.' This is a monumental disaster." Carly and Jacob were private people. They wanted to keep their wedding special, focused on them and those who were close to them.

A media circus would be the opposite of that.

"What are we going to do, Cassie? I should rephrase that to 'What are *you* going to do?' I just make wedding dresses and talk you off the cliff when things get too steep."

"That you do. Thank you for that." Cassie rubbed her temples again. "I'm going to have to think about this. Her wedding's in just a few weeks, so I'm not sure if I can get a venue they'd like, or one at all at this late date." Cassie glanced at the stack of mail on her desk begging for attention and knew she'd also have emails in her inbox that she'd ignored while she'd been gone. "Let me plow through everything else this morning, then I'll start checking around. Have you talked to Simone lately?"

"I have. She said everything's on track for all of her weddings, so that means you're in good shape with cakes."

"I'm thankful for that."

"Lunch today?"

Cassie checked the time on her phone. "Only if it's a late lunch. I have several hours of work to get to before I can leave this office even for a short while."

Bella agreed, and they settled on a place to meet at two.

Romeo curled up on an upholstered chair beside Cassie's desk as she handled most of her mail and inbox. After setting up first appointments for tomorrow with two potential clients, she went through the details from her own wedding. A few calls later, she'd confirmed that her loyal vendors had taken care of everything once they'd realized she'd run.

It seemed this wasn't the first time they'd had to deal with a last-minute wedding cancellation. It was the first one in her business, however.

A couple of the vendors had hinted at wanting to know the full story. Settling on "we realized we weren't well-suited" gave them little information, but it seemed to be enough. One even replied, "At least you found that out before the ceremony!" Cassie had wholeheartedly agreed with her.

That was the one shining light in all of this. She was not Mrs. Jonathan Albach right now. Make that two shining lights: without Jonathan's duplicity, Two Hearts would have always been a dot on a map to her.

Instead, it had started to feel like a second home. Maybe it was just that her heart had been shattered into a million pieces before she'd gotten there. The people in that town had helped put it back together.

Cassie scrolled through the photos on her phone and stopped on the yellow house. Would it make sense to own a weekend getaway? She laughed. Wedding planners, at least successful ones, worked almost every Saturday of the year. The last thing she needed was a vacation home. She kept scrolling.

A photo of Greg on the steeple showed next.

She put her phone facedown on her desk. Enough of that. Her life was here in Nashville, in the city.

Romeo got up and had a bite to eat and a drink of water.

"Will you be okay alone for a while?"

He dove for the pen again, continuing his game. He'd settled in well here. Should she bring him to her office every day? He'd be at home when she had to be on site for a wedding. More than that much alone time felt wrong to her.

Then she dug into the Carly and Jake venue problem. Five, then ten phone calls later, she'd confirmed what she expected.

Purse in hand, she stood. Romeo now snoozed on what he apparently saw as his chair.

She was supposed to meet Bella at their favorite downtown restaurant, one that Jonathan had dismissed as having "chick food." She looked forward to one of the trendy spot's many salads as she walked. Passing a church she'd called brought her back to her problem.

She'd redouble her efforts this afternoon.

Bella waved from a table, so Cassie smiled at the hostess and hurried over.

"How has your day been?"

Cassie frowned as she sat. "Good and bad. I have a couple of possible new clients. My wedding mess isn't a mess anymore." She took a sip of the water with a slice of lemon in it, which Bella must have already ordered for her.

The server stopped at their table. "Do you have any questions about the menu?"

Bella grinned. "We could help *you* answer questions. I think that between us, we've had everything on the menu. I'm ready to order. Cassie?"

She nodded. "I'd like the fruity festival salad and a sweet tea."

Bella handed him the menus. "I'll have the same salad, with the dressing on the side. I'm fine with water."

When he'd left, Bella turned toward her again. "What about Carly and Jake's wedding?"

"Disaster. Complete and utter disaster."

Bella raised an eyebrow. "I suspected as much when you ordered sweet tea."

Their server placed a glass of iced tea in front of her, and she downed about half of it.

Cassie shrugged. "It often tastes like sugar with a hint of tea, and I do try to watch my diet, but not today."

"Some might order alcohol. Your crutch is sweets."

Cassie finished the tea and signaled the server to bring her another.

"Are you sure you want that much sugar flowing through your body?"

"One more. Then I'll switch to unsweet." She grinned at Bella. "To answer your question, I haven't found another church for their ceremony."

"Not one?"

Cassie shook her head. "I have called every church that fits their needs within a five-mile radius. I plan to broaden that to the whole county when I get back. The problem is that more newly developed areas—and by that I mean in the last fifty to seventy-five years—don't have churches with the character she wants." The Two Hearts church came to mind. "I need something exactly like the building I just helped paint. Where am I supposed to find that in the city?"

"There's a beautiful historic one in East Nashville."

"Called it."

Bella opened her mouth to speak, and Cassie held up her hand in a *stop* motion.

"I'll bring up the list on my phone, and you can see everywhere I've called."

Bella scrolled through it. "I think you've reached out to every historic church I know of." Handing the phone back to Cassie, she added, "And I know you've searched online."

Their food arrived. While they ate, they caught up on everything else that had happened in the last week and made plans for a get-together with Simone and a couple of their other wedding-industry friends. They parted, with Bella promising to think about any places she could add to the list.

That afternoon, Cassie called every other chapel with character and charm within the city limits. Then she started to contact those in nearby towns.

Her phone rang, and it was Bella. "Hey, did you call that cute church in Franklin?"

"Uh huh." Even Cassie heard the forlorn tone in her voice. "They're booked. On the flip side, I do have good news."

"Okay," Bella said slowly. "Please share that."

"I now have a comprehensive list of every historic church within this county and in the surrounding area. This could prove useful in the future."

"When you're scheduling a wedding in advance?"

"Yeah." Cassie blew out a breath and leaned back in her chair, startling Romeo out of his nap. "Bella, this is a problem. We absolutely cannot have the wedding where it's scheduled. I predict a three-ring media circus."

She leaned down and picked up Romeo, who sat on the floor staring up at her. He curled up on her lap, purring. "I'm going to keep digging for the next couple of days. I *will* find a perfect location for them, one that will make the couple just as happy or happier."

"That sounds like my friend Cassie. She doesn't give up."

Cassie chuckled. "No, I don't. Speaking of giving up, I will admit, though, that I'm not looking forward to going to my condo tonight. I'd rather check into a hotel. Do you think Jonathan will show up there, or has he given up?"

"Word hasn't really gotten out about why the wedding was called off. I've actually checked his social media to see what's been going on. He's grieving the loss of his wedding, which was unexpectedly canceled at the last minute."

"So he's trying to save face."

"That would be my guess."

"And talking me into coming back to him would help him do that."

"Not to mention—as he assumes—line his pockets with some of your daddy's cash."

Romeo jumped onto Cassie's desk and began exploring.

"Well, let's just hope he stays away. I certainly won't answer the door for him or for anybody else I don't know."

"Good plan. And by the way, there's one thing that you may have forgotten, something that you'll need to deal with when you get there."

Cassie pictured her home and everything that was in it. Her dining room table was piled high with gifts from well-wishers. Gifts that she had happily unwrapped not long ago. "The wedding gifts." She'd pictured where they could put each thing when Jonathan moved into her condo after their honeymoon. "Those all have to be shipped back to the gift givers." She leaned on her desk and groaned. "I had to have a large wedding."

"Maybe you can just put each one of them in a bag, tag it with the recipient's name and address, and drop the bunch of them off at a parcel store for them to pack and ship."

"Thank you! That sounds like an amazing plan." It didn't shrink the number of gifts, but it certainly would cut down on the time it took.

"I can come over Saturday night, and we can work on it."

Cassie checked her schedule. "I have a wedding Friday night and nothing Saturday, so that sounds like an excellent plan to me. I'll even provide ice cream."

"If it's peanut butter fudge, you know I'll be there."

"What else?" They hung up with the promise to see each other then.

Cassie gathered together everything, put Romeo in his carrier, and reversed this morning's process. This time, she walked out with the litter box at a busier time and got some curious glances.

They soon arrived at her downtown condo. It had seemed so wonderful, in the past, to be downtown for everything, but now, walking through the underground garage toward the elevator, she could hear the honking and other sounds from the dense traffic. Two Hearts had been free of traffic jams and noise. She'd get used to it again, though.

Before she opened her door, Cassie peeled five flower-delivery stickers off. Apparently, Jonathan had moved to a different florist after she'd contacted the first one. She'd deal with that later.

With the door closed behind her, she let Romeo out of his carrier. When she straightened, the tower of gifts on the table was in front of her. It was startling, even though she'd known it was there. Crystal and silver sat next to a blender and towels. Some things, she'd been thrilled to receive, but with others, she'd wondered where she'd even store them.

Romeo hopped up onto a chair in the corner. "This is it, handsome. This is home." *For now* came into her mind.

Maybe it was time to move to a place that had fewer memories of the relationship that hadn't worked. Maybe somewhere in the suburbs where she could have a small lawn. Romeo might like to play outside while she sat in the yard. Her balcony could barely hold a tiny table and two equally small chairs.

~

Greg had noticed a blue Hyundai leaving the motel. Not that he'd been waiting to watch when she left. He'd just been driving the roads of the town as he usually would.

Her brake lights came on as she went around the curve south of him, and then her car disappeared. Cassie had left. Not that she'd said otherwise, but he'd hoped she'd decide to stay longer, as she had a week ago.

But she had a life to get back to in Nashville. And he had a life in Two Hearts, one he'd enjoyed before she'd arrived and would enjoy again. Turning on Main Street, Greg drove toward Dinah's Place. Coffee and a piece of Dinah's pie would help ease the surprising amount of pain he had felt from seeing Cassie drive away.

The place was empty when he arrived, and Dinah sat on one of the stools normally reserved for her customers.

From the time she opened the doors until she closed at night, someone was always here. "Where is everyone?" he asked as the door closed.

She spun around to face him with a frown on her face. "They've all gone over to the church to finish painting it."

He could be on duty with a paintbrush in his hand. Besides, physical labor would help him forget the loss of his new friend, Cassie. "I'll have a cup of coffee and pie to go."

"I have apple, cherry, strawberry, and chocolate cream."

"Dinah, you make the decision difficult."

"It wouldn't break my heart if you had one of each. I don't think any of them will get eaten. I'll have to freeze them and eat them myself later."

She was right. Her customers were working on a project he'd helped build momentum for. Guilt rushed through him. "Box them all up, and I'll take them over to the painters. My treat."

Her face lit up, and he realized she was actually quite pretty when she wasn't pushing hard and focused on work. "Thank you, Sheriff!" She scurried around and soon set two large bags in front of him, both stacked with pies and one topped with plates, forks, and napkins.

As he paid, she asked, "Do you know if Cassie will be back?"

He cleared his suddenly choked-up throat before speaking. "I don't think we'll see her again."

"Oh, Sheriff, I'm sorry she hurt you."

He unnecessarily glanced around the still-empty restaurant to make sure they were alone. "She was a guest in our town. As the sheriff, I showed her around."

Dinah cocked her head to the side and watched him for a

moment before speaking. "You don't know, do you?" She patted him on the hand. "I'm sure you'll figure it out. At least, I hope you will."

As he exited the restaurant with his bags, she said what sounded like, "Men can be so stupid." That didn't sound like the kind of thing Dinah would say, so he must have misheard.

When he neared the church, two brothers he knew were dairy farmers climbed out of a truck. Unfortunately, he couldn't remember their names.

"We heard you needed help painting," one of the brothers said to him. "I can't draw a straight line for anything, but he's an expert."

The second brother said, "I spent a summer with an uncle who was a painter." He looked up at the top of the church. "This is already much better than it was."

Greg asked, "Inside or outside painter?"

"Portraits. But my uncle painted house interiors for extra cash sometimes. I did all of those jobs for several months so he could focus on his art. In June, my work wasn't what you'd want, but by August, I'd learned the skills well."

"Then you're the perfect man for the job. We've made progress on the exterior, but the interior is dingy. We saved so much money doing the rest of the work ourselves that we have enough money left for the interior paint."

The painter brother grinned. "But you need free labor."

"We do. If you wanted to spearhead the interior . . ."

"I'll come over every day when the cows are all milked. It shouldn't take but a few days." His gaze dropped to the bags in Greg's hands. "Are those pies from Dinah's?"

"They are. Everyone was here, so I took pity on her and bought the lot of them to share."

"Count me in, too, if there's free pie," the other brother said. "Need help with those bags, Sheriff?"

His brother rolled his eyes as Greg handed over one of them.

"You were always going to help with this job, bro, but you won't be holding a paintbrush." To Greg, he added, "He truly is a pitiful painter."

The man's cheek twitched. "That hasn't proven to be my most useful skill."

"You know most of the people here. I've noticed some are better painters than others."

The good painter said, "What about our visitor? I heard she was a hard worker, and pretty, too." The man's gaze searched back and forth as they continued toward the church.

Greg swallowed hard. "She left today."

They stopped at the bottom of the church steps. "When will she be back?"

"Never." The word lodged in his heart as he said it. He would miss having her around. She'd added a much-needed spark to this town.

A voice Greg recognized as Michelle's called out, "Did you bring treats from Dinah's?"

Pasting on a smile, he held up the bag. "Anyone ready for a pie break?"

The sounds of feet pounding down ladders and tools being set down made him smile. The town would be fine without Cassie. He ruthlessly shoved the little voice to the side that asked, *Yes, but will you?*

# CHAPTER FOURTEEN

*T*wo days into her work week and her relentless search for Carly and Jake's wedding venue, Cassie thought she had struck historic-church gold. Online, it looked perfect. It was old, seemed to be in a beautiful setting in a forest, and was only about a half hour from the city. She ordered a sandwich to be delivered to her office and ate it on the way as she headed out of town, going north.

Near the church, the surroundings changed from residential to industrial, with large metal buildings housing manufacturing plants and warehouses. The road curved as her GPS told her she'd almost arrived. As she came around the bend, there sat the cutest little church. It must have been built in the mid-1800s, when the area had only had farms and houses. It had survived wars and other conflicts.

Unfortunately, it hadn't survived urban sprawl.

A large warehouse sat to one side and a commercial office building to the other. This would not work. Without stopping, she pulled through the parking lot, rolled back out, and headed toward home.

Tomorrow, she could look forward to meeting with new

clients, and that would break things up a bit. Tonight, she'd scour the internet again for historic churches—and if that started to drive her crazy, she'd take a break and have fun browsing online wedding sites to see what the next trends might be and make note of ideas.

She had both online folders and actual printouts of ideas. You never knew what a bride might want. Her file folder for "unusual" weddings had come in useful last year, when a couple had said their vows in an airplane and parachuted out of it soon after. Thankfully, the wedding planner had not been required to jump with them.

Thursdays were special because Cassie tried to schedule all new client consultations for that day. Those were often fun, as she learned about each bride and what she wanted. Grooms attended those meetings . . . sometimes.

This morning, she and Romeo went to work. Now, he had a litter box hidden in a special side table built for that purpose. She'd placed it next to a chair in the corner of the room. He'd already used it, so it seemed that she and the only male in her life had worked everything out to their satisfaction. She'd also bought some toys for him, but kept most of them at home.

Cassie had always liked the fact that each day brought a fresh start. Today, though, came with some trouble. If she couldn't find a new place for Carly and Jake's ceremony, she'd have to call them and admit defeat. She still wasn't sure what Plan B would be, but it would be a letdown for them.

Her first clients of the day were a bride and groom, Etta and Charles, with both sets of mothers in tow. The first words out of Etta's mother's mouth were "How much does this cost?"

"Mother!" The bride rolled her eyes. "She's come highly

recommended. We can talk money later." Her glare at her mother was kind but firm.

Cassie definitely wanted to work with a bride who kept control over the mother of the bride and wasn't a bridezilla as she did it.

Once they were seated around her desk, they discussed their ideal wedding, which sounded quite normal.

"So you'd like a wedding ceremony conducted by your father, Charles, who is a judge and so is allowed to officiate here in Tennessee. And both the wedding and reception will be held in your uncle's backyard, Etta." She almost felt guilty being paid for a wedding this simple.

"It's a large piece of land. Do you think it's five acres, Mama?"

"At least. They're south of the city, off Hillsboro Road."

Cassie knew that area well. They were either wealthy with a house on a large piece of land, or owned a farm. Either way would work.

"The next question is a big one. When are you planning to get married?"

Both the bride- and groom-to-be shifted in their seats, making Cassie so nervous she had to fight the urge to do the same thing.

"Twenty-eight days from now." The bride's mother's eyes narrowed as she said it.

Cassie almost didn't want to ask why the hurry, but she needed to. Pregnancy and leaving for military service usually topped the list when she had a rush job. "May I ask why?"

Etta leaned forward with an earnest expression on her face. "Charlie got a job in Paris. That's Paris, France, not Paris, Tennessee."

If anything, the bride's mother's eyes narrowed even more. "I *suggested*"—she emphasized the word with a strength that said she'd probably done that loudly—"that she stay here in the US to see how things work out before taking such a big step."

Cassie wasn't sure if she was referring to moving or getting married.

Etta grabbed Charlie's hand. "We dated all through college, Mother. We're as ready as we'll ever be." Her sweet smile changed to a smirk. "Unless you'd like to be made a grandmother first?"

Silence fell over the room. As the mediator for all things wedding, Cassie stepped in. "A wedding in a month is possible. You have the venues planned. Do you have a dress?"

Etta's eyes filled. "I haven't found anything I like yet." The formerly calm bride began a meltdown. "On the TV shows, they have to order them months in advance. I'm in trouble, aren't I?"

Bella had worked more than one miracle for Cassie's brides. "I have some great options for wedding dresses. Those are dependent on budget."

The groom's mother spoke for the first time. "They can have almost anything they want—within reason, of course." She named a high figure that made Cassie's eyebrows raise.

"I'm going to step out for a moment to talk to a wedding dress designer I know well." She went out the door and into the hall with a bounce in her step that slowed when she remembered Bella had been busy recently.

Her friend answered on the first ring.

"I have a client in my office right now," Cassie said. "She needs a dress."

"Perfect! Do you want to set up an appointment now?"

"There's a catch to it."

"Oh, no. You don't have another parachutist, do you? A dress that wouldn't tangle up as she dropped from the sky came with numerous challenges."

"No. This one's getting married in twenty-eight days."

"Two words: Not. Possible."

"*Please.*" When Bella didn't say anything, Cassie added, "She's sweet and keeps her mother on a tight rein."

"She's nice? The bride that just left . . ."

"You can help her?"

After a pause so long that Cassie knew she'd say 'no,' she replied, "Only if she can meet with me today. I have to get started on this ASAP."

Cassie ended the call and stepped back into the room. "I consulted with a custom wedding dress designer I often work with. She says she can make the dress in time—"

Etta jumped up and hugged her mother. "I told you Cassie could help."

"*If* you can get to her studio today."

"I can. If we're done here, I can go there now."

"Let's sign the paperwork. I'll get started right away."

The bride and her entourage left, and Cassie texted Bella to tell her they were on the way—without the groom. Bella had firm rules about the groom seeing the dress before the wedding day.

Cassie's own wedding came to mind. She wouldn't have caught Jonathan with Giselle if she hadn't opened the door a crack, but just a crack, so he couldn't see her. Yes, it was a good rule to not show the groom the dress.

She greeted her second client of the day not long after the first one left, a designer-dressed twenty-something woman and her mother, Charlene and Odelia.

When the bride-to-be stepped into the room, she screamed and stepped backward into the hall when she saw Romeo. "It's a cat!"

He raced under the couch to hide.

"Yes. That's my new kitten, Romeo." She wanted to add: *And I don't appreciate your scaring him.*

"No cats." She sniffed.

A vision of her client itching and sneezing came to mind. "I hadn't thought to ask if you were allergic. I'm sorry!" Cassie reached for her coat. "There's a wonderful restaurant next door where we can have our meeting." She pushed her laptop and other materials she'd prepared into her tote bag. Supplies in hand, Cassie turned back to her potential clients.

Charlene stayed near the door. "I'm not allergic. Cats are dirty." She wiped her hands on her skirt as though Romeo had contaminated them from across the room.

"Romeo is a clean cat."

The woman shuddered, and the mother answered, "You've been highly recommended. Let's go to the restaurant, Charlene."

Cassie checked on Romeo before following her clients out. When she put her hand under the couch, he licked it, so he was fine. The meeting went well in spite of the fact that she didn't like either mother or daughter by the end of it.

The soup had been lukewarm, the salad—what Charlene had eaten of it—had too much salad dressing on it, and the coffee was too hot. Nothing seemed to be good enough for her. The mother thought every suggestion for a reception—even the highest-rated hotel in the city—not good enough.

When they wrapped it up after what seemed like the longest meeting of her career, Cassie said, "I'm not sure we're a good fit. We need to share the same vision of your day, but I don't believe we do." She stood. "There are other excellent wedding planners in Nashville."

With a smile she hoped appeared genuine, she left and went back to her office and Romeo.

Before her week in peaceful Two Hearts, she would have put up with almost any client, but now she knew two things. One: nice was her new normal. She would seek nice people and avoid the unpleasant ones as much as she could. Two: Charlene could never be happy, so she'd avoid her.

Surely her day would go better after this.

A knock on her door a half hour too early for her next client made her sigh. When she opened it, expecting to greet another mother and daughter like the last pair, she found herself face-to-face with one of the largest bouquets of flowers she'd ever seen. The pink, yellow, and white roses couldn't have been prettier.

A male voice she didn't recognize spoke from the other side of them. "Flowers from Music City Blooms."

Her anger grew as she stared at them. Pretty they may be, but she knew a weasel had sent them. Jonathan had moved on to her office address.

He said, "Um, this is a surprisingly heavy floral arrangement."

The poor man was only the delivery person, not the sender. Pulling the door wider, she said, "Please set them . . . on that table." Romeo wouldn't mind flowers on his table. Would he tear them up, though?

When the delivery man left after receiving a tip from her, she reached for the card. Opening the small envelope, she got a surprise. *Two Hearts thanks you for helping us see our church as we should have all along.* The mayor had signed it.

Tears began running down her face, and she brushed them away. She'd managed not to think about Two Hearts today. Well, not often. The emotions whooshed in so intensely that they startled her.

Instead of pretending that she didn't care about the town or people, she needed to choose a day to visit. Maybe she'd see the sheriff when she was there. Not that she cared. No, she didn't. He was the past. The future she had been building for years could only be here, where her business was.

Her next client arrived on the hour. She hoped this mother and daughter would be nicer, that her day would end on a better note. That would be an easy threshold to reach after Charlene and Odelia.

When she invited the duo inside, she noticed Romeo lounging on his favorite chair.

"A kitten!" Amelia, the bride-to-be, exclaimed.

*Oh, no, here we go again!*

"What's its name?"

"Romeo."

"He's adorable. Can I pet him?"

Cassie shrugged. "Sure. If he's okay with it, I'm okay with it."

This meeting began on a much happier note. Not that she expected every client to be a cat lover, but Amelia didn't just love cats: it soon became clear that she was genuinely kind.

The wedding ceremony's setting would be easy. Amelia simply wanted flowers as a backdrop. When they got to the point of the meeting when they discussed the venue, Cassie had high hopes for being able to give this woman the wedding of her dreams.

"I want a country theme."

Cassie nodded. In a city known for country music, weddings with that theme were common. "Casual, maybe cowboy boots on the groomsmen and a circlet of wildflowers in the bridemaids' hair? And a country music group? I can do that."

Amelia shook her head. "No. Well, those things could work, but what I really want is a barn."

Cassie sat back in her chair. "As in an actual barn with animals in it?"

Amelia cocked her head to the side as she considered that. "I think the animals would need to be moved for the day. And I don't want a modern barn that looks like it was built for events. I want a genuine barn."

Where would she come up with that in Nashville? People in other places often thought Nashville was a small town, but it was a large city with many tall buildings and not a lot of large, in-use barns. "Can I ask why?"

The perky brunette's cheerful expression became more

intense. "My grandfather is a rancher in Texas. My happiest memories growing up were visiting him, and I met my fiancé there."

"He's a cowboy?"

She even laughed in a cute way, but she was so nice that it drew Cassie to her instead of being over the top and pushing her away. "He's a lawyer who was working for my grandfather's business. He's in the process of moving here."

So, her client wanted to get married in a certain kind of barn, one that would be even harder to find within the city limits than an available historic church had been.

"Can we search nearby counties for the right barn?"

Amelia looked at her mother.

"I told you, honey, that it might be hard to find what you wanted." To Cassie, she said, "We're fine with a location outside the city as long as it isn't too far. Amelia had her heart set on a barn wedding even before she met Evan."

"They show barn weddings in magazines, but they're often in the country, or they fly somewhere to get to the place. Will my idea not work here?" The sparkle left Amelia.

Cassie knew she had to put it back. "I will find a barn for you."

Amelia perked up. "Are you sure?"

"Trust me. I will find the right place for your reception." Cassie gulped. Had she just made a promise she couldn't keep? She hoped not because the pair left smiling.

To save on loads to the car, she left the flowers in her office. They would brighten it tomorrow, too. Her focus then would be last-minute details for a Friday night wedding. And she'd probably work a while on Saturday to finish catching up from her week off.

$\sim$

Greg stood across the street from the Two Hearts church and snapped a photo with his phone. Then he took a few more from different angles.

He'd told himself he needed to document the newly painted church. In reality, he planned to send one of them to Cassie, and he wanted it to be right. After hitting the shutter button what must have been fifteen or twenty times, he scrolled through the shots.

Which one would make her smile? He did love her smile. Her eyes came to life and added more sparkle to an already sparkling woman.

His friend Micah stopped his truck in front of him and rolled down the window. "What still needs to be done?" He gestured toward the church.

"A small amount of painting inside. Just the trim, I think. After a deep cleaning that my mother is arranging, it will be good as new." He shrugged. "As new as a hundred-and-fifty-year-old building can be."

"I wouldn't have guessed that it could look this pretty. That woman worked a miracle."

"That she did."

"She's gone and not returning?"

Greg nodded. "I think so." Every time he thought about Cassie, sadness slammed into him. He heard it in his voice, and so did his friend.

"Ever thought about moving to the city?"

Greg stared at him. "Are you suggesting I chase after a woman who was here for a week?"

Micah sighed. "Sometimes that's all it takes."

Greg knew his friend had loved his ex-girlfriend deeply. He'd bought the ring and planned the proposal when he found out she'd taken a job in Boston.

"Talking about Celeste?"

"Yeah. I should have chased after her. Now she's dating a Bostonian. His family arrived on the Mayflower."

"I see. Maybe you could find someone new in town."

Micah shook his head. "Just like you did? No. Besides, I enjoy single life."

"Me too," Greg said firmly.

His friend grinned. "Are we playing poker Saturday night?"

"Of course. I ordered sandwiches for the group from Dinah."

Micah drove away with a promise to see Greg then.

# CHAPTER FIFTEEN

*H*er Friday evening wedding went without any major hiccups. The mother of the bride had tried to take over, but Cassie's persuasion skills had won out. The bride had argued with the groom at the reception, but they'd left together and happy. She counted it a success.

Bella knocked on her door right on time Saturday night.

"I hope you have a hearty dinner planned. I'm starved!"

Salads with shredded chicken, lettuce, nuts, and blueberries might not be what her friend wanted.

Bella leaned on the kitchen island. "You went healthy on me again, didn't you?" She sighed.

"I did stop for croissants to eat on the side."

"I'm feeling a little better about this."

"And I bought not only peanut butter fudge ice cream but also chocolate chip."

Bella slapped her hand on the counter, and Romeo meowed. "Now you're talking. How's life with your kitten?"

Cassie looked down at him and grinned. "Great. He makes my life better. We've been going to work together every day."

"You're bringing a cat to your office?"

"Yes. I've figured out that he's a client filter. If they don't like him, they turn out to be clients I wouldn't have wanted to work with, anyway. Not that I wouldn't move a meeting for an allergy. That's completely different."

Romeo grabbed one of his new toys, a small, catnip-filled orange mouse, held it in his front paws, and beat it with his back feet. Yikes! She'd hate to be a real mouse on the end of that.

She pushed one salad toward Bella and one toward the chair beside her at the kitchen island. When she went to the counter to get the croissants, she realized she missed being able to stop at Dinah's Place when she was hungry. The small-town connection was real, and she already felt its absence in the big city. At least tonight she had a friend here.

Bella dug into her meal, and they ate in silence for a few minutes. "This is better than I expected. You may not be a great cook, but you've become a great salad maker."

Cassie laughed and almost choked. She reached for her glass of water and took a big drink. "I appreciate your compliment."

Bella chuckled. "That didn't sound like one, did it? It's just that you've been light on cooking skills, and you know that. This shows finesse." After a few more bites, she asked, "Anything new with you and your sheriff?"

Cassie choked again. When she'd recovered, she said, "Stop that!"

With an innocent expression, Bella said, "Asking simple questions while we eat?"

"You know what I mean. Two weeks ago today, I found my fiancé in the arms of another woman." She tapped her chest. "My heart isn't ready for romance."

Bella picked up a croissant and watched her.

"What?"

"I'm trying to decide if you really believe that."

Cassie rolled her eyes. "I said it. Of course I believe it."

Halfway through her salad, her phone chimed with a text.

Picking it up, she expected one about a wedding or one from her mother. She couldn't have been more wrong. The photo she'd taken of Greg showed on her phone. With her friend watching her closely, she smiled and set the phone to the side.

"Aren't you going to see what they said?"

"It can wait."

"Oh, it's business."

Cassie didn't like to lie, even by omission. "No, it isn't business."

"Family?"

Cassie grimaced. "No. It's Greg. Okay?"

Bella's eyebrows shot upward. "Why wouldn't you want to open a text from a man who doesn't interest you even a little?"

To prove the point, Cassie grabbed her phone and opened the message. A photo of the Two Hearts church filled the screen along with the words: *The outside is complete, and the inside will be done in a day or two. I thought you would like to see it.*

Willing herself not to cry now, she took a deep breath and held up the phone so her friend could see it. "He snapped a photo of the church I helped with. See, no sentiment there."

"But it is sweet that he thought of you and sent it."

That was true. "Greg is a good guy." And he was. If only she'd met him a year ago, before she'd loaded herself up with tons of baggage.

"So—"

"He's a long way from here." Setting down the phone, she pushed aside thoughts of Two Hearts and the town's sheriff. "I'm done with dinner. Should we have dessert before or after we tackle the mountain of gifts?"

"Definitely after. Ice cream is our reward." Bella put her last bite of food in her mouth. "We'll finish faster with an incentive."

They began bagging and labeling each wedding gift. As they worked, Cassie said, "Have you thought of any other places for Carly and Jake's wedding?"

"You've contacted every historic church within the city and near it. I doubt I have anything to add to that." Bella set one bag down and picked up a blender. "Why would anyone give you a blender as a wedding gift? Don't most people our age already have one if they want one?"

"Buyers seem to picture 'just starting out' when they go wedding shopping."

"True. Back to Carly and Jake, when are you going to tell them you couldn't find what they wanted?"

Cassie sat on one of the dining room chairs and rested her face in her hands. "I don't know. I guess Monday."

"What is your Plan B for the ceremony?"

"Other than a modern church or outside under a tent, I don't have one." She grabbed a crystal vase off the table and put it in a bag. "If only there was a church like the one in Two Hearts."

Bella set another completed bag on the floor. "Hey, Cassie, what *about* that church?"

"What?" Cassie labeled the bag and set it in the growing pile of ready-to-return gifts.

Bella stared at her. "The Two Hearts church would be perfect for them, wouldn't it?"

Cassie laughed so hard she snorted.

"That's what I love about you, Cassie. You've got class."

That sent her into another peal of laughter. "How would we have a high-end celebrity wedding in a small town in the middle of nowhere?"

Bella shrugged. "There's a church exactly like the one Carly wants in that little town. You even said before that it's exactly what you're looking for."

Cassie thought it over. "You're right about the church. But there's nothing else there." She shrugged. "Where would we have the reception? How would we do any of it? It's a town that's sadly dying. I gave them some hope, Bella, but I wonder if it was false hope. They have a sweet little church in their sweet little town. One building has been restored. But what else can I do?" Cassie shook her head.

"Then, it's time to come up with a Plan B. Or maybe Plan C, because I just gave you Plan B."

"Okay, let's go with Plan C. Maybe we could find a beautiful modern church that Carly would love. I know there are plenty of those in this city."

"There are. But that isn't what your bride wants."

Cassie sighed. "I'll keep thinking about it this weekend." She looked around at the stack of completed bags and the small pile that was still left on the table. "Thank you so much for coming. This made a tedious job so much better."

Romeo took that moment to leap onto the table, landing on all fours and looking around like a tiger on the prowl.

Bella laughed. "He is cute, isn't he?"

He batted the pen off the table and watched it drop to the floor.

"I told you he was."

They finished up their task, then Cassie went into the kitchen to get out the ice cream. "Do you want a scoop of each?"

"Of course. To start with." Bella had an evil grin.

"You talk about me and sweet tea. What about you and ice cream?"

"Hey, you and I work hard enough with our jobs that we burn off all these calories."

As Cassie scooped the ice cream into bowls for them, she pictured the photo Greg had sent. Bella was right. That was exactly what Carly wanted. The old-fashioned wooden pews with the aisle down the middle for the bride. Beautiful stained-glass windows. And the brick steps out front, which would be wonderful for Carly's bridal photos and go well with the look the singer always portrayed on her albums and in her music brand. But what about the reception?

A spark of an idea flashed into her mind, quickly growing to a brighter and brighter flame. "Bella, what if we did the reception under a tent on a farm with a view of a field of blooming flowers?"

"Are you kidding? That would be beautiful. Where is this idyllic location?"

Cassie handed her a bowl of ice cream and sat down on the chair across from her. "Two Hearts."

Bella slid a bite of the peanut butter fudge ice cream into her mouth and closed her eyes. "Oh my, this is so good."

"Forget about the ice cream. What do you think about Two Hearts?"

"You were there. The downtown is boarded up." She leaned forward. "It's ugly. There. I said it. The people are sweet. The town right now is ugly." Bella took another bite of the ice cream, sighing. "If the buildings were cleaned up downtown—you know, all the windows sparkling and shiny—wouldn't that change everything?"

Cassie thought about it. In many ways, that was what she'd considered when she'd walked up and down that street, every time. If only someone cleaned it up.

"And the overgrown yards on the way into town, we could have someone trim those," Cassie said. Justin came to mind. That could easily be taken care of out of the wedding budget. Jake had given her carte blanche on it.

"Cassie, you have a faraway expression. Is it going to work?"

Cassie gave a firm nod. "I believe it can. I'm used to walking into a venue and having everything done exactly as I ordered when I get there. This will take more work, but I think Carly and Jake might just love it. She's done all those songs about small towns, and it's perfect."

"Are you ready to suggest it to the bride and groom?"

Cassie stared into her bowl of chocolate as if it held all the answers.

She had no idea.

Cassie tossed and turned all night as she pictured the wedding in the town. One perk of being there was that she would see Greg again. Was that good, though, or bad? Did she want to pull the splinter out slowly or yank it out? She was going to have to say goodbye to him again either way.

She finally fell asleep before dawn and woke up later than normal. She hauled herself out of bed, got dressed, and decided to take a road trip. After a brief stop for a cup of coffee, she ate a snack bar on the way to Two Hearts. Mrs. Brantley always made Sunday lunch for her family and would be happy to feed her, so she knew she wouldn't go hungry.

Cassie pulled into town as everyone was going into church, so she parked her car and hurried over and up the steps, walking in just as the singing began. Michelle looked up and waved her over, so she slid into the pew beside her.

As the service went on, she listened, but she also looked around. She could envision flowers decorating the aisle and Carly walking toward Jake. The stained-glass windows on either side were beautiful, and with everything freshly painted and cleaned, Bella was right: this was her client's dream location.

The logistics threatened to overwhelm her, though. They would have to load guests on buses to transport them there. Since they had no idea where the leak had come from, no guests could know the location until the wedding day or this would be another circus.

When the service ended, Michelle nudged her with her elbow. "I'm surprised to see you back. But I'm glad." She impulsively hugged her, and Cassie hugged her back.

"I have an idea, and I want to talk it over with the mayor. Is he here?"

Michelle scanned the crowd, stopped, and pointed. Cassie

waited outside for the mayor and walked up to him after Michelle left.

"Mayor?"

"Cassie? I didn't expect to see you again, especially not this soon." The man's voice was strong, more so than she'd expected. "You have a serious expression. Is everything okay?"

Cassie chewed on her lip. Was she proposing something ridiculous or wonderful? "I have a client who wants to have a wedding in a small historic church. My team would take care of everything, but I wondered how you and the town would feel about a big wedding being held here." It was a far-fetched idea, but right now, this was the one she had to get Carly what she wanted. She hoped everyone would be on board.

The mayor gasped. "Are you telling me that you want to bring hundreds of people—you are talking about hundreds of people, right?"

Cassie nodded.

"Then, hundreds of people to our town?"

This wasn't going well. "Yes, sir."

The man she'd seen as standoffish suddenly hugged her. "My goodness! This is the best thing that's happened to Two Hearts in decades."

As the mayor's words sank in, a slow smile spread over Cassie's face. "You're okay with my plan?"

"Okay with it? Just tell me what I can do to help. Tell all of us what we can do to help. Will they stay in the motel?"

She planned to bus guests in and out in one day, but she would need space for her team members. A cabin for the bride and one for the groom to get ready would be helpful. "I think we'll book the whole motel."

"Could Dinah provide some food?"

"Of course. I can sit with Dinah, and we can come up with the parts of the menu that she's able to supply."

The mayor looked thoughtful. "If you'd use as many of our people as you can get involved, I would appreciate it."

"I was planning to have Justin put together a group to do some maintenance on the yards coming into town, and also get a team to clean the windows in the boarded-up downtown area. I'd like the town to look . . . *alive*. I hope my choice of word doesn't offend you," Cassie added in a hurry.

The mayor laughed. "You didn't say anything I haven't been saying to myself for years. Just let us know what we need to do." He cocked his head to the side and looked at Cassie. "Someone famous or just someone with a lot of money?"

Cassie laughed. "It's someone famous *and* someone with a lot of money."

"Will there be paparazzi?" The man clasped his hands together excitedly.

"There may be. But I'm doing my very best to avoid even a whiff of where this wedding is going to take place. They may descend on the town afterward, though, to learn all about the destination."

The mayor clapped his hands with glee. "Wonderful! I have always wanted to see paparazzi in action." The man might be getting up in years, but he had energy.

Cassie felt like shaking her head to try to get her bearings in this strange new world, one where paparazzi were not only accepted, but welcomed.

Greg stepped out of the church and froze. Someone who looked exactly like Cassie from the back was talking to Mayor Jordan. He blinked, then closed his eyes and opened them back up. She was still there. His heart started to beat faster, but he took deep breaths to quiet it down.

They'd parted as friends, and he had to respect that. Besides, the woman was right that she'd just had a narrow escape from an ugly relationship. No, the only answer was that someone from Two Hearts had liked Cassie's hair color enough that they had dyed it that shade. That exact shade of red.

He continued down the steps toward her. "Hello, are you having a good morning?"

When he became level with them, the woman turned to face him.

Greg's tongue stuck on the roof of his mouth. When he jarred it loose, he said, "Cassie?" He knew he was staring, but he couldn't help it. She was even more beautiful than he remembered.

When the mayor cleared his throat, Greg turned to find him smirking at them. That would not do.

Greg said, "I didn't expect to see you again so soon, Cassie. What brings you to our town?" That sounded sufficiently sheriff-like.

Cassie blinked for a few seconds and then said, "It's also good to see you, Sheriff. It's good to see everyone in this town." She put on what he had to assume was her professional smile, the one she used with wedding parties, and gestured to the area around them. "I'm so glad to be back in Two Hearts. I didn't expect to miss it, but I did. Even with my busy week after taking time off."

"Greg, Cassie has come to us with an interesting proposition. She'd like to do a wedding here." The mayor dropped his voice a notch. "A wealthy celebrity's wedding."

Greg could feel the mayor's excitement, and he fought a grin at his enthusiasm. "A big wedding here in Two Hearts?" He looked around the area. Since he'd spent years away from here, he had a feeling he saw it with different eyes than most of its residents. Those who had never left pictured it as it used to be. But to him, the town had fallen into disrepair, and almost every house and store needed work.

Two houses, each with different landscaping, sat right across the street from the church. One belonged to Dinah, and she kept hers in pristine condition. How she did that, given the hours she worked in her business, he had no idea. The other house had been abandoned for years, and the house and yard reflected that.

But he didn't want to be the one to burst their bubble.

He must have shown his horror-struck view of the situation because Cassie said, "We're going to have yards tidied up. I thought Justin would be good in charge of that, and we'll have a team clean up the downtown area."

"How many people are you expecting for this event?"

"Two hundred and four. I counted the pews and the space in the church, and it looks like it can accommodate more than that."

The mayor nodded. "It's a small church, but we can comfortably seat about two hundred and fifty. I don't think we'll have any problems, do you, Greg?"

He imagined hundreds of strangers coming to their town, consuming alcohol and probably driving. How was he going to take care of that security issue? "I'm going to need to bring on some additional help."

Cassie hit her forehead with the palm of her hand. "Of course. In my excitement about the plans I forgot about that, but I often have to bring on more security. It's in the budget already, Greg. How many extra do you need?"

"I'm not sure what to do about a patrol on the road—"

Cassie held up a hand. "You don't need to worry about that. I'm bringing almost everyone in on buses."

"Why would people with enough money to plan a wedding like this have their guests ride a bus?"

Cassie sighed. "At some point, someone who has been invited leaked the original location of the wedding. It was supposed to be in a small church in Nashville. The bride wants a church like this one. She also wants it to be very private."

Which meant she really was a celebrity, and that came with all sorts of other problems. "I'd like five additional security members on my team."

"Done."

Her response startled him because the expense would not be small. "When is this taking place? And please tell me we have a lot of time to get this ready."

Cassie winced. "Unfortunately not. This wedding is happening two weeks from yesterday."

Greg rubbed his hand over his mouth and chin. "I'd better get to work."

"We'd all better get to work," the mayor added.

"I have to run this by the bride and groom first," Cassie said. "I'm sure they're going to approve it. They don't have much choice at this point if they want a historic and charming church. Once I've done that, Mayor, should I talk to Cherry and Levi or is that something you would do in your role?"

The mayor asked, "What do they have to do with this?"

"I think the fields of flowers would make a wonderful backdrop if we set up the reception tent at their farm."

Greg could see that. And it would be a lot easier to maintain order in a controlled setting like that than it would be all over his town.

Cassie looked up into his eyes again, and he struggled to keep his police demeanor.

The mayor said, "I'll leave contacting Cherry and Levi to you, Cassie. I think I'm going to run now since you don't seem to need me for anything else. Let me know the second you've got confirmation on this, though."

Cassie didn't say anything when the mayor waited for a few seconds and then left. He noticed that same smirk on the older man's face. Fortunately, Mayor Jordan was one of the few people in this town who wasn't a gossip. But the longer they stood outside the church, the more the potential there was for it.

"Cassie, are you heading back to the city, or can you come to lunch at Mom's?"

She grinned. "I was hoping you would invite me to lunch. Your mother is an excellent cook."

He reached out to put his arm around her to direct her down the stairs but quickly pulled it back. When he turned around, he saw Dinah, and she raised an eyebrow.

"Let's head over there right now. Mom will be so excited that you're back in town."

On the way to Mrs. Brantley's house, Cassie decided Two Hearts was the *only* place to have the wedding. She just needed to ask Carly and Jake about it. After she pulled up into the driveway, she sent Carly a text.

*I found a great church for you. But it's a little out of the way. Give me a call when you have a chance so we can talk about it.*

As she reached to open the car door, her phone rang.

"What's your crazy idea?"

Cassie chuckled. This woman was so much fun to work with. "I found the cutest little church in a small town. But it's about an hour and a half outside of Nashville."

Silence greeted her. "How are we going to make that work, Cassie?"

At least she hadn't said "no."

"I think the best thing to do is load everyone into buses and bring them in from Nashville. They'll get an excursion to a charming area, with bucolic country scenes out the window on the way there. And Carly, you're going to love this church. Just a sec." Cassie brought up the photo Greg had sent and fired it off to Carly.

A few seconds later, she heard, "Oh my goodness! That is so cute. Does it have what I was looking for?" Guitar strumming began in the background. Carly must have put on music.

"It does. Stained glass. Old-fashioned wooden pews. It's exactly what you want, only completely in the wrong place. And I have an idea for the reception. We were going to do it in a luxury hotel, which is fine, of course. Lots of people have receptions there. But I was at a farm outside of town that grows flowers for florists. They have the most beautiful fields. What would you think of a tent set up with a field like that as the view out the open side?"

Carly gasped. "That sounds wonderful! Can we do all of this on the budget that Jake set for the wedding?"

Cassie burst out laughing. "Carly, we can pretty much do this wedding on the moon with the budget that Jake gave me. Don't worry about it. I'll get rolling on everything. Do you want to come out here one day next week to see it before things go too far?"

The guitar playing had now been joined by other instruments. "I have rehearsal this week," Carly said into the phone, much more loudly than before. When the volume kicked up even louder in the background, Carly shouted, "I have a concert next weekend. It's the last one. I'm going to trust you on this, Cassie. Because I truly do trust you. I have to go now." Cassie's phone went quiet.

Whoa. This was a huge responsibility. Should she ask Jake if he wanted to come out? No, he was busy with his business as well. Carly knew exactly what she wanted, and Cassie had found it. She'd make this the best wedding Carly could have ever imagined. Like a lot of grooms, she suspected that Jake was just along for the ride and happy to be humoring the woman of his dreams. He didn't really care what color the flowers were or how many layers the cake had.

With that settled, she happily got out of the car and walked toward the house. But with each step, her footsteps got heavier and heavier.

When Mrs. Brantley answered her knock, Cassie cried out, "What have I done?"

She had taken on the most monumental task in the history of wedding planning. She needed to relocate a wedding from the city, where things could be challenging anyway, to a small town that had never done this.

She had to figure out the logistics for food and cake and flowers and security. At least Greg had taken over that bit.

"What's wrong, Cassie? Greg came in here today on his phone, and he's been on it the whole time. Is something wrong in Two Hearts?"

Greg hung up his phone at that moment, having heard his mother's words. "Nothing is wrong, Mom. Cassie is going to do a celebrity wedding in our town two weeks from yesterday."

The expression on his mother's face changed from confusion to the realization that money was coming to her fair town. "Cassie, that's wonderful. Can I do anything to help?"

Could she? Cassie was still standing on the front step, and the older woman seemed to realize it at that moment. "Come in. Come in! Lunch is ready. I'm glad I made extra today."

Greg laughed. "Mom, you always make extra."

"Well, that may be true. I do love leftovers, though."

Cassie sat down and was treated to homemade chicken and dumplings, and broccoli.

"Do you need a place to work from, Cassie? I don't know how much space wedding planning takes. Will you simply work out of your car, or do you need a remote office?"

Good question. She'd never done anything like this. The idea of having an office and a space to store things like the wedding favors sounded like an excellent plan to her. "I'd like that, but I'm not sure where I would go."

"I have an idea." Mrs. Brantley grinned. "You know that yellow house you've mentioned a couple of times?"

Cassie sighed. "I do. It's a cute house."

"I realized that I hadn't talked to Mabel in months, so I reached out to her. It turns out that she loves living near her family. I also learned that the family has decided to sell the yellow house. I have a feeling that they would rent it to you short-term, with the idea that you could help clean it up a little bit for them."

Cassie pictured herself sitting in that adorable house, looking out the windows as she worked. It was fantasy come true. "If you can negotiate that, I would be very grateful."

Mrs. Brantley got up and started taking care of the dishes. "I will, just as soon as we have dessert." She brought over a cake. "This is Greg's favorite." She gave Cassie a look that said she needed to remember that fact, and Cassie felt her face grow hot.

Greg, as men often were, seemed oblivious to the remark. "Chocolate cake with cherry filling?"

"Yes, I made a Black Forest cake. I must have known we would be having special company today."

As they ate the dessert, Greg said, "I contacted a firm I know of, and they're going to send security people the day before the wedding. They've assured me that everyone can stay until the day after it. Does that sound okay, Cassie?"

"Of course."

"I called Marisol Estrada, too. She said she's always wanted to see Two Hearts, and she was excited to come down here. I'll need to get her one of the cottages over at the motel."

"Your old partner? She can stay in the guest room here, Greg."

He nodded. "Okay, I'll give her a choice in case she's someone who likes to be alone."

Mrs. Brantley turned to Cassie. "I had high hopes for a romance between the two of them when they were police partners." She shook her head sadly. "But nothing came of that. And now my boy is sitting here at my table in Two Hearts as the town sheriff."

Cassie's head whipped around toward Greg. His old flame was going to be coming here to help with the wedding?

"You know, Mom, that you don't date your partner."

But they weren't partners anymore, were they?

"Besides, we were simply officers sitting beside each other in a car. We became friends, but there was never a hint of anything more." He held up his plate. "Can I get another little slice of the cake?"

Mrs. Brantley laughed. "Of course."

As soon as she had finished tidying up after their lunch, Mrs. Brantley went down the hall to her room and closed the door, Cassie assumed to make the call about the yellow house. Excitement rushed through her at the thought of being inside it. Having a place of her own to work would be a godsend during this job.

# CHAPTER SIXTEEN

*C*assie glanced at Greg across the table. The realization that they were alone sent a flutter of happiness through her.

He said, "I haven't had a chance to talk to you privately, but it's good to see you, Cassie. I wasn't sure I would ever see you again."

How did she answer that? Her heart beat faster. She felt the same way, but she shouldn't pursue whatever this was between them. She couldn't. Pushing aside any romantic ideas, she used her wedding planner smile. "I'm glad to be able to bring this opportunity to Two Hearts."

His face fell. Hurting him had never been part of her plan.

Wait. What plan? She'd been winging it since she ran out of that church. Cassie put her hand on his. "Greg—"

At that moment, his mother burst out of the room at the end of the hall and barreled toward them. "It's a done deal. You can go there right now, and we can start getting it ready for you. Utilities are off, so that's a negative, but we should be able to get those on for you first thing in the morning."

Cassie looked up at him with words unsaid. Maybe it was better that way.

"Well, what are you waiting for? Let's get over there and see what this place looks like." Mrs. Brantley grabbed her purse and started for the back door. "Mabel was always an excellent housekeeper. But she lost some mobility about when she turned ninety-five. Or maybe it was ninety-six."

If Cassie's only problem when she was old was that she couldn't clean as well, she'd be set. She'd never liked cleaning in the first place.

They walked down the street, with Greg's mother setting the pace and them keeping up. When this woman was on a mission, she was a force to be reckoned with. She'd actually make a great mayor.

To Greg, Cassie said, "Why do you have a mayor who is desperately old and doesn't seem to want the job very much?"

"He doesn't want it at all. He's been in the position for a long time. The problem is that no one else wants the job, either. It doesn't pay much, and there always seems to be something to be fixed. It's more of a burden than a joy."

As were too many things in Two Hearts.

When they approached the yellow house, Cassie felt a smile begin from inside and work its way out. Something about this little yellow house charmed her. As they walked up the path to the front door, dodging overgrown weeds that had tried to consume it from both sides, nerves kicked in. What if her fantasy about this place from the outside had nothing to do with the reality of the inside?

Mrs. Brantley reached above the doorjamb and pulled down a key.

"She's storing a key in plain sight?" Greg groaned.

"Son, it's only in plain sight if you're tall like you are. Otherwise, it's sitting above the doorjamb at the end of a path no one has used for years."

"That much is true."

The older woman turned the lock, pushed the door open, and stepped to the side. "Cassie, you're the one who saw the potential in this house. I think you need to go first."

Cassie cautiously stepped over the threshold. While it was true that dust was everywhere and dead bugs were garishly strewn here and there across the room, light was still filtering in through the front windows with their diamond-shaped panes, and the original hardwood floors peeking out around the area rugs said this home had been a beauty in its day. Spinning in a circle, she saw what appeared to be stained glass in the transom window above the front door. It was so grimy that she couldn't tell for sure.

She picked her way through the mess, having to step around a stack of newspapers, a few boxes, and other things the old woman had left behind. When she got to the kitchen, a shriek built up inside of her, but she tamped it down. Dishes had apparently been left in the sink. Several years ago.

"Oh, my," Mrs. Brantley said from near Cassie's ear.

Looking up instead of at the sink, she saw white cabinets rising toward a tin ceiling. An old-fashioned white stove, one that must now be a coveted collector's item, stood in the corner. The newish refrigerator must have been bought not long before Mabel had left. "It has good bones."

Greg pointed toward the sink. "There are probably bones in that sink."

She nudged him with her elbow. "Be nice. This building is my new office."

"Yes, ma'am. I think you'll need a couple of people in hazmat suits to take care of the kitchen, though." He chuckled.

He was making a joke, but Cassie would want to be covered from head to toe before she took on that sink or—heaven forbid—the refrigerator. She shuddered just thinking about it.

Down the hall, they found a bedroom and bathroom. The

bathroom could use a good scrubbing of its fixtures and the black-and-white tile, but it wasn't as scary as she'd expected, and the bedroom's lavender color would be fine for her office.

Up the back stairs from the kitchen—she'd always found an air of romance in having both a back stairway and a beautiful front staircase—there was a landing with wood floors edged with an inlaid pattern of other woods that must have been quite a luxury when the home was built. In total, there were three additional bedrooms—one with French doors that opened to a back balcony that she immediately adopted as hers—and a bathroom with questionable green tile with black trim. Everything had an authentic vintage feel to it, including the clawfoot bathtub.

"I don't see any evidence of the roof leaking. That's good," Greg commented.

When they were back downstairs in the living room, Cassie said, "I know there's a lot to do to get everything ready for the wedding, but I wonder if a couple of people could come help me clean this place up tomorrow."

"Of course we will," Mrs. Brantley said. "I'm working on a list of people for each of the tasks. Justin's team can mow this lawn so you can at least use the sidewalk to the front door. Then he's going to work on the town. Albert should know who we can get to clean up Main Street. We need to take down any boards that cover windows and wash the glass."

"We should probably power wash the outside of the buildings and the sidewalks, too," Greg said.

Cassie envisioned the amount of work that had to be done to get this town in shape. Had she taken on too big of a task when she'd moved the wedding here?

Her face must have shown the panic she was starting to feel inside, because Mrs. Brantley said, "Don't worry, Cassie. We're going to get this place ready for you. Your yellow house and everything down Main Street. At least when the guests head out of town toward the reception, there isn't much city left, and we don't have to take care of any grooming of farms."

That was an upside. "I guess I'd better call Cherry and ask if they are interested in having this event there," Cassie said. Half her plan hinged on that.

"Don't worry. Cherry has wanted to hold events there for years," Mrs. Brantley said. "They did host one small wedding last year, but it was for a cousin. She'll be thrilled. And I know, with the new baby, that the extra income will be much appreciated." She stared at Cassie. "You are going to pay them for using their farm, right?"

"Of course." Cassie nodded. "And I will have a generous sum to pay the town for everything that has to be done to clean up. I know you'll have to board the windows over again when we leave."

A pall fell over the room.

She shouldn't have used those words. "Not that this won't be something that's a turning point for the town."

Mrs. Brantley sighed. "I certainly hope it is, Cassie. At least you're showing us what's possible. Maybe some of us can get together and start promoting it once we see how it's done. Do you think anyone else would want to have a wedding here?"

Cassie tried to think about her client list, but details from this wedding crowded everything else out. "Give me some time to consider it." For right now, at least, Two Hearts was about to have its most prosperous two weeks in decades.

True to their word, Cassie found work underway the next morning when she and Romeo pulled up to the yellow house—a.k.a. her temporary office. When she went inside through the back door with Romeo in his carrier, she found a crew hard at work washing dishes.

"You just keep on going, Cassie. Mrs. Brantley said you weren't allowed to work in this kitchen until it was clean," Michelle said.

A woman she didn't know—at least she didn't think she did; she was becoming overwhelmed with new faces and names— was up to her elbows in soapy water at the sink. She deserved a medal for hazardous duty.

A running faucet also meant that water had been turned on. The old-fashioned single light overhead wasn't lit, so Cassie flipped the switch, and it came to life.

"Oh, good," Michelle said. "That didn't work when we got here. Mrs. Brantley has been busy."

The disgusting smell had already diminished. "I can never thank you enough, all of you." Turning toward the one modern appliance, Cassie asked, "Has anyone opened the fridge?"

Michelle gave it a glare that implied it was evil personified. "We did. We closed it up just as quickly. My uncle has a gas mask, and I'm going to wear that. We'll leave the back door open, too. Mrs. Murth's family is lovely, but I cannot imagine why someone didn't think to clean out the kitchen when they moved her away."

Maybe Mrs. Murth had a daughter like Sandra Van Bibber, a woman who wouldn't touch a dirty anything with a ten-foot pole. Cassie continued on through to the living area.

"Greg?" She found the town sheriff rolling up rugs in the living room, and the furniture pushed against the walls. When he looked up, her heart did its happy dance. After setting Romeo's carrier on a side table, she walked over to Greg, her smile growing wider with every step.

"I have about an hour before my shift. I think we can get this knocked out pretty quickly." He pointed to the opposite end of the rug that he had just finished rolling. "Let's carry this outside. Then I'll clean up this room, shake out those rugs, and put everything back together."

"Hey, I can help with all of that."

He stopped mid-roll on the last rug. "Cassie, I don't know a thing about the wedding business, but my guess is that you have a lot to do before this wedding. Am I right?"

He certainly was. "I have some initial calls to make and then a lot of mountains to move to make this happen on schedule and here."

"If you'll help me with this one thing, I'll get someone else to help me with the rest. Mom thought you'd want to use the bedroom at the end of the hall as an office, so her team cleaned it first. You do your work, and I'll do mine. Does that sound fair?"

Cassie loved this little town and its people. "More than fair."

After they'd hefted the rug—which weighed far more than she'd imagined—and deposited it on the lawn, Greg followed her back inside.

"Thank you for your work on my temporary quarters." She stared at him for a moment longer than she should. "We'll get to work, then."

He raised an eyebrow as he looked at her. "We?"

"Romeo and I." She pointed toward the cat carrier.

He leaned down to look inside the carrier. "I forgot you had adopted him. How's the little guy doing?"

"He's fine. I bring him to work every day, and almost all of my clients adore him. I fired the one that didn't."

He rocked back on his heels, looking up at her when she said that.

"Love me, love my cat."

Chuckling, he stood. "It's that simple to win your love?"

Why did his words feel so packed with emotion? Looking into his eyes, time stopped. The sparkle in them and the dimple from his smile should be declared dangerous weapons for all womankind. The kindness and caring beneath his appearance made him even more attractive.

Swallowing hard, she struggled not to lean toward him. When her eyes dropped to his lips and she all but groaned out loud, she knew she was in trouble.

"Yuck!" a voice shouted from the kitchen.

"I told you not to open the fridge," a voice she recognized as Michelle's said.

Looking down at her, he shook his head and said, "Cassie, what are we going to do about this?" He moved closer to her, so close that they almost touched. Almost.

She knew exactly what he was talking about, but she wasn't ready to sort it all out. His warmth pulled her closer.

He reached up and put his hand on her cheek, rubbing his thumb across it.

Cassie closed her eyes. "Greg, I don't know. But—"

"Miss Cassie, do you want me to save the storage containers from the fridge?" The voice grew louder with each word as the speaker drew closer.

Cassie leaped back from Greg and hurried toward the kitchen. "Do not, under any circumstances, open those containers, ladies. I don't care if it looks like they are genuine antiques. The substances that have been locked inside there for years should not be released." She turned back to Greg with what she knew was a longing glance, grabbed Romeo's carrier, and escaped down the hall to her temporary office.

Behind the closed door, she could forget about Sheriff Greg Brantley. She hoped.

As soon as she was alone, she picked up the phone to call Bella.

Her friend answered, "I hope your day's going better than mine. No, that fabric will not work for the dress. Sorry about that, Cassie. We had somewhat of a crisis here this morning when a bride announced that she wanted a different fabric for her wedding gown. Yes, that one's much better."

"Should I call you back later?"

"I think everything's settling down now. I need a vacation. You had that lovely week off in your small town."

Cassie gurgled with laughter. "You mean the week that began with me wearing someone else's clothes? And I didn't have a vehicle and had to rely on strangers to feed me? *And I* was only there because of Mr. Cheater and his pretend cousin. That week?"

"That's only how it started. Besides, you were able to step away from your business for a while. I think I need to plan something like that into my life. I'm going to go into my office now. Just a sec."

Cassie heard heels tapping on the tile floor and then a door closing.

"I think—make that *I hope*—we have resolved the fabric issue. So, what's new with you? I didn't hear from you yesterday, so I figured you were just relaxing or thinking about the Carly and Jake wedding."

Cassie looked around her new office. "Do you remember that photo I showed you of the yellow house in Two Hearts?"

"Sure, I do." Cassie could hear rustling papers. "It looked like a huge mess, but it did seem to have hidden cuteness."

"I'm sitting in it right now in a temporary office because Carly's wedding has been moved to Two Hearts."

Bella yelped. "Are you kidding me? How did you do that in a day?"

"It's a long story. Let me say that the people in this town are very excited, and I think it's going to all work out."

"Maybe I can escape for a day or two right before the wedding and bring the dresses with me. Just in case Carly's dimensions changed again."

"Again?"

"She's been working out because she wanted to have more stamina for performing. That means we've made a few tucks and tweaks to them."

Cassie envisioned her celebrity bride wearing a dress that did not fit properly. Photos of this wedding would probably be in major publications—if the couple chose to share them after the service. "In that case, please come here to make sure her dress is right for the wedding."

"And the *reception*. Oh my gosh, Cassie. She wants to change into a different dress for the reception, and hers was designed for a high-end hotel's ballroom. Will that work in a tent in the country?"

Would it? "We've been calling the wedding 'formal.' But if someone has to walk around in dirt or gravel to use the restroom, maybe we need to change that." Cassie leaned forward and closed her eyes. "Why didn't I think of this, Bella?"

"You mean why didn't you think of this among all the other things you had to do with this wedding? Don't beat yourself up over it, Cassie. The dress is beautiful. Absolutely beautiful. If I say so myself."

"I'm going to run this by Carly for her opinion, and I will get back to you. But, Bella, you have about a week and a half before the wedding. Can you make a new reception dress in that amount of time? I already have you working on Etta's gown."

"Etta is a sweet girl, and her design is very simple. It's a satin silk sheath with a small amount of embellishment on it. She's the dream client to work with on a short timeline. Carly, on the other hand, as a music performer—especially a country music performer—enjoys her sequins and pearls and every other extra I can put on there. I need to know today, Cassie."

"Okay. I'm on it."

She fired off a text to Carly and waited for the immediate call back that she'd gotten yesterday. A few minutes later, she decided she needed to move forward with other chores. She'd call Jake to help track down his fiancée if needed.

But now, it was time to secure the venue where Carly would wear that dress. A quick trip to Cherry and Levi's farm brought the answer she needed. They'd been thrilled about what businesswoman Cherry had called a "second income stream." The new mother—who must be busy even by Cassie's definition —presented her with a loaf of homemade banana bread.

~

Greg finished his work and hurried away before he could do anything stupid. The second Cassie had stepped back into his life, he'd lost whatever good sense he'd had. He nodded to the teenagers working in Cassie's yard. Between them and the ladies inside, this place would be a home again by sunset.

He glanced back. He hadn't said a word about it, but he'd always had a soft spot for Mabel's yellow house. She'd baked cookies for the boys after school a few times when their mothers had been busy. It was too much house for a bachelor, though. No, he was better off where he was.

At home, he quickly changed into his uniform. This apartment over the garage had been a temporary solution. Everything still felt temporary, even though he'd been back in Two Hearts almost two years. How many men chose to live in the apartment over their mother's garage?

Somewhere along the way, he'd given up and accepted that this would be his life. Cassie had shaken that up. That was all.

Going down the stairs, he jammed his hat on his head with unnecessary vigor. *Then why do you get all fuzzy-feeling when she is near? Why do you want to kiss the woman whenever she steps close?* Someone might have spotted them today, and they'd have been the talk of the town in ten minutes.

He'd even used the word "love" earlier with Cassie. If there was any word in the English language that must be avoided around a single woman, it was that one. That was part of every single man's code. They all knew that.

But he'd broken that rule. And she'd noticed it.

Greg drove his usual pattern through the town's side streets. Everything seemed unusually quiet. No one was out working in a yard or walking their dog. There were a fair number of people helping at Cassie's house, so that could explain part of it.

When he turned onto Main Street south of town, he understood. Justin had assembled an army of workers. Several yards were already more groomed than they'd been in recent memory.

Main Street's business district—what was left of it, anyway—showed an equal amount of activity. Men pried plywood off windows he didn't remember any other way.

Albert's old truck was ahead of him on the road. When he parked on the side of the street, Greg pulled up behind him.

The older man stepped out of his truck. "Sheriff, help me unload this power washer."

Greg went to help, and the two of them muscled it onto the ground.

Albert closed the truck's tailgate. "I never thought I'd live to see this."

Someone scraped peeled paint from a door on one of the storefronts, but he couldn't tell who he or she was. He didn't even remember anything being in that building. Only a few of the buildings had been used in his lifetime.

"This must have been a nice town when all of these shops were filled and customers went from shop to shop."

Greg didn't realize he'd said those words out loud until Albert replied. "That it was."

"I'd better get back to work."

Albert laughed. "Don't you mean that it's time for lunch at Dinah's Place?"

Greg grinned. "You're right. It is lunchtime. Can I get you anything?"

Albert said, "I'll stop by later for pie. I do that almost every day."

During the short distance to the restaurant, a call came in about Mrs. Marshall's cat, who liked to climb the tree next to the house that her elderly owner was sure she could not come down from.

Last time, he'd climbed the tree, only to have the cat exit it onto the nearby porch roof, then dart through a window into the house. There would be no more tree climbing for him.

It looked like he'd have a late lunch.

Fortunately, Mrs. Marshall's baking skills hadn't diminished. Seated at her kitchen table, he ate all the warm chocolate chip cookies he could hold and a glass of milk.

By the time he went to Dinah's, lunchtime had come and gone.

"Missed you today, Sheriff. Busy with the wedding and all that's going on?" She poured him a cup of coffee before he reached his chair at the counter. The place was once again empty.

"Mrs. Marshall."

"Oh, no! Lucy's been up the tree again?"

After a sip of coffee, he nodded. Before he stopped to think about it, he asked, "Has Cassie been in today?" For someone who didn't want people to think he was interested in her, he sure sounded like he did. "I just wondered if she was working so hard that she hadn't stopped for lunch." He winced. That sounded even more like he cared.

Dinah's smile said she'd caught that, but, like a bartender who heard many secrets, she kept these things to herself. "I haven't seen her. My guess is that she'd like a break about now with coffee. And a piece of pie."

Would she get the wrong message if he brought her a snack? If he was her friend, which he thought he was, he would be doing something kind for her.

"Please fix coffee for her however she drinks it, and your guess is better than mine on the pie." The list of pies on the board showed lemon meringue, coconut cream, pecan, and cherry. She'd had a big bowl of fruit in her motel room. "Make that a piece of your cherry pie."

"Good choice." Dinah prepared his order.

"You'd say that about any of your pies, wouldn't you?"

Glancing over at him, she grinned. "I would. But I also know that Cassie orders things like strawberry pancakes and fruit pies. You did make a good choice."

"I'll take a cup of coffee to go, too."

Driving over to the yellow house, he rehearsed his words out loud. "Cassie, I thought you might be thirsty." *Did that sound strange?* "Cassie, you've worked hard all day and need to stop for a minute." *Did that sound caring or pushy?*

When he arrived at the intersection past the house, he realized he'd been so wrapped up in his own thoughts that he'd passed it. He turned around and cruised slowly down the street, doing a double-take when he saw the house.

Overgrown flowers and grass had become a neatly groomed yard with graceful clumps of flowers that seemed appropriate to the era of the house. Hanging baskets with brightly colored blooms flanked each side of the porch.

Justin could have a bright future in this work. Maybe an influx of money from this wedding would help create work for him and convince him to stay here instead of moving to a city.

His hand on the doorbell, an old-fashioned one that twisted to ring, Greg wondered if he'd made a mistake doing this. The hot cups in his hand convinced him to hurry up and ring it. A minute later, when he didn't hear any noise from inside, he knew he'd been a fool for trying this. What did he want, anyway?

Her car was in the driveway, but maybe she'd walked somewhere instead of driving. On the way to his car, he heard Cassie's laughter. He'd know it anywhere. Following the sound, he went around to the back of the house and found her on a wooden chair in a garden that appeared purposefully wild, like an English garden.

Cassie dragged a bright pink ribbon on the ground. Romeo pounced on it, trying to grab it in his teeth, but the elusive toy pulled away as Cassie tugged on it.

When he jumped on it again, Greg laughed at the cat's antics.

She jumped back with her hand over her heart.

"Sorry! I didn't want to startle the two of you, while you were playing."

"Is that coffee for me?" She pointed to the cup in his hand with her ribbon-filled hand, and Romeo leaped up to catch the end of it.

He handed it to her. "It is. And cherry pie."

"Then you're forgiven." She took a sip of the coffee and reached for the bag. Only seconds passed before she had a bite of pie in her mouth. "Please have a seat, Greg." After another bite, she sighed. "I needed this, especially the coffee."

As he relaxed on the chair, he took off his hat and set it on the table at his side. It struck him now that he had a way to spend time with Cassie: he'd bring her coffee and get one for himself, too. This could work.

# CHAPTER SEVENTEEN

$\mathcal{C}$assie took a long sip of her coffee.

"Have you made much progress with the wedding?"

"Are you kidding? Everyone has been so helpful. Justin came by early. He had assembled a group of teenagers he knew and borrowed the equipment they'd need for the job. He'd even created a timeline." She'd like to find a place for him in her business when he finished school. "He had a buddy drive slowly down the road and wrote down the address of every yard that needed work."

"I hope Two Hearts is able to give him the future he should have."

The town would rather he stayed, and she respected that. This wedding needed to revive the town enough that someone like Justin could stay. Another notch of pressure went onto her tally. She had to make this wedding a success. "Then I called Albert at the hardware store. You'll never guess who had consulted with him and come up with plans for the Main Street cleanup."

"Gasp!" Greg had an expression of mock surprise. "Could it be my mother?"

She did like a man with a sense of humor. "Of course. I have the utmost respect for her ability to run a project."

"I drove down Main Street hours ago, and they were already making great progress."

"Whew." With that going well, would she be able to make everything else fall into place as easily?

"You seem . . . concerned. Is there a problem?"

"Are you asking as the sheriff? If so, everything is fine."

"I'm asking as a friend."

Were they friends? Maybe they were. "Then as a friend, I will tell you that I have many mountains to move to make this happen. An outdoor event always has more steps." She caught herself frowning, but turned it into a smile.

"Cassie, what's really going on?"

"I'm a planner. I like doing everything according to plan, and that trait has helped me thrive in the wedding industry. Sure, I know how to fix last-minute problems, but I prefer to schedule everything a year in advance and make it happen."

"This isn't going to plan, is it?"

"The plan went up in massive, glorious flames a week ago." She brought her hands together and pushed them out like an explosion.

He took her hand in his and squeezed it. Knowing she should pull away didn't make her do it. His touch somehow comforted and excited her.

"Know this: the people of this town will do whatever it takes to make this wedding come off perfectly." His thumb rubbed her hand, making tingles zing up her arm.

She sighed. "Thank you. That helps." Even she didn't know if she meant his words or his touch.

"Can I take you to dinner tonight?"

No. She could not allow a romance to develop between them. Slowly sliding her hand away from his, she said, "Romeo and I need to settle in here tonight. I think I'll run to the grocery store and pick something up." For someone whose palate could tell the subtle differences between seasonings when it came to helping bridal parties choose foods, you'd think she could cook like a dream. Not so. A sandwich was on the menu. Again. She could put almost anything between two slices of bread or roll it in a wrap and have it taste decent.

Picking up his hat, he stood. "Then I'll see you later." He placed his hat on his head, gave her a nod, and left.

"What are we going to do about Greg Brantley, Romeo?"

Her kitten jumped on her lap as though to say, "You've got me."

"Are you saying I don't need another male in my life?" He purred in response.

The next day, work went well, and by mid-morning, she'd made sure everything on Main Street was on track. When this town embraced a job they did it with gusto. They'd completed far more than she had expected in so little time.

Cassie found a storage container on her back step when she got home, with a note from someone she thought she'd met once taped to the top. She pried it open in her kitchen. The scent of warm chocolate chip cookies wafted up, and her mouth started watering. In the next two hours, knocks on her door brought apple muffins from one woman and chicken salad sandwiches for her lunch from another. She grabbed a sandwich and went back to work.

If this continued, she'd have to add an exercise bike to her office to burn up the calories. Two Hearts had been good for her soul, but not her waistline.

Cassie and Romeo spent the next couple of hours in her home office, sorting out details such as the scheduling of buses for guests to use from Nashville to Two Hearts and back, and the rental of portable toilets.

At noon, she answered the doorbell to find Greg standing there with two cups of coffee.

Being nice to him for his kindness was the right thing to do, and maybe he could take some of the treats she'd amassed. "Please help me in here."

"I'll have to leave if I get a call."

"No problem." She grabbed his arm and pulled him forward, toward the dining room. "Greg, I have been overrun with sweets."

He burst out laughing. "The Two Hearts welcome committee has been busy."

"There's an official committee?"

"It's simply small town life at its finest." He checked out the offerings. "Did anyone bring you something savory? I had a call earlier and missed lunch."

"The best chef's salad I have ever eaten." After the chicken salad sandwiches had arrived, someone had brought a huge bowl filled with lettuce, cold cuts, cheese, hard-boiled eggs, and veggies, along with a container of ranch dressing.

He followed her into the kitchen, where she fixed him a bowl of it. She could feel his eyes on her while she worked. She added a sandwich to the side.

"Grab whatever you want from the treats." When she looked up, his heated expression tore through her. This man could do to her what no other man could. She gulped and handed him his lunch. "Let's go outside."

"You aren't eating?" he asked as he followed her out.

"You saw that pile of treats. I felt like I needed to taste each one so I could tell the person I liked it. Someone even made my favorite—iced sugar cookies. I had to eat two of them. Just to be sure."

He sat, grinning, and took a sip of his coffee. "Was everything good?"

"Promise you won't tell?" She sat in her chair and put Romeo on the ground next to her.

Greg nodded.

"I didn't like the—"

He interrupted. "Raspberry coffee cake."

"It's well known?"

"It is. The woman responsible for it found that recipe in a magazine years ago and thinks everyone loves it. We don't have the heart to tell her the truth."

Birds chirped, and a squirrel in a tree chattered, both making Romeo crazy as he tried to reach them. Cassie and Greg sat, and she enjoyed the peace of being here with him.

A short time later, Greg had to respond to a call. He left, and she watched him go, wanting to call him back.

The next day, he showed up about noon with her coffee.

"I'm glad you're here. We're friends, so please come inside and share my lunch." She started for the kitchen. Her heart sang when she heard his footsteps behind her.

After that, Greg showed up every day at lunchtime—the time varying because he had to answer calls some days. When the gifted food ran out, she made sandwiches for them.

Saturday, she looked up from her work to find the grandfather clock showing it was almost three p.m. She wasn't sure exactly when the grocery store closed, but she had a feeling it didn't stay open much later. It had been closed when she'd first arrived on a Saturday evening.

"I'll be right back, Romeo." This time, she didn't have to buy anything for him. She'd come well prepared for her stay—at least as far as her cat went. Her, not so much.

A while later, she added a dozen eggs to the basket she had looped over her arm. Deciding to make more of a meal, she added in tortillas and cheese for a breakfast burrito. Then she decided to be wild and crazy and put in an onion and bell pepper. Could she manage to cook an actual meal without a recipe? With some grapes, cheese, and crackers, she had everything she needed to get by.

When she checked out, the woman said, "If most of these things are going together, this looks really delicious."

"If it is, then this will be one of the few delicious meals I have ever produced in my kitchen."

The woman looked at her as she paid. "I don't know you." Then she gasped and put her hand over her mouth. "Wait! You're the woman who's doing the fancy wedding, aren't you?"

She liked that much better than "runaway bride." "Guilty as charged. I hope you don't mind the inconvenience."

She grinned. "Are you kidding? This is the most exciting thing to happen in this town in . . . well, forever. My kids are as excited as they can be."

Cassie waved as she left, and she drove home.

*Home.* She had been in this little yellow house for a short time, and she had already come to think of it that way. When she was almost there, she called Bella.

"How is life in small-town America?"

Cassie looked at the little yellow house as she pulled into the driveway. "It's great. I couldn't be happier." As soon as she said the words, she realized they were true.

"Hey, Cassie, you aren't leaving the city for a small town permanently, are you?" Her friend sounded distressed.

"Of course not. I own a condo in the city. I have an office—a very nice office, if I say so myself—there as well. I have friends. Nashville is my home."

"Whew. That's quite a drive out there, and I wouldn't want to have to do that every time I needed ice cream with a friend."

Cassie's heart twisted when she thought of the friends that she had in the city and was making here. She would have to leave one set of them soon.

"How's Mr. Handsome?"

"Are you referring to the sheriff?" She refused to fall into this trap of Bella's, or her idea of an imagined romance.

"You know who I mean. Tall, dark, and handsome. Available. And he comes with an awesome mother."

"Bella—"

She sighed. "I know. You're going to tell me it's too soon, aren't you?"

Was she? "Honestly, I wasn't. I rarely think about Jonathan. When I do, like right now, I realize that I would have had a wonderful tan from the beach."

"So if I'm reading this correctly, you aren't missing Jonathan so much as you need a beach vacation?"

Leave it to Bella to get right down to the nitty-gritty. "I guess that is what I said. I miss what should have been. But I will eternally be grateful for catching them in the act before I married him."

"The rat," they said at the same time.

Cassie chuckled. "When are you coming here?"

"I'm almost done with Carly's new reception dress, but I had a couple of last-minute alterations. One bride lost weight, and one bride is pregnant. I'll be there early the day of the wedding."

Cassie gasped. "The day of the wedding?"

"I'll get up predawn. Carly isn't going to be there before then, is she? I only need to be there when the bride is."

As disappointing as that was, Cassie understood. When your business was busy, you had to take care of it. "You're right. Carly's on tour now. I'll see her the day of the rehearsal dinner. Do you want to spend the night here in my house or do you want me to get you a room at the motel? Because I am making you stay overnight. You know that, right?"

Bella's voice became concerned. "I wouldn't have it any other way. Of course I'll stay with you. But do you realize you just called it 'your house'? Not 'the little yellow house' or 'the house that belonged to whoever' or 'my temporary office.'"

When had it become her house?

～

Wednesday morning, Cassie checked her watch. She had an hour or so until Greg arrived. Correct that: until she ate lunch with her friend. As the clock ticked down the time, she knew she was more hungry to see him than she was hungry for food.

Everything for the wedding was coming together nicely. In two days, they'd have the rehearsal dinner in Nashville as planned. Then, the next morning, guests would be bussed here for the wedding. A mere four days from now, and everything would be over.

The house she'd come to see as hers would be closed up again and put on the market. But would anyone buy it when so many houses were already for sale here?

A while later, she checked her watch again. Greg was late. A knock on the door at about two had her racing to it. Pulling it open with a smile on her face, she found Michelle with a Dinah's Place bag in her hands. Cassie leaned to check one side of her and then the other. She'd come alone.

"The sheriff called and said you needed lunch. I needed a break, so I volunteered to bring it over."

Disappointment washed over her. "Thank you, Michelle." When the woman turned to leave, she realized she might be the answer to a problem she had. Not every team member had wanted to come out to Two Hearts and she was shorthanded.

"Michelle, I need someone to go stay at the church after the wedding to make sure the photo shoot goes smoothly and that everything is tidied up. Would you be interested? I would pay you, of course."

The waitress stared at the ground, then looked up. "I would like that."

"But? I sense a 'but.'"

"Is this Carly Daniels's wedding?" Michelle burst out and stared expectantly at her.

Cassie blew out a long breath. "Even if it was, I couldn't tell you. I've signed an agreement to keep it secret."

"Yeah, I thought so." Michelle frowned for a moment, then perked up. "What do you need me to do?"

"Stop by tonight after work. I'll walk you through it. And think about your wardrobe. We all wear black while we're working."

As Michelle walked down the sidewalk, Cassie felt the other woman's disappointment. "Michelle, if this *was* Carly's wedding, what would you wear?"

She turned back. "That's easy. A dress and hot-pink cowboy boots."

"You own pink cowboy boots?"

She blushed. "They looked so cute on her that I saved up for some."

"That sounds like a great outfit." She let her words sit there.

"Do you mean . . . ?"

"I didn't say anything. And if you're going to work for me, you'll have to be able to keep secrets." Cassie rolled her eyes. "I've seen and heard some doozies. You can start out in your black outfit for the ceremony."

Michelle smiled. "Thank you for your faith in me. I'll bring my boots Saturday."

Cassie nodded. "Good plan."

A call came in later that afternoon from Mrs. Brantley. Cassie was invited for dinner—something she always enjoyed—and to meet a friend of Greg's who was in town to help with the wedding.

That night, she changed into jeans and a cute deep-blue top. She'd been striving for a professional look during business hours but wanted to relax at the Brantley's home. She chose this top because Bella had told her that shade enhanced a redhead's natural beauty. Whatever that meant. Not that she wanted to impress Greg.

The more she told herself that, the more she wondered about the truth of her words.

As she went up the front walk to their house, loud laughter rang through the screen door.

"Hello?"

Mrs. Brantley hurried over. "Cassie, I'm so glad you could come. I made one of your favorites, poppy seed chicken casserole, and Greg's former police partner is here from Chicago."

Cassie turned toward the laughter, her eyes resting first on Greg. His eyes crinkled up with happiness. Then her gaze moved to the left, landing not on the woman with an average appearance that she'd expected to find, but instead on a gorgeous woman her age with wavy dark-brown hair; big, beautiful blue eyes; and a figure that wouldn't quit.

Greg stood when the room went silent. "Cassie, this is Marisol. She's helping with security this weekend."

Cassie stood rooted to the spot, then her years of training came into play. Stepping forward, she said, "It's a pleasure to meet you. Have you visited Two Hearts before?"

"No, and it's such a cute town!"

Greg smiled at Cassie and eased some of her tension. "We have Cassie to thank for most of what you're excited about."

~

Pulling onto Main Street the next day, Greg slammed on his brakes and stared at the scene in front of him.

"She's done amazing work in a short time."

Greg didn't need to ask who "she" was. "The town is actually charming."

His mother laughed. "Don't sound so surprised. It looked like this when I was a girl. It just hid its charm for a while."

"Hah. A long while." Moving down the road, he glanced from right to left. Sure, there was still work to be done—some doors and trim appeared to have primer but not paint—but overall, it had been transformed into the quintessential small town everyone wanted to live in or at least visit.

Vibrant pink, blue, green, yellow, and red, invigorated the street. "Mom, I see a lot of bright colors on the finished doors and the wood frames around windows."

His mother smiled. "That was Cassie's idea. She said it would make the buildings seem more welcoming and the town happier. I think she's right."

He had to agree. A rush of community pride hit him for the first time in his life. He'd loved the people but had never felt this sense of being in a thriving place.

"We have a truck full of flowers arriving tomorrow. There will be pots of them here in the business district, and some will be planted in yards along the road. Cassie and I discussed it, and we're only planting flowers in yards with occupied houses. That way, someone will take care of them."

With two days until the wedding, it all looked remarkably good. "How did you manage to get everything done on time?"

"Not me. *We*. Many of the folks around here spent hours helping. Cassie made us believe we could."

Cassie never stopped amazing him. "I'll get her coffee, drop you off, and take it to her."

"She's gone."

He almost slammed the brakes again. "Where?"

"She said she needed to have 'boots on the ground' tomorrow morning for last-minute rehearsal dinner preparations."

"So she'll be back?" He strived for casual, but his mother saw right through him.

"Not that you're interested in her. Greg, a wedding is being held here Saturday. Of course, she'll be back, you idiot."

"Excuse me? Are you insulting my intelligence?"

Laughing, she shook her head. "You're one of the smartest people I know, and I'm not saying that because you're my son. Well, maybe a little. But when you open your mouth to talk about Cassie . . . it's like it vanishes. Poof!"

She had a point.

"Greg, she *will* leave after this wedding."

His head knew that, but his heart stayed hopeful. He somehow needed to convince Cassie that she'd be happy here. *Right, Brantley. A sophisticated woman like Cassie who enjoys city life wants to give that up to live in Two Hearts, Tennessee? Keep dreaming.*

The tall buildings of Nashville in the distance always let her know she was almost home after a long drive. When she reached them, they would comfort her as she drove the rest of the way.

But every time she returned from Two Hearts, the city noises were a little louder, and the traffic was worse.

The hotel she had scheduled for Carly and Jake's wedding reception had kindly not penalized her for the last-minute cancellation, as it had another event that wanted the space. And she'd kept the rehearsal dinner there. Carly, after a comment about having done years of choreography, didn't miss a beat when they walked through the ceremony. The groom's job of standing at the front of the church waiting for her took so little explanation that they were able to begin the dinner early.

The evening ended on a bright note, with promises to see her in Two Hearts the next day.

~

Cassie met with her team members at the church at nine a.m. They were all people she had used before with her weddings, except Michelle.

"Everyone, you'll take your usual positions. Jasmine, this time, you'll be with the bride. Michelle, you'll stay behind, as we discussed, to make sure the church is in good shape."

Michelle nodded her head up and down so much that Cassie was surprised she didn't complain of it hurting.

"Okay, everyone, let's make this an amazing wedding for Carly and Jake. As always, remember: this has nothing to do with us. It's all about the bride and groom today, and making sure that things go flawlessly, that neither they nor any family or guests see anything except the wedding of their dreams. Come to me with any problems, and we'll find a way to solve them. Okay?"

When no one commented, Cassie said, "Let's get to work. I'm going to go out to the farm and stay there all morning to receive deliveries and make sure that everything is set up properly. Those of you who are on wedding detail, get everything established here."

She handed Michelle an apron. "We keep some of the most commonly needed things tucked in the apron's pockets. During the ceremony, I'll have you wear this. You do want to come to the reception, don't you?"

"Are you kidding? I get to go to Carly's reception? And I'm being paid for it?"

Cassie grinned. "I'll take that as a yes."

"You can safely do that."

As Cassie drove toward the farm, she thought about the security arrangements for the day. Greg and his former partner would stay wherever the bride and groom were and follow them out to the farm. The other security team members would arrive in time for the wedding and then follow the couple out after the service.

So Cassie got quite a surprise when she showed up at Cherry and Levi's farm and found the sheriff's car parked there. "Greg?"

He popped his head out of the barn. "You're here early."

Cassie laughed. "I've already been to the church and working. Wedding day is a long day for a planner. But what are you doing here? I hope nothing is wrong."

"No, we're just looking through the barn and walking the perimeter to make sure we understand where everyone will be. Talk me through it one more time, Cassie."

She strolled beside him to the open area that would soon be covered with the tent. Pointing around them, she gave him the complete layout. As they stood there, a large vehicle came down the road. When it drew closer, she realized that the portable toilets had arrived.

"The greatest need is being taken care of now. That is a load off my mind."

She directed the delivery person to the correct area, and they dropped the toilets off and left. Minutes later, another two vehicles pulled down the driveway.

"I see what you mean about being busy."

"Greg, this is nothing. There are thirty to forty vendors involved in most of my weddings, and many of them are going to be bringing their products to me today. I'm just thankful that it isn't a hot day, so we don't have to worry about air conditioners under the tent. Or worse—so, so much worse—a stormy Tennessee day with wind and rain."

"I was concerned about that when I heard that you were doing an outdoor reception. Has there ever been a problem?"

"You're joking, right? I have stories that would make your hair curl. We always make it work, though."

～

Cassie certainly was earnest in her endeavors. "Have you ever had a disappointed bride?"

"Never. I do everything I can to make sure that my bride is as thrilled with the wedding and reception as she is with her groom. Sometimes, that takes more effort than you would imagine. But we always get it done," she said, raising her voice over the sound of the tent stakes being hammered into the ground.

Side by side, they silently looked out on the field of flowers.

He knew he was losing her soon, but she'd gone far and above anything he could have imagined for this location. Turning he said, "This truly is beautiful. It's going to be a beautiful event."

"I hope so. I think it's exactly what Carly would want." She leaned against him, and he enjoyed having her at his side. Too much. He put his arm around her and pulled her closer, and she didn't fight him. At least, not for a moment, and then she stepped away.

Cassie stared up at him with sad eyes and said, "I live in Nashville," as though those four words said everything that needed to be spoken between them. They probably did.

"Greg! Where did you run off to?"

Cassie whipped around as Marisol came out of the barn. "Everything looks good in there. I think we can head over to the church now, don't you think?" The other woman looked from him to her, then at the ground. "You know, I'm going to walk the perimeter one more time. I'll meet you back at the car, Greg."

"She is beautiful," Cassie said.

"What?" He looked back at his former partner. "I guess so." Was she asking if he was having a fling with Marisol? "I've trusted her with my life many times, but I do not want to spend my life with her."

Another delivery truck came down the road toward them.

"I'll see you at the church," he said.

She shielded her eyes from the sun to look up at him. "Yes, I'll see you then."

She couldn't seem to stay away from that man. Tomorrow, she would drive away—permanently, this time. She doubted she'd have another wedding for a long while that brought her to Two Hearts.

When the truck came to a stop, she hurried over to it. She recognized the logo on its side before she reached the vehicle. Her favorite florist, Henri, stepped out. But he'd arrived much sooner than Cassie had expected.

"The drive took less time than I thought it would, Cassie. Am I too early for the reception flowers?"

"You have a refrigerated truck, correct?"

"I do."

"Do you need to be anywhere else soon?"

"There's no way I could have scheduled another event for today with all the flowers Carly wanted for her service and reception."

"Then you're right on time." After leaving Henri, who said he had a book to read to keep him busy, Cassie checked on progress.

The tent was almost up, and the portable toilets had arrived, so Cassie could step away for a short time. She tapped on Henri's door, and he set down his book and opened it. "Follow me to town, and I'll take you to lunch at Dinah's. After that, it will be time to start getting flowers set out at the church." She called an assistant over. "I'm going to leave you here to receive other deliveries. As always, make sure that you check every box and bag to make sure everything is correct. And if you have even the smallest question, don't hesitate to call me."

The woman nodded in her efficient way.

"I saw that sheriff driving off as I arrived, and he kept his eyes on you longer than he should have for safety," Henri said when the other woman had left and taken up her post. "Did you and he—"

"I can't have any relationships here. I'm leaving, remember?"

Henri whipped his head around and turned toward her. "Oh, my, you have it bad for him, don't you?"

Cassie hoped not. She left, with the florist following behind. Ignoring Henri's comment, Cassie focused on the countryside, hoping it would calm her wayward thoughts.

# CHAPTER EIGHTEEN

While they were eating, Cassie received word that Carly and Jake had arrived and were each in their respective cottages. She shoved a final bite of soup in her mouth and hurried over to meet with them.

"Carly?" She knocked on the door.

"Cassie! I'm so glad to see you!" The music performer pulled her in for a hug. Clients who became friends were the best. "Come inside."

As Cassie entered the room, she asked, "Is your room okay?" She had personally gone over everything in each of the cottages.

The wedding gown lay draped over the bed. Bella's creation would stun everyone, especially the groom. Lace to the hips, the white, mermaid-style dress had off-the-shoulder cap sleeves and a V-neckline. The fitted bodice stayed snug to Carly's upper thighs before flaring out into a skirt with chiffon and more lace. Subtle beading caught the light, so the whole gown shimmered.

"Bella is amazing." Carly fingered the dress. "I described what I wanted and showed her pictures, but this . . ."

"I agree. What will Jake say?"

Carly giggled. "I want a tear out of the man when he sees me walking up the aisle."

"I think you'll get more than one."

"Thank you for suggesting her. I also want to thank you for finding this adorable cottage to prepare in. It's so much better than being in a big hotel."

Cassie wasn't sure what to say because that would have been the opposite of what most people thought.

"I spend so many nights a year in hotels, you know? In the beginning, I was in small towns, places like this. People are kind in small towns." She sighed. "Maybe I'm feeling jaded right now."

"Are you sad your farewell tour is over?"

"I had never planned to do one, but Jake wanted me to go back out there again to make sure I wanted to walk away from it." A dreamy expression lit her face. "I am. I'm going to teach music privately and start a new life."

"I assigned someone to take care of you right up to the wedding. She's also going to be working with your bridesmaids. If there's anything you want, we'll do our best to get it. If we were in Nashville, I would tell you if there's anything you want, just let us know and we *will* get it, but that may not work in Two Hearts."

Carly laughed. "That's fine. I'm not a diva."

"Jasmine should be here soon," Cassie said. "She's worked with me for years and will make sure everything is taken care of. The limousine you arrived in will take you to the church and then to the reception. Afterward, the driver will deliver you to the Nashville airport for your honeymoon flight. Are you still going to the Caribbean?"

"Jake said since I planned most of the wedding—with your help, of course, Cassie—he wanted to surprise me with the honeymoon. All he told me is that we're going to a private island in the British Virgin Islands." The sentence ended with a sigh. "A beach alone with Jake sounds heavenly. It's almost show time, isn't it?" She sounded less enthusiastic now.

Every fiber of Cassie's being clenched. *Please, don't let this be a remorseful bride.* "Are you sure everything's okay?"

Carly said, "I'm just amazed at where my life has gone in the last year. I never mentioned this and most people don't realize it, but I was left without a cent. I lost my house and everything in it. It's amazing where your life can go in a single year. Even without Jake and his wealth, I was still finding a new way for myself." She took a deep breath. "It's realizing what you're capable of and how strong you are that feels good."

Cassie wondered if she was on a path of similar changes in her life. Everything felt like it was in such chaos.

"But what about you, Cassie? How was your honeymoon?"

Shock vibrated through Cassie. This was the first time she'd had to address her situation with a client. "You must not have heard. I was a runaway bride."

Surprise registered on Carly's face. "I don't know what to say. I know that you must have had a good reason."

"Thank you, Carly. Almost everyone has assumed I just didn't want to marry the man. He didn't turn out to be who I thought he was, and I found out at the last minute."

Carly nodded. "Cheater, right?"

Had her story gotten out after all? "How do you know?"

"Are you kidding? Do you know how many country songs there are about cheating men?" She laughed. "I know your situation isn't a laughing matter, but I've heard that story before and sung about it more times than I can count."

Cassie chuckled, surprised that she could laugh about this subject.

"The right man will appear when you least expect it."

An image of Greg popped into Cassie's mind, but she quickly dismissed it. He wasn't the right man if he was in the wrong place. Those sounded like the words to a country song.

A knock sounded on the door.

"I'm going to leave you in Jasmine's capable hands," Cassie said. "Bella will be here soon, too. I'll see you at the church." She opened the door. "Carly, this is Jasmine."

The women exchanged greetings, and Cassie left.

When she checked in on Jake, he was perfectly fine. Even relaxed. He told her, "I'm marrying the woman of my dreams. Why would I be nervous?"

That was a good thought. She hoped she would have a groom who appreciated her that much at some point in her life.

Time flew, and before she knew it, the countdown for the ceremony had begun. She'd run out to the reception site, and everything there had looked good. A welcome sign with the wedding party's names on it had been placed at the farm's entrance, evidence that the signage vendor had arrived.

Then she got the kind of call she dreaded.

"Cassie, the groom's grandmother wants to make a change."

Panic went through her with every word. "I'm on my way."

When Cassie entered the church, she found a petite senior citizen glaring at her assistant.

"Is something wrong, Mrs. Miller?" Cassie had memorized all family names.

"This person"—she glared at Cassie's assistant, Taylor —"won't let me substitute birdseed for rose petals to throw when the bride and groom leave the church."

Putting on her most reassuring smile, Cassie said, "I asked Jake and Carly their preference, and Jake strongly preferred the rose petals. He said he'd been pelted with bird seed at one wedding and didn't want to get smacked with it at his own." She winced at the last part, but those had been his words.

The older woman relaxed. "Jake wanted that?"

Cassie nodded.

"Then that's fine."

Cassie sensed the older woman needed to help in some way.

She leaned closer to her and glanced around as though she was sharing a secret. "I could use someone to help with the bridesmaids when they leave the church. They're young and need guidance."

The older woman looked intrigued. "I can understand that."

"Would you go with them to the farm and make sure everyone stays out of trouble?"

"You've got it. I'll watch over them as though I was their grandmother." She marched off, a woman on a mission.

"But, Cassie, I don't think—"

"She needed to feel useful."

Taylor gave a slow nod. "I think I understand. I should keep an eye on her to make sure she doesn't take her job too seriously?"

"Absolutely. You'll make a great wedding planner when you branch out on your own."

"I don't know how you do that, Cassie. I'm so glad you do, though."

With that taken care of, the wedding went off without a hitch. The bride was stunning. She had musician friends play the bridal march as she slowly walked down the aisle toward Jake.

He wore a black suit Cassie knew he'd had custom made. Jake looked so good that he had turned every female eye in the room his direction, but he only had eyes for Carly. The groom wiped his cheeks when his bride neared. Her friend had gotten her wish: he'd thought her so beautiful he'd cried.

When they said the vows they'd written themselves, Carly promised to love him, honor him, and be his best friend. Jake said he would take care of her forever and dream about her every night. The entire church sighed, and Cassie noticed quite a few people reaching for tissues.

Carly and Jake truly loved each other. When the minister pronounced them husband and wife, Cassie's eyes filled with tears. The wedding planning had come with challenges, but she suspected the marriage would be solid and last.

The pair stepped outside to the rain of rose petals while the photographer snapped photos.

Cassie left them with Jasmine and Michelle and hurried out to the farm. Buses soon began arriving and offloading guests, many of the people exclaiming with delight when they saw the location.

She stood waiting as Carly and Jake arrived in their limousine. Carly stepped out wearing an adorable white dress that had a snug bodice, flowed freely from the waist, and landed just below her knee. The last time they'd spoken over the phone, Bella had described the dress as "country wedding chic," and now Cassie understood exactly what she had meant.

The bodice, covered in sequins, would light up with tonight's candlelight in the outdoor room. Bella had done amazing work in the short time she'd had to make a new dress. On her feet, the bride wore her signature hot-pink cowboy boots.

"Cassie, this venue is even more beautiful than I could have pictured." Carly turned in a circle to look at the farm.

Jake agreed. "Yes, you've outdone yourself with our wedding. Thank you so much."

Cassie flushed at their praise.

"I want to have a quick word with Cassie." Carly kissed her new husband on the cheek. "It's a secret."

"Okay. Will I like it?"

"Time will tell."

Carly stepped to the side, and Cassie followed her.

"I have your microphone ready and have done a sound check."

Carly glanced at Jake. "I hope he likes it."

"He will *love* it."

Cassie could not have asked for a better day for the event or for one that went off better than this. Everyone was minding their manners and not drinking too much. She stood off to the side when it was time for the first dance, giving Carly a nod that the stage was hers.

Carly took the microphone. "I have a special surprise for you. I've written a song for my man. My new husband." She turned toward the band and transformed in an instant from a happy bride to a professional performer. "Let's do this."

Cassie grinned as she watched Carly perform the song about falling in love with a man named Jake. She didn't think there was a dry eye in the place when Carly finished and held out her hand for Jake to join her onstage. Standing with their arms around each other, Carly said over her shoulder, "Are y'all ready to dance?"

A bunch of yeses and a few whoops went up around the room.

"Then these boys are going to entertain you, and I'm going to get down off the stage."

Cassie understood the deeper meaning behind what she'd said. This might be the last stage she was on for a while. Could a singer-songwriter completely walk away from performing, though?

The band, which was surprisingly versatile, switched from Carly's country song to a traditional first-dance love song. The couple took to the floor, Jake doing pretty well for himself, and Carly, of course, getting every step right after years of performing.

Throughout the evening, Cassie checked in with her assistants and security team. She finally sought out the head of security. Not because she needed to see Greg but because she needed to do her job.

As soon as she caught a glimpse of his familiar broad shoulders, she knew she'd just lied to herself. She found him and Marisol watching the crowd, but also talking and smiling.

They looked like good friends. She had to remember that. He had told her that was all they were, and she needed to believe him.

But again, why did it matter? She would drive out of town for the final time tomorrow—she checked her watch—today. He had no interest in keeping up a relationship with her long-distance, and why should he? She didn't even know how she felt herself. Sure, she knew she liked him, but was it more than that?

After checking outside the tent to make sure her team had everything under control, she came around the corner of the tent at the same time as Greg approached from the opposite direction. When he put out his hands to steady her, something to the side caught his attention.

"What?" She turned that way, missing his touch after she turned and his hands slipped away.

A man approached her, she assumed someone from the wedding—until the moment the lights hit his face.

"Jonathan?"

She felt Greg tense beside her. Her former fiancé shouldn't have gotten past security.

Anger surged through her. "Why are you here?"

His boyish grin no longer felt genuine. "Your mother thought I deserved another chance."

Her mother had watched the video, so this made no sense.

"What does my mother have to do with your being *here*?" Cassie hadn't spoken with her in quite a while, so she couldn't know about Carly's wedding in Two Hearts. Besides that, why would she expect her daughter to reunite with a man who had hurt her?

"I didn't know you were doing a wedding tonight, but she told me you'd come to this dreary town. I asked one of the townspeople, and he told me where to find you."

At those words, Greg stalked off, but she heard his footsteps stop after ten or twelve steps, so he must be watching out for her. Jonathan shouldn't have gotten through security, so Greg would have to figure out how he'd done that after the man left.

"I will ask you again, Jonathan. Why are you here?" She caught herself as her voice rose, dropping it lower in case a guest could hear their conversation through the tent wall.

He reached for her hand, but she jerked it back.

"I must need to apologize for something," he said. "You've never told me what I did that caused you to leave."

Cassie's jaw dropped. "Are you kidding? Wait." She'd only shared the video with a few people. "You don't know, do you?"

"Don't know what, sweetheart?"

She recoiled at what she'd once thought of as his endearing word for her. Leaning forward, she said, "Don't *ever* use that name for me again." How had she fallen for his lies? Pulling out her phone, she brought up the video, then realized she'd deleted Jonathan's contact information from her phone. "What's your phone number?"

He rattled it off, and she entered the digits and hit Send.

"Have a nice life, Jonathan." She frowned. "No, I don't think slime can have a good life, so that may not be possible."

As he stared at his phone, his eyes grew wider. "I can explain—"

"Don't try. Goodbye, Jonathan." When he stood still, staring at her as though he might try to change her mind, she added, "Please leave now, or I will have security remove you."

Taking deep breaths, she watched him vanish again into the night, and she felt . . . nothing. He hadn't broken her heart, because she'd never given it to him. They were acquaintances who had planned to get married.

His voice in the distance said, "It didn't work," and a female voice replied with words she couldn't make out.

He'd brought Giselle.

Walking around the tent, Cassie hoped a few minutes alone

would restore her professional demeanor, because she didn't feel very friendly right now.

Jonathan Albach had left her life forever. Feeling lighter with every step, she knew he'd given her a gift by coming here.

Each time love had been mentioned tonight, and it had been mentioned often, Greg had thought of Cassie. She made his heart beat faster whenever he saw her. He smiled whenever he saw her. And he'd been so distracted by her when he'd driven away this afternoon that he'd almost gone off the road and ended up in a ditch.

It was time to admit to himself that he loved Cassie Van Bibber. He'd wondered about it a time or two, but he'd been able to push those thoughts away when she left. Then she'd come back to Two Hearts.

It made no sense. Her life was in Nashville, and his was here. He'd moved before, though, and for less of a reason than what he felt for Cassie. He loved this town, and, as the sheriff, walked in his father's footsteps. But maybe he could talk someone he'd worked with in Chicago into the job of sheriff in a quiet, small town. Most larger cities' police forces would be interested in someone with his experience, so he could try Nashville and the cities around it. If not, he'd go into private security.

None of that mattered: he needed to tell her how he felt.

Several hours into the reception, he found the florist off to the side speaking with a man he didn't recognize.

"How did these end up in here?" The florist did not sound pleased.

The man raised his hands in a very Italian shrug. "I have no idea, Henri. After everything was unloaded from the van, we found a box of red roses in the corner."

He folded the flaps on the box. "Make sure these aren't put out. The bride doesn't want red anything here."

"Of course."

Greg stepped forward. "Henri, could I buy a rose from you?"

He turned his head to look up at him. "You're the sheriff, aren't you?"

"Yes."

"Take the whole box. No charge." He glanced over to his left and seemed to notice something, because he was on his feet and moving in a hurry.

Greg opened the box and pulled out a single, long-stemmed red rose.

When the event was nearing the end, he searched for Cassie and finally discovered her outside with a clipboard. "I was hoping to find you."

Cassie rubbed her eyes. "Greg, I'm exhausted. You heard most of my conversation with Jonathan, so you know about that little diversion. And a wedding this size always leaves me tired by the end. Please tell me there isn't a security crisis."

There had been one. He'd discovered that Jonathan had driven through the fields of flowers to avoid the main entrance and security. She didn't need to know that now, though.

He had something personal to say.

"What do you need?"

Maybe talking to her tonight would be a mistake.

"I *need* sleep."

"Fine. I'll make this as quick as I can." He brought the rose from behind his back and handed it to her. "I love you."

When she didn't respond, but simply stared at him, he turned and walked away.

With every step toward his car, he became more convinced that his mother's words were true: he was an idiot.

The event came to a close soon after her odd conversation with Greg. Everyone left—the guests in their bus, the bride and bridegroom, their family, and their close friends in limos. Cassie's former fiancé must have left, too, because she hadn't seen him since their chat.

She stood to the side and watched as the tables were loaded up. Everything under the tent would be packed up tonight, and the tent itself would come down tomorrow.

Cassie watched Greg's car drive down the gravel driveway and out onto the highway, his taillights disappearing into the night. Maybe she was so tired that she'd hallucinated the conversation with him. She'd once been so exhausted that by three a.m., the remains of a cake had appeared to bend and twist. She'd had someone drive her home that night.

Lifting her hand, she found the long-stemmed red rose. Holding it to catch its scent, she winced when a rose thorn nicked her finger. Greg had been here, and he'd handed her a rose.

That probably meant that he'd told her he loved her.

As soon as she had enough brain cells active, she'd figure it all out.

She'd done all she could in the dark. Tomorrow morning, she'd be out here to do a final walkthrough. Someone would have inevitably left something behind that she'd need to retrieve. The tent rental company and others would be here around noon to get everything.

Then she would pack up and go back to her life in Nashville.

When she got back to the yellow house, Romeo greeted her at the door.

"Sorry I was so late." Without stopping, she picked him up and went upstairs to her bedroom. After stripping off her clothes, she grabbed a T-shirt and slid into bed.

# CHAPTER NINETEEN

*C*assie peeled open her eyes and yelped. Romeo stared at her from inches away.

Blinking, she did her best to focus on him and then the room around them. That's right; she was back in Two Hearts. In her yellow house. She picked Romeo up, sat, and put on her slippers. Right now, she needed one thing, and that was coffee.

It was too bad she made the world's worst.

Once she had her robe on, she trudged downstairs with Romeo at her heels to get some liquid caffeine in her veins. When she stepped into the kitchen, the rose lying on the counter stopped her in her tracks, and she gasped.

"I wondered about that when I came in."

Cassie whirled around and found Bella at her kitchen table.

"There weren't any red roses at the wedding. Everything was in the colors Carly loves, and those don't seem to include red."

"Coffee?" Cassie formed the one full word she could manage.

Bella laughed. "I'm a tea drinker, remember? I haven't been up long myself, and I made a pot of it. You're welcome to a cup."

She could have bad coffee or excellent tea. It was a tough call. Tea wasn't her favorite substance. "I'll take a cup."

Bella made a *tsk-tsk* sound. "You must be groggy. Here." She poured it into a pretty china teacup. "I love all the beautiful things that are in this house."

Cassie held onto the cup with both hands because she didn't think she could manage it with just one. Taking a deep, fortifying drink, she felt like she could handle the day after all. "Please tell me there's caffeine in this."

Bella laughed. "There is. It's Earl Grey."

Whatever. She took another gulp.

"Want to tell me about that rose?" Bella watched her over the top of her teacup as she drank more of her tea.

"I'm trying to put together the pieces myself. Greg gave it to me." She put her hand on the side of her head to support it. "I was so exhausted, Bella. But I'm certain that he said . . ."

"Yes? Come on, I need to know."

After another long sip, Cassie set the mug on the table. "Bella, he said he loved me."

Her friend started choking on her tea. Coughing, she patted her chest before saying, "Are you sure?"

Cassie nodded. "Almost a hundred percent. What do I do about it?"

Bella laughed, her head tilting back and her body shaking.

"I don't see anything funny about this. I don't want to break the man's heart. And I certainly can't live here." Hadn't that been the main problem all along?

"The biggest question is: do you love him?"

"Of course, I do. I've known I loved Greg for days."

Bella stared at her, her eyes wide. "Did you just admit that out loud?"

Cassie sat down hard. "I did, didn't I? I guess I do."

"You guess? It's not a guess, Cassie. It's a yes or a no."

Her friend was right, of course. "I haven't wanted to admit it to myself. I mean, weeks ago, I was supposed to marry another man. What kind of woman does that make me?"

"You weren't in love with the first man." She held up her hand to stop Cassie from talking. "You're a wedding planner, and you were in love with the *idea* of love."

"I know you never liked Jonathan."

Bella sadly shook her head. "It isn't that I disliked the man. I didn't trust him."

Cassie wasn't hearing anything she hadn't sorted out for herself. She gestured at the kitchen. "This house, this town, is all temporary for me. This isn't my real life."

Bella poured more tea in her cup. "How did the wedding and reception go yesterday?"

Cassie blinked at the sudden change of subject. "You know it went well. What's your point?"

"Did the vendors bring everything out as they needed to?"

"A few of them grumbled. A couple of them grumbled loudly. But everyone did cooperate." Cassie thought over the wedding. "It went remarkably well considering I was on new territory."

Cassie popped open the window and heard birds singing outside. "I've come to love this little town."

"And this house."

"Yes, and this house. I wish I could stay here."

"You can."

Cassie sputtered as she tried to speak.

"Everything you want is here. Do you think you can get ten to twelve high-end clients who want a wedding in the country each year?"

Cassie answered without hesitation. "I could if that was my specialty."

Requests for high-end, country-themed weddings were frequent in this country music capital. She'd have venues to choose from including fields of flowers, the Christmas tree farm, and many, many barns. And, unlike in the city, she wouldn't be competing for spaces booked a year or more in advance.

"I *know* I could." Cassie stared at Bella.

"I will miss having you in Nashville, but I wouldn't be your friend if I didn't say this: Go get your man."

Grinning, Cassie knocked back the rest of her tea and stood. "I'm going to do that right now." She started for the back door.

"You might want to change your outfit and consider taking a shower. Not that he won't see you like this after you're married, but it may be a bad idea to surprise him with scary morning Cassie."

Cassie burst out laughing. Turning around, she went toward the stairs. "You know, I'm going to get back at you for all of these comments when you find someone you're interested in."

As she went up the stairs, Bella yelled, "Not going to happen anytime soon." A moment later, she said, "I'll feed your kitten."

She wasn't even a good pet parent today. But at least Romeo loved her, anyway. Had Greg said what she thought he had? Did he love her?

# CHAPTER TWENTY

*C*assie ran out the back door, down the steps, and straight into a man's chest. She steadied herself by grasping both of his arms and looked up to find none other than Greg Brantley.

"I was on my way—" she said.

"I wanted to say—" he said.

"You first." Greg took a step back.

"I'm sorry for how I responded last night. I was exhausted."

He gave a single nod. "You don't need to apologize. I shouldn't have tried to talk to you then, and I'm sorry for what I said."

Cassie looked up at him. Did he mean to take back his words of love?

"I may be a fool for saying this, Greg, but I was on my way to find you so I could tell you I feel the same way. Are you here to tell me you changed your mind?" She said the last words so softly that even she could barely hear them.

His face lit up. "Are you telling me you love me?"

She nodded. "I love you, Greg Brantley. Let me say that out loud so there's no mistaking what I mean."

He pulled her close and swung her around. "I love you, Cassie. I thought I'd overstepped my bounds last night."

He set her down and leaned forward, putting his lips on hers for a quick kiss, but she wrapped her arms around him and pulled him tighter, deepening the kiss.

When he stepped back a moment later, blinking, he said, "I guess you mean it, don't you?"

"I do."

"It may be too early for those words."

Cassie thought over what she had just said and put her hand over her mouth.

Greg turned serious. "But that would be my plan for the future."

Had he just proposed? An image of her walking down the aisle toward him in the church they'd restored brought a smile to her face. "Greg, if that's your proposal, it might be the worst one I've ever heard."

He laughed and got down on one knee. Reaching for her right hand, he held it in both of his. "Cassie Van Bibber, would you do me the honor of becoming my wife?" He gazed up at her nervously. "With the wedding yesterday, I haven't had time to go to Nashville to buy a ring."

*A ring.* Cassie closed her eyes. She'd done this once before. She wanted to say yes, but . . .

"It's a little crazy, isn't it?"

Greg was the right man in so many ways that Jonathan had never been. She couldn't stop a laugh from bubbling up. "It is, but I don't care." As soon as she said that, she realized it was true. "I don't need even another day to know you're the man I want to bring me coffee every day for the rest of my life."

"Is that a yes?" He shifted his knee on the lawn. "Help me out here. I knelt on what must be a rock in the grass, and this is starting to hurt."

Cassie tugged on his hand to pull him upward, and he

winced as he stood. "I would love nothing more than to marry you, Greg Brantley." When he leaned forward to kiss her again, she pulled back and added, "But we may need to wait a year for the wedding. I need to plan it, and I was almost a bride recently—"

"Say no more. But I may try to talk you into something faster."

"I won't argue when you're trying, especially if your tactics involve this." She leaned forward and kissed him one more time.

Continue reading for the Epilogue . . .

# EPILOGUE

*C*assie set the large vase of pink and yellow flowers on the food table and stepped back. "Do you think that's the right place for it?" Decorations in the same pastel hues were throughout the outdoor room.

Bella put her hands on Cassie's shoulders and nudged her around to face her. "It's fine. This will be the best engagement party in the history of engagement parties."

She laughed. "I may be overthinking this." Then she pictured her mother entering the tent they'd set up in the park. No, she wasn't.

Turning slowly in a circle, she gave a final review of every detail. The white tent covered a buffet table laden with Dinah's sandwiches and pies, and a large bowl filled with an old-fashioned pink punch Mrs. Brantley had made. Tables were ready for guests to sit and eat. Yes, it was informal—and that would annoy her mother—but Cassie wanted everyone to feel welcome here.

"Do you think Sandra Van Bibber will approve?"

Bella raised an eyebrow. "Does that matter?"

Cassie considered her friend's words and exhaled with a

*whoosh.* "More than it should. I want her to like Greg, but I'm marrying the man no matter what she says."

"He will be relieved." Bella shrugged when Cassie rolled her eyes. "You went with the man your mother approved of, and look where that got you."

Her new fiancé entered the tent wearing a suit he'd donned for the occasion. Without meaning to, she sighed like a teenager.

"You made the right choice when you decided to marry that man."

"I couldn't agree more." Cassie watched him approach.

"Are you sure you want to move *here*, though?"

"I have never been more sure of anything." Greg reached her, and she stared into his eyes for a moment then leaned forward to kiss him.

"Everything ready?" He moved beside her and put his arm around her waist. Glancing around, he added, "It looks good . . . to me."

Cassie chewed her lip. "I hope it's good enough."

Bella laughed. "This event is ready for royalty. You've created a beautiful get-together. But you do know that no one plans their own engagement party, right?"

"This is the first event I've planned since I bought the house, and officially moved here." *Her* yellow house. "I want everyone to know I care about them and the town."

"They know. I'm the only one who matters, anyway." Greg grinned, and she swatted at his arm. "Micah's here." His friend came toward them wearing a black leather jacket over jeans.

Bella leaned closer to Cassie. "Who's that?" she asked with interest in her voice.

"That," Greg answered, "is my friend." He glanced from Bella to Micah and a slow grin spread over his face.

Cassie had briefly wondered about matching them up. Then she'd dismissed that idea in a hurry. Micah had no desire to move elsewhere, and Bella oozed *city girl*. She wouldn't be happy anywhere that didn't have high-end shopping, endless restaurants, and constant busyness. Besides that, the more time she spent with Micah, the more she realized that he and Bella would be like oil and water: they'd never mix together well.

Cassie nudged Greg. When he turned toward her, she gave a slight shake of her head. His brow furrowed, he turned forward as Micah reached them and slapped his friend on the back.

"I'm glad you could make it."

Micah's eyes stayed on Bella. "I wouldn't want to miss it." To Bella, he said, "Micah Walker. I haven't seen you here before."

Cassie winced. Bella wouldn't respond well to a classic line like that.

"Isabella Bennett. Do you live in Two Hearts?"

"Most of my life."

"That's nice."

Micah seemed to be waiting for her to say more, but Bella simply stood there with a polite expression.

He wisely gave up and addressed the three of them. "Can I get everyone some punch?"

Cassie jumped in. "I think we'd all love some. Why don't you help him carry it, Greg?"

Her fiancé and Micah headed toward the table.

"Why are you treating him that way?"

Bella blew out a breath. "He lives here."

"I do too."

"Cassie, you know I can only take a small town for a short time. A few hours. Overnight at most. Then I need to get back to a city." She faced the men again.

Greg and Micah soon headed back toward them, each carrying a cup of punch.

Bella smiled—or did her best job of faking a smile. "I'll try to be pleasant to him," she said before the two men reached them. "He is attractive."

"And nice."

"And in Two Hearts."

Bella didn't have the usual passion behind her words. "I've never seen you act so lukewarm with a handsome man. Something else must be wrong."

Bella sighed. "Sorry. I'm distracted by something else." Before Cassie could ask for more, her friend added, "I'll tell you about it *after* your party."

As Cassie debated pressing her for details, a black-and-white puppy shot through the tent's entrance and toward them. Cassie raced over to scoop it up before it could topple decorations, but it swerved and headed right for the men.

"Greg, Micah, look out!"

They jumped to the side and right into the puppy's path. It slid onto its rear and tried to stop, but ran into Micah. The pink punch in his cups flew up out of them and down onto Bella's dress. Cassie finally grabbed the dog, glad she'd chosen a harder-to-stain navy-blue dress and not the soft-peach her friend had worn.

Bella held the sodden dress away from her body. "Yuck. This will never come clean."

The puppy wiggled in Cassie's arms. "At least my mother isn't here yet. Let's try to get everything straightened up and find this dog a place to stay before she does."

Sandra Van Bibber took that moment to enter the tent. Dressed as one would for a garden party with a hat embellished with flowers and a coordinating floral print dress, she glanced up and around, gave what seemed to be a nod of satisfaction, then came toward them. About halfway across, she paused, her eyes going first to Bella's dress, and then stopping on the puppy.

The event wasn't going as Cassie had planned.

But she did get the man of her dreams.

❧

Thank you for reading Cassie and Greg's story!

If you enjoyed this fun book, MARRIED BY MONDAY is the next book in the Wedding Town romance series. Bella and Micah aren't a good match. When Micah needs to get married to fulfill the terms of a will, and Bella needs help with something, the two make a pact. They'll get Married by Monday. There's no chance they'll fall in love.

Carly and Jake have their own book: HOW TO MARRY A COUNTRY MUSIC STAR. She's a down-on-her-luck country music star, and he's the wealthy man who hires her to be his housekeeper. Get it FREE at cathrynbrown.com/marry.

# ABOUT CATHRYN

Writing books that are fun and touch your heart

Cathryn always loved reading. When she was in college, a friend gave her a paper grocery bag filled with old romance novels. She read them, her first romances, and asked for more.

A few years later, she found a romance novel with humor in it. She knew then that she wanted to write a book like that. It wasn't published, but she learned a lot.

After that, she applied her communications degree to writing and publishing hundreds of articles, becoming an award-winning journalist.

But she still wanted to write romances. *Falling for Alaska*, the first book in the Alaska Dream Romances, became her first published romance. There are currently nine books set in her home state of Alaska.

She now lives in Tennessee with her professor husband and adorable calico cat. It isn't surprising that she wanted to write a series set there. The stories in small-town Two Hearts, Tennessee, begin with *Runaway to Romance*.

And if you have kids, she also writes middle grade mysteries as Shannon L. Brown, which start with *The Feather Chase*.

For more books and updates, visit cathrynbrown.com

Made in the USA
Middletown, DE
09 January 2023

21763269R00146